ONE DEADLY LESSON

A DI SCOTT BAKER CRIME THRILLER

JAY NADAL

INKUBATOR
BOOKS

Published by Inkubator Books
www.inkubatorbooks.com

ISBN (eBook): 978-1-83756-065-3
ISBN (Paperback): 978-1-83756-066-0
ISBN (Hardcover): 978-1-83756-067-7

Previously published by the author as Retribution.

PROLOGUE

Christopher Johnson gazed out the window of his study at the dark night. The warmth of the summer sun still hung in the air long after its orb of light had disappeared below the rolling hills of the Sussex Downs. A tall, brass antique night lamp near the back illuminated the room. Its soft glow cast a shadow across the hundreds of books that filled the built-in bookcase. Rows upon rows of worn volumes were displayed on wooden shelves that extended the full width and height of one wall.

As the evening wore on, he found it increasingly harder to concentrate. He recalled the countless hours he'd already spent reviewing those books.

How many bloody ways are there to explain the impact of conflict and change in the Middle East c.1914–1995 on modern-day society in the region? Such dull research, he'd decided.

Many hours at his desk had left his muscles tight and knotted. He leant back in his vintage chesterfield, dark-red leather captain's chair. The leather squeaked beneath him as he shifted. The 1940s wooden frame creaked like the timbers of an old sailing ship from a bygone era.

He cracked his back and shoulders, and the tension eased. But his aches were the least of his worries. His weak arthritic hip had locked, forcing him to lean to his right to release the seized joint. It clicked, and he rubbed the tender area.

To the left on his desk stood a tall pile of books that he still needed to work through. To his right a half glass of Merlot, his third tonight, which was helping to numb the monotony of his work and melt away the stresses of the day.

For company tonight it was just his books and the relaxing sounds of *Tristesse* by Chopin drifting from his well-worn mini-CD player positioned on a small mahogany coffee table. The energetic and atmospheric tones of the music left him sated. The dramatic rise and fall in tempo stirred the air, taking his mind on an intoxicating journey.

The music was loud enough to mask the sound of the intruder. His footsteps were softened by the thick, plush red hallway carpet that led to the study. He'd chosen his footwear carefully; the bare, wooden parquet floors in the hallways and walkways of the main building magnified sound, making it impossible for a silent approach.

Johnson remained deeply engrossed in his work, flicking through pages and humming along to the music whilst tapping the end of his pen on the dark mahogany desk. The sweet smell of mellow Virginia pipe tobacco lingered like a mist in the air. Faint clouds of smoke swirled and danced around the room in no particular direction, their trails illuminated by the glow of the light.

The intruder turned the ornate, brass handle on the old mahogany door millimetre by millimetre. He then opened the door just wide enough to peer inside. From his vantage point, he could see Johnson sitting at the far end of the room in front of the window.

The intruder crept forward, his steps in perfect synchronisation with each slow, steady breath. He was just a few inches behind his target when he raised his left hand. The thin blade he gripped glinted under the light.

Johnson froze when the cold steel blade was pressed to his neck. Terror gripped him, but his drowsy senses, loosened by the wine, sapped all will to fight back.

He swallowed hard as he stared ahead at his reflection, eyes fixed wide. The reflection of the intruder standing behind him in the darkened window was clear, his face covered by a balaclava.

"Get up," the intruder said in a calm and measured tone.

"What is it that you want?" Johnson's voice quivered.

"Retribution."

The intruder repeated his demands again as he pressed the blade harder against Johnson's neck. With his other hand he yanked the man's collar up, pulling him out of the chair.

"You're coming with me."

"Retribution?" Johnson asked, terrified. "I don't understand..."

Sweat trickled between his shoulder blades as he tried to keep his body from shaking. "My w-wallet is in my jacket. Take it. There's fifty pounds in there. Here, you can take my watch. Take anything you want. Just don't hurt me."

The intruder yanked Johnson harder, who stumbled and almost fell. "Come with me."

He marched Johnson through the hallway and downstairs, pulling him out the back door and into the darkness of the night. Johnson squinted hard, desperate to adjust his eyes to the blackness. Confusion and panic forced bile into his throat.

The intruder had planned this moment for many years. He'd chosen his exact spot in the forest, a place isolated enough that no one would disturb them or hear Johnson's screams.

The masked intruder pushed Johnson ahead. The half-crescent moon provided enough brightness to illuminate the edge of the forest. Johnson struggled to keep pace as he was pushed and shoved along. The speed had him stumbling on the uneven ground; a mixture of heather and gorse tried to tangle in his feet.

The two men arrived at a small clearing. On their way there Johnson had remained insistent he had done nothing wrong. His bravado had surfaced occasionally to demand an explanation. He'd receive none.

The intruder shoved him to the ground and loomed over him, holding the knife just inches from Johnson's face.

"It's your fault. You're to blame. You let it happen, and you did nothing." The intruder recited the Latin phrase. "*Ignavus iners timidius tu mori debes.*"

Johnson, well versed in Latin, challenged the intruder. "I'm not a coward. I don't deserve to die. What the hell is this all about?" He bucked upwards in a futile attempt to unsettle the intruder.

"I want you to admit your guilt, Johnson. I want you to beg for forgiveness."

Johnson started to cry, his frustration boiling over as he pleaded for his life. "I can't. I don't know what you're talking about."

"You're going to die anyway." The intruder removed his balaclava. "You don't recognise me, do you?"

In the dark, Johnson studied the man's face. "You?... But you're..."

The steel blade pressed harder into Johnson's neck.

"No, think back...much further back," the intruder replied.

Johnson studied the man again. He bore a resemblance, a striking resemblance in fact, to someone he once knew.

The realisation hit him, and his eyes widened.

Johnson's jaw dropped, the danger of the situation sinking in bone-deep. Tears welled in his eyes as fear knotted his stomach. "I can't say anything. They'll kill me. I swore I'd never say anything."

The intruder waved the knife in Johnson's face before pressing the tip into his cheek, causing a small nick. Blood glistened under the moonlight.

"You have a choice. You die by the sword, or you hang," he said, looking at the noose he had looped over a strong branch.

Panic consumed Johnson. His head spun; his chest heaved. Bile raced up his throat once again, and he struggled to breathe. He was old now. He'd been a junior wrestling champion once, afraid of no one, and had fought opponents older and bigger. Now he was just a shell of his past virility. He had little chance of overpowering this man and an even slimmer chance of outrunning him.

The desperate plight of his situation spun his mind like a tornado as his thoughts collided. Submerged in a dire hole of his past mistakes, he tried to rationalise it. Perhaps he could talk his way out of this. But the wine had dulled his ability to think clearly.

"This can't be. No. This is ridiculous, but...but...no, you won't get away with this." The words tumbled out as he drew in ragged breaths. Even though he wasn't making much sense, he continued to plead. "You can't make me do anything. I won't choose. You're just trying to scare the shit out of me!"

"You're right. I can't make you do anything, so I'll make the decision for you."

The intruder tossed the knife away, then punched

Johnson hard in the face, dazing him in the process. He grabbed him by both collars and hauled him to his feet before delivering several more blows to the man's stomach. Johnson doubled up in agony and crumpled to his knees.

Ignoring Johnson's cries for mercy, he dragged him along on his knees to the noose. He stuck the loop over Johnson's head and took up the slack before Johnson could wriggle free. Johnson kicked and flailed. The intruder pulled hard on the rope, and it tightened around Johnson's neck. Johnson screamed as he gripped either side of the rope. Ragged breaths caused him to convulse as his lungs fought to take in oxygen.

The intruder used all his strength to haul the rope up just high enough to lift Johnson's feet off the ground. His muscles tensed; he gritted his teeth and poured every last drop of energy into the pull. The forest floor offered little grip; the overgrown grass and vegetation robbed him of a firm footing.

Johnson kicked and fought with every ounce of energy. Spittle sprayed from his mouth. His eyes bulged as the pressure increased, crushing the veins in his neck and starving his body of oxygen. His mind swirled like a dark vortex as light-headedness confused him and blurred his vision.

His body kept thrashing for release as the pain intensified, every fibre of his being fighting to stay alive. But the intruder was proving far too strong for him, and he was fast losing the battle to live.

With one final pull of the rope, Johnson was jerked violently into the air; his legs flailed as though he were running. Blood leaked from his eyes as the pressure built in his neck. His final few gasps of breath came short and sharp as he scratched and clawed at his neck.

In the space of a heartbeat Johnson's body stilled. With his head bowed forward, his arms and legs limp, his body swayed gently like a human pendulum. The only sound, the creaking of rope as it slowly came to a stop.

He stood and watched for a few minutes. Johnson deserved the last few minutes of suffering. The others would feel the same pain when he met them.

1

The undulating slopes proved a challenge for the most competent of runners, and for Matthew, the hills presented the ultimate test in endurance, pace and strength. He'd been running for twenty minutes. The reputation of the house was at stake, and the risk of facing the wrath of the sports teacher and housemaster proved enough of an incentive to spur him on as he languished behind.

The summer heat was only a few hours away, but the cooler conditions of the morning offered a refreshing respite that prevented him from overheating as he tried to keep up with the rest of the pupils.

The route took him east towards the hamlet of Westmeston. He travelled along single-lane tracks that were barely wide enough for a car let alone the farm vehicles that crisscrossed the land as they headed from one field to the next. The lead runner frequently shouted a warning about oncoming vehicles to those behind. The message was relayed in sequence down the line as everyone puffed out their cheeks and carried on.

They barely had time to take in the beauty of the landscape, or the tall green hedges that skirted the road, or the traditional stone walls that enclosed the few dwellings that made up this small community. The eleventh-century parish church was just another spectator as the runners passed. From there they headed north-west towards Ditchling cross country. The rough terrain and inclines forced the group of boys to thin out, with the strongest taking the lead and the weakest beginning to trail.

Matthew Edrington was one of the last. Running had never been his forte; he was more into reading spec fiction, creating music on his laptop, and keeping his Facebook fan page "All Things Ginge" going. He'd spent most of his life being the butt of jokes about his bright ginger hair. His recent attempts to stop the jibes and digs by growing his hair longer and sporting the unkempt mop look hadn't worked. His bright blue, piercing eyes, pale complexion and high cheekbones had attracted taunts about his soft boyish looks.

"Poof", "gay boy", "you big girl", and "grow a pair of tits" were comments he took on the chin daily.

His Facebook page had been an attempt to face his issues head-on and embrace his traits. In reality, it was his alter ego running the page. He hid behind the buffer the page created between him and the world. Matthew was weak; he knew it, rarely felt comfortable in his own skin and lacked self-confidence. And for that reason he never sought out attention.

"Edrington, you're not a team player. You're a waste of space," his housemaster would say.

Matthew puffed out his cheeks and stared at the ground as he plodded on. As each minute passed, his pace dropped off a fraction more. The heavy panting of the other stragglers grew nearer as they caught up to him. They levelled with him briefly, then threw him exasperated looks that suggested he was once again going to be responsible for the house coming in last in the weekly cross-country competition.

Despite the feeling that he could do this, his pencil-thin, pasty legs wouldn't carry him any faster. His mind willed him to speed up, to turn things around.

Come on, you can do it.

But his body was failing him fast. His tight lungs fought to take in air. His throat was drier than a desert plain. His thighs stung, feeling like two heavy concrete blocks stuck in mud.

Time seemed to stand still. He was sure that he'd travelled a few hundred yards farther, but his surroundings remained strangely familiar in his eyes. The other pupils ahead were fast disappearing and now looked like tiny dots on a radar.

Matthew had to think fast. He couldn't come in last again and endure the usual humiliation from those gathered at the finish line.

He slowed to a walking pace in an attempt to familiarise himself with the landscape. He had no choice; he'd have to find a shortcut.

He looked around, desperate to find the fastest way back to school. He bent forward, his hands resting on his knees, as he tried to catch his breath. Sweat beaded on his forehead and dripped into his eyes, causing them to sting.

To have any chance of making it back in a place other than last, he would need to cut across the fields, climb the brow of the hill, and then cut through the forest that surrounded the school on three sides. Urgency hastened his thoughts, coupled with doubt as to whether his body would carry him that far.

Matthew turned off the road and fought his way through the hedgerow. Sharp bramble bushes scratched his exposed limbs. His shorts snagged as he fought his way through. In places, the hedgerow was as tall as Matthew and certainly not designed for easy transit through.

He pushed on, calling on every ounce of energy to carry him over the hill. He gritted his teeth. His mouth was parched. His feet barely trudged over the brow. Downward momentum carried him into the dense woodland that surrounded the perimeter of the school. The forest had an identity of its own, a thick tall canopy that created a darkness that only added to its ghostly, unwelcoming atmosphere.

There were a few well-trodden ramblers' routes that criss-crossed the forest. For Matthew, the trails offered him little relief. He had never ventured into this part of the woodland in all the time he'd been at the school. He stopped for a moment to catch his breath, his gaze darting in all directions.

Everything looked the same. Brown, natural barriers rose from the ground, blocking his line of sight. Birdsong high up in the trees was drowned out by his heavy breathing. From the direction in which he had come, he figured that if he continued to run forward, he was sure to find his way out.

In the distance through the trees, he saw what appeared to be the edge of the forest and the first signs that he was close to the school. A mixture of adolescent shouts, whistles, and clapping marked the finish line.

He struggled to move, the crushing pressure on his ribs pushing the air out of him. His asthma kicked in and caused his chest to heave violently. He had to stop; he couldn't carry on, even though he was only just a few hundred yards away from safety. Cold fear spread through him as his lungs lit on fire. Stopping for just a few seconds wouldn't harm his effort to be second last, he decided.

Matthew fell to his knees and used his hands to steady himself. His stomach heaved as he fought to take in oxygen. A whistle of breath and phlegm rattling in his throat warned of an imminent asthma attack. He needed his Ventolin inhaler, but he'd foolishly left it back in his room, thinking he wouldn't need it.

Oh shit, I can't breathe. I need to move on. I have to move on.

Each exhale he made was accompanied by an eerie howling cry.

An odd sound caught his attention. His mind whirled as he tried to identify it. It was coming from behind him. He realised too late that it was a sound of a branch creaking. A slow, hypnotic and rhythmic creaking.

He turned to look over his shoulder. The sight that greeted him caused him to recoil. He shuffled around, and his eyes widened in fear. He gasped, unable to comprehend what he'd found. Matthew tried to make sense of it. His mind must be playing tricks on him, a hallucination or a consequence of the fatigue that racked his body.

This can't be real. My mind is creating this horrible scene to scare my body into running again.

But as the seconds passed, the trick remained. It wasn't a dream. He was in a living nightmare.

Before him was a man swinging from a rope. His face was swollen, with bulging eyeballs that stared off into the distance. The body slowly rotated like a musical ballerina in a jewellery box. The taut rope rubbed repeatedly on the branch, making the creaking sound he'd heard.

Matthew fought the bile that hit the back of his throat. His breathing came in shocked pants as fear raced through his veins, sending shock waves through his body. He trembled violently as he clambered backwards, desperate to get away from the hideous scene in front of him. He glanced around. Terror contorted his face. Frightened whimpering screams escaped from him. He scrambled to his feet, but his mind moved faster than his body, causing him to stumble several times on to the uneven, overgrown forest floor.

With each step he increased his speed. His fear provided

him with enough momentum to run. His trainers snagged on exposed tree roots and slipped on lichens. Stumbling once again, Matthew's arms took the full brunt of the impact. Blood seeped from the deep scratches.

Soon, he cleared the forest and entered the grounds of the school. He was met with a cacophony of whistles, boos, and the usual cries of "loser!" Except this time he didn't care.

He needed to get away fast and as far as he could from the scene he'd just witnessed.

"Edrington, get a bloody move on," his housemaster shouted at him.

The welcoming party was as hostile as he'd expected. Some of the pupils glared at him with hate in their eyes. Others, leaning on each other's shoulders, pointed at him, the state of him giving them plenty to laugh at. He fell to his knees by his housemaster, who looked down at him in displeasure, his brows pulled forward. The man shook his head slowly at Matthew.

Pain and fear stopped the words from leaving Matthew's dry throat.

He raised one arm and jabbed in the direction of the forest.

"Body," he whispered, his words drowned out by the barrage of abuse from the other pupils.

Drawing on all his reserves and taking one huge breath, he made his voice loud enough to be heard by those within a few feet of him.

"Body."

Jabbing his finger in the direction of the forest, he tried a third time. "There's a body in the forest."

2

Scott and Abby swept through the imposing black wrought-iron gates of the school. It was inadequate to merely call this a school – a luxury hotel or retreat seemed more fitting. A long sweeping drive took them up one side of this sprawling estate. On their left, a long line of tall, established oak trees offered natural privacy.

Scott noticed how every twenty yards or so, the border of oaks was broken by ornate weeping willows with long flowing branches that gently grazed the grass. A light breeze rustled through the branches, breaking the silence in the area.

To the right, a row of small wooden stumps were set out at evenly spaced intervals. Thick boundary rope connected in perfectly symmetrical loops from one stump to the next. Scott guessed that the lawns beyond them stretched for some distance, as he couldn't see where they ended.

A uniformed officer waved them to the left of the main building, gesturing towards the rear. Driving around the back, Scott saw even more open land that stretched into the distance a few hundred yards until it met the edge of the forest that surrounded the school.

"Shit, this is a big place," Abby said and whistled. "Can you imagine how much it costs to send a child here?"

"I hate to think. Way more than our salaries combined... including overtime," Scott replied.

"And the rest."

The presence of two white scientific services vans, several police cars, a silver Ford Focus belonging the Cara, the pathologist, and an ambulance was visible near the forest.

As he and Abby kitted up in white paper overalls, he looked up at the school. He couldn't help but admire how the building looked just as imposing and elegant from the back as it did from the front.

This was a completely different type of schooling experience. It wasn't your average comprehensive school found in the sprawling suburbs of every town and city across the country. This was a fine example of a privileged educational system reserved for the elite and wealthy dating back generations. Pupils who attended had their lives mapped out and place booked at the school long before they were born.

You wouldn't find kids from poor backgrounds here or unruly disruptive teenagers looking to start a fight at every opportunity. Places like this taught an honours education and guaranteed successful university placements. Many would likely head to Oxbridge and then go on to be leaders and CEOs in industry, or one day become future politicians or ambassadors in far-flung countries.

"Why do I always end up in forests?" Abby grimaced as she trampled through dense undergrowth. She adjusted her body cam to begin relaying footage back to the office. "You would have thought I'd have learnt my lesson after the Newland murder a few weeks ago. Lack of preparation on my part...again." Abby thought back to when she'd got caught up on thorns visiting a crime scene.

"Stop whining. You're starting to sound more like an old bag as each day passes. Seriously, what's up with you?"

"Nothing, I hate getting messy, and Lord knows what's beneath this undergrowth. I could be stepping in shite or on decaying rodents and I wouldn't know." Abby scrunched up her face as if she'd sucked on a lemon.

The forest offered a cooling respite from the midday sun heat. July was shaping up to be a warm month with temperatures regularly hitting the mid-twenties. The crime scene was much deeper in the forest than Scott had anticipated. Scott wondered if this had been a deliberate act, an attempt to hide the scene and the body from prying eyes for as long as possible. If that was the case, then that strategy had failed.

He and Abby were puffing a bit by the time they reached the blue and white police cordon tape. Scott could clearly see the suspended body still in place whilst forensic officers logged and photographed the scene. Having already signed in to the crime scene log, Scott headed in the direction of the crime scene manager, Matt Allan.

"Matt, how're things going?"

He nodded. "We should be ready to cut him down any minute. We don't want the poor sod up there any longer than is necessary. Cara can then get stuck in. Looks like a suicide on the face of it. It's going to be a lengthy job mapping out the scene and gathering any evidence."

"Have we got an ID?"

"We understand he's the assistant head of the school," Matt replied. "Poor lad in the ambulance found him. Gave the kid an asthma attack."

Scott glanced around, trying to get a feel for the geography. It was a dense secluded spot, not the easiest to get to, but the spot where they stood offered a clearing of some sorts. He assumed that it had been chosen deliberately rather than randomly because of its inaccessibility.

"Okay, mate, keep me informed," Scott said. He headed off to track down Cara, who was now engrossed in a cosy conversation with Abby.

"Inspector," Cara called to him. She and Abby stopped to look at him. He saw a playful glint in Cara's eyes.

"What are you two up to?"

"Nothing, just making sure you're all right," Cara replied, a hint of mischief in her tone.

"Yes, why wouldn't I be?"

"Just thought you might be tired after all the late nights you've been having?" Cara winked and waited, knowing Scott would be squirming after her loaded question.

Abby smiled as she watched the natural banter between him and Cara. She raised a questioning brow at Scott.

Scott ignored Cara's question. "Guess you've not had a chance to do much yet?"

Cara replied, "No, I'm up shortly. I can give you an initial assessment not long after. On first impression though, it does appear as if he's taken his own life. There's no evidence of other injuries other than a small nick on his cheek, from what I could see, but then again he's hanging from a rope, so my visibility is limited."

"Abby and I will go and have a chat with the lad," Scott said. "There's nothing much for us to do around here at the moment."

Abby breathed a sigh of relief when they stepped out into the warm sunshine once again. She tucked her golden blonde hair behind her ears, smiled, closed her eyes and lifted her face towards the sky.

"What do you make of that, then?" Scott asked.

She didn't move as she pondered the scene.

"Sounds like Cara keeps you busy at night!" She laughed.

"You know what I mean, you cheeky mare."

"Seriously, it does look like he took his own life, and the fact that it's out here and not indoors suggests it was premeditated."

Scott nodded as he entertained his own theories, but Abby had a point. The man certainly hadn't wanted to be discovered.

3

Matthew Edrington sat shaking in the back of the
ambulance. Wrapped in a red hospital blanket,
his chest heaved as he sucked hard on a nebu-
liser. His ginger hair was matted with sweat. His dirty arms
and legs were scabbed with dried blood. His frightened eyes
looked at the officers as they peered in the back.

A woman in a two-piece matching, grey check suit and
white blouse comforted the boy. She had one arm around
Matthew's shoulders, pulling him closer to her. She lightly
dabbed her moist eyes with a tissue.

"I'm Mary Harrison, the deputy head," she announced.

Scott gave her a nod of acknowledgement before turning
his attention to the boy. "Hello, Matthew, I'm Scott." Scott
spoke gently as he held up his warrant card. "This is my
colleague Abby. How are you feeling?"

Matthew shrugged, his small frame making him look
helpless and weak beneath his red shroud.

"Can we ask you a few questions?"

The boy hesitated for a moment before nodding once.

"Did you see anyone else when you found...erm, when

you found the body?" Scott struggled to find the right words without upsetting or alarming the boy any further.

Matthew shook his head once.

"Did you notice anything out of the ordinary or odd as you approached the forest?"

Matthew shook his head again.

"How about when you came out of the forest, anything odd?"

"No." A crackling, muffled reply came from beneath his plastic oxygen mask.

"Well, you've been very brave, and I know what you saw was very upsetting. We'll make sure you're looked after and that your parents are notified." Scott asked Mary Harrison, "I understand that the man was the assistant head of the school. Is that correct?"

"Yes." She nodded weakly.

"And his name?"

"Mr Johnson. Christopher Johnson," she replied.

"I let the house down," Matthew wheezed through deep gasps of air. He glanced at the officers. "I came in last again."

Mary Harrison gave him a sympathetic hug. Her red bloodshot eyes were focused on the police officers. She opened her mouth, about to say something, but then stopped herself. Perhaps she had decided that now was not the best time to be discussing the tragic death of her colleague.

"You'll find Mr Collier, the head, over in the main building."

Scott gave Matthew a reassuring smile before he and Abby left.

"Poor bugger, he's as white as a ghost." Abby sighed.

"That's going to stick with him for a long time; poor lad will need some counselling."

MATT ALLAN, the crime scene manager, caught up with Scott and Abby as they were walking back to their car.

"We've taken the victim down; there are no further visible injuries that we can see other than some swelling to his face. Cause of death looks like strangulation by hanging. We're still sweeping the ground for evidence. The area has been disturbed quite a bit, so we're not sure if that's as a result of the boy, foxes or those who investigated the area before calling it in. Cara will know more. I think the post-mortem is for tomorrow." Matt added, "He had his school ID card on a lanyard in his trouser pocket. It says Christopher Johnson, Assistant Head."

"Well, at least we know who he is," said Scott.

Matt continued, "There's something else worth noting, Scott. In one of his pockets was a folded piece of paper with what looks like Latin written on it...and a white feather," Matt said, holding up a clear plastic evidence bag.

Scott was sure he looked perplexed. "Despite my many talents, I can't admit to being a professor of Latin, so the words would mean nothing to me."

Abby looked equally blank. "Me neither."

Scott nodded. "We'll look at that later, thanks, Matt. Abby, let's head over to the main building to see what's what with the head."

4

S cott couldn't help but admire the magnificent architecture of the Edmunston-Hunt boarding school. Nineteenth-century additions complemented an impressive eighteenth-century Gothic-style grey stone design, added on as the school grew. It was a well-proportioned building set over three floors. Directly over the main entrance was a fifty-foot-high steeple topped with a spire. A large black and gold clock with Roman numerals dominated the frontal aspect of the steeple.

At either end, the building had two large extensions with elegant stained-glass windows. The design had created a horseshoe-shape building. Scott admired its ornate stone features, its early Christian influences apparent.

Scott and Abby exchanged glances as they entered one of the few bastions of elite education. He glanced back at the large green lawns that fronted the school. From what he could see, they were being used as cricket pitches. The lawns were perfectly cut and striped in true British fashion. A distinctive smell of freshly cut grass hung in the air. The setting, the school, the lawns and smell of grass all were quintessentially English in Scott's eyes.

Silence appeared to reign at the school, lending a sense of isolation to the place. For any school, there should have been a bustle of excited children hurrying from one class to another. Nothing but an eerie silence filled the halls as pupils attended class.

"Guv," Abby said, catching Scott's attention. She nodded to the far right-hand side of the building.

A sliver of a man appeared wearing dark blue overalls, carrying a broom in his hand. He was leaning on the top of the broom handle, observing them. Scott couldn't tell if the man was curious or concerned. He studied the man's drooping shoulders and loose, limp arms that hung by his sides. He was a man with short, dark hair that had no particular style, but was neat and tidy. His face was impassive. His lower jaw jutted out farther than usual. The character Bubba in the film *Forrest Gump* sprang to mind. He had a small mouth, and the edges turned down to give him a forlorn appearance.

Even a cursory wave from Scott didn't prompt a reaction. He made a mental note to find out his identity.

The school reception area carried on the dark theme. Dark wood parquet floors stretched in all directions as far as the eye could see. A thin lady wearing a tweed skirt, white blouse and choker chain greeted them. She peered over the top of half-rimmed glasses.

"I'm Mrs Hilary, *senior* receptionist," she said in a refined voice that was clear, crisp and sharp.

Scott smiled as he noticed the intonation in her voice.

"Mr Collier has been expecting you for some time." Mrs Hilary's tone carried an undercurrent of dissatisfaction.

Scott hated being talked down to. There was no need for it. He wondered if she was even capable of being pleasant or welcoming. Mrs Hilary either loved her job too much or thought she ran the school.

"I appreciate your concern, Mrs Hilary. As you must know, we needed to review the scene first. I'm sure even *you* would want to make sure that Matthew, the teenager who found him, was safe and well *before* we spoke to Mr Collier," Scott replied.

Mrs Hilary huffed and led them to the head's office without further comment. Her short, quick steps echoed through the old corridors. A pungent aroma of ancient Asian spices wafted out from the school kitchen. It smelt more like an Indian takeaway than a school. The pupils would no doubt be tucking into a curry of some sort later today.

Abby frowned at the old historic paintings and pieces of artwork on oak panelling. Scott didn't recognise them either. He had no idea what century the paintings belonged to or who the artists were who'd created them.

Scott found it strange that, despite the death of a senior colleague, the head was holed up in his office. He assumed that following such a tragedy, the head might walk the corridors to reassure the pupils and teachers.

Mrs Hilary knocked firmly on the large oak door, which had a gold plaque inscribed with *Mr Collier – Head.*

They entered the room after a sharp "Enter."

"Please come in and take a seat. I'm Adrian Collier, the head."

He was a tall chap with a large frame. He had lost most of his hair, and what little remained was grey-white around the sides and back of his head. His thick, frameless glasses were perched high up on his nose, and his thin lips were straight. He was bland in appearance but smart looking at the same time. His grey, two-piece suit coordinated well with a light blue shirt and matching blue tie.

Scott shook Mr Collier's hand. "I'm Detective Inspector

Baker, and this is Detective Sergeant Trent. We need to ask you a few questions."

"Yes, yes, of course," he said. His firm, deep voice was more befitting of a man from the military than education. He sat behind a large, leather-topped mahogany desk. "Yes, it's a terrible tragedy. It's shocked all of us." He shrugged. "Unfortunately, I haven't got much to add. I'm hoping you can shed some light on what's happened, Inspector. Can I assume he took his own life?"

"We're not at liberty to discuss that at the moment. We are still conducting our preliminary investigation."

"Yes, of course, I understand." Collier rested his elbows on the armrests of his chair, his fingers steepled beneath his chin.

Abby pulled a notepad and pen from her bag and began taking notes.

"What can you tell us about Mr Johnson?" she asked.

Collier paused for a moment, gathering his thoughts. "He was a hard-working, likeable chap. A real grafter, and a stickler for rules and regulations."

"And how did he get on with other staff members?"

"In all my years here he'd never had a major spat with anyone. Of course, when you're working in such close proximity to others, you can sometimes grate on each other's nerves. But I've personally never seen any behaviour that was a cause of concern for me."

"Do you know of any worries that he had?" Abby continued.

Collier shook his head. "Nothing I'm aware of. In my time as head, I haven't seen the staff unburdening their troubles on each other. I guess it's mentality and upbringing...We remain strong and steadfast and deal with our problems in private."

Scott leant in. "Was Mr Johnson in a relationship?"

"He was single as far as I know. He lived on the grounds; we provide staff accommodation, you see. A small row of cottages behind the main building. All staff members are entitled to guests if they're not married. And I do know in the past that Christopher had the odd lady staying over. But that's going back some time now."

"Did he have any financial problems?" asked Scott.

"I'm afraid I wouldn't know, Inspector. That's something you'd need to look into."

"How long had Mr Johnson been working here?"

"Off the top of my head, I think just over five years or so."

"Do you know of any reason why anyone would want to harm him?"

Collier sat up, his body tense. "Are you suggesting that something more untoward is going on here?"

"Not at all, Mr Collier. As part of our investigation, we need to explore all avenues. Personal, professional, financial, and even psychological."

"Well, then my answer is no, Inspector. Let me make it perfectly clear, I run a tight ship here."

"Just one last question," Scott said. "What was his state of mind in the last few days?"

Collier furrowed his brow. "I'm not sure what you're implying. He wasn't weak-minded if that's what you're suggesting. None of my staff are."

"Okay, Mr Collier, you've been very helpful. We need access to his personal file and his cottage."

"That goes without saying. You'll have our full coopera-tion. Mrs Hilary can see to that. I'll inform her." Collier stood up, signalling their meeting was over. "If you make your way back to reception, I'll arrange for her to meet you there."

He showed them out the door, then shut it swiftly behind them.

"Can't quite make him out, guv," Abby said. "He seemed

very matter-of-fact, and a bit blasé at times. Judging by his reaction, you wouldn't think that he'd just lost a member of staff. I'm not being funny, but the deputy head, Mrs Harrison, showed more emotion than that old codger."

Scott thought back to Collier's words: mentality and upbringing. What had that meant?

"Something doesn't sit quite right there," Scott said. "On the one hand he was helpful, but on the other, he knew very little about a senior member of his management team. I think we've only touched the surface with Mr Collier, and I'm certain time will tell us more."

5

Scott's opinion of Mrs Hilary descended fast from tolerable to a pain-in-the-arse battle-axe after she'd left them waiting for fifteen minutes whilst she went in search for the spare keys to Johnson's house. She annoyed Scott further by insisting on accompanying them, commenting that, "I'd hate for anything to go missing," and, "You just don't know who you can trust these days."

A jobsworth was too nice a title for her.

Johnson's property was one of a series of two-bed, three-storey period cottages set back away from the main building on the sprawling estate. Accommodation had been provided for members of staff who didn't live within easy commuting distance. From the outside, the cottages had a quaint look about them. An assorted row of potted plants with ornate Greek-style vases decorated each front.

Clearly, the owners had taken great care in maintaining their homes. The brown brick weathered fronts were suitably maintained. Pristine, white sash window frames with matching windowsills added a symmetry that spanned the block. Each property had a matching stable door, all sporting the traditional racing green colour.

Scott warned Mrs Hilary to stay outside and under no circumstances to enter, lest she disturb possible evidence. The woman glared at him over the top of her glasses perched on the end of her nose. With crossed arms, she shot Scott a scornful look as he and Abby pulled on latex gloves.

The inside of the property was just as impressive and cosy as the outside. It was rich with traditional and contemporary features, with exposed oak ceiling timbers, oak floors, doors and frames. An exposed brick fireplace offered a contrasting look to the plain, white plastered walls.

Johnson appeared to live a tidy life. The ground floor was tidy and functional and perhaps a little impersonal. Absent were any family photos, flowers and ornaments. The bare theme continued throughout the first floor.

Abby searched the ground floor while Scott explored the first and second floor. He found the first bedroom, which had been converted into a study. A bathroom was situated to the right. The top floor of the property housed the second bedroom. Everything appeared to be packed away, neat and tidy. His feet sank into the thick red velvet carpet, which was a style change from the oak floors downstairs.

A faint smell of tobacco hung in the air, instantly transporting him back to when he was a boy. His uncle, who lived around the corner to their family home, used to stuff tobacco in his pipe. Scott had watched in fascination as he used his Swan Vesta matches to light it, then take short, sharp puffs. He'd enjoyed the woody smell. Uncle Tom had been a great storyteller; he'd entertained Scott for hours with stories that rambled on as he puffed on his pipe.

The design of Johnson's study appeared to be the hub of the house. An oversized desk had been piled high with student workbooks, notes and random pieces of paper that left very little working space. A well-worn metal ashtray on the red leather surface was half-full, and an unfinished glass of red wine sat beside it.

Scott cast his gaze around the room, looking for any evidence of anything untoward that may have been the precursor to Johnson taking his life. An open laptop was perched precariously on the edge of the desk; its screen was blank. A bright orange power light gave the only indication that the laptop was still on.

"Nothing down there, guv," Abby said as she walked into the study. "I couldn't find a phone downstairs, but there's the usual collection of bills and receipts on the kitchen table. I bagged them up to look at later. The back door is unlocked though. Perhaps he felt a degree of security and privacy here on the school grounds that he didn't lock his doors?"

"I didn't think you'd find much down there. It looks like Johnson spent most of his time in here," Scott replied, glancing around the room. "I need you to bag up that laptop, and the wine glass and bottle; we need to get them to forensics." There was a suit jacket on Johnson's chair. He fished around for a few seconds, then pulled out Johnson's wallet. It contained an assortment of credit cards and bank cards, plus a driving licence.

As he peered into the notes compartment, he counted two twenty-pound notes and a ten-pound note. But also there were three pieces of paper, neatly folded. He inspected each one in turn.

"Looks like Johnson was in a relationship." Scott passed the notes to Abby.

Abby read aloud, raising her brow. "'You make me feel so alive and wanted. Can't wait to see you again. My body is aching for you. S xx.'"

"That's kind of you to say, Abby. I didn't know you felt that way about me," Scott replied with humour.

"In your dreams, mate," she fired back, sticking two fingers in her mouth and pretending to gag.

"The other two notes are signed off in the same way," Scott added. He made a mental note to bring the signatory up with the head next time they met. "We could do with tracking down who this person is. They might be able to shed some light on his final few hours and his life in general."

Scott placed the wallet and notes into a clear evidence bag.

"I don't see a phone anywhere," he said, looking around.

He walked over to the grand bookcase that filled one wall. It was obvious that the majority of Johnson's books hadn't been used in a long time. The spines were worn, tatty and cracked, but it was the thin layer of dust that indicated they had not been moved for a while. Scott ran his finger along one shelf, and a pile of dust collected on it.

Abby rooted through the first drawer of a grey filing cabinet in the corner. "Most of the files contain the performance records of various students he taught," she said. "A few other folders contain invoices for purchases, but the rest of the filing cabinet is empty."

"Wait a sec..." Abby knelt down by the small space between the filing cabinet and the wall. "Found it."

She pulled out a phone that was connected to a charging cable.

"That's handy. The phone's on, and there's no screen lock." She scrolled through the text messages. "The mysterious S seems to have had the hots for our man. There are dozens of messages on here, and some of them are X-rated enough to make a nun blush. Judging from some of them, she was a frequent visitor here."

"Even more reason to find her," Scott said.

"Back to the office, guv?"

"Yes. Let's get a briefing organised."

They returned to the car.

Just as Scott was about to drive off, he noticed the caretaker they had seen earlier. He was slouched against the wall and was slowly puffing on a cigarette. He didn't move, and his eyes were firmly fixed on them.

He kept watching as Scott turned the car around and headed for the main entrance.

Scott glanced in his rear-view mirror and saw the man turn and walk away.

6

The late afternoon sun poured through the windows, making the briefing room decidedly uncomfortable. The air conditioning had broken down some time ago, and attempts to repair it were being delayed due to the station's refurbishment programme. In the meantime, it meant that any meetings were held in a stuffy hot room with the pungent smell of *eau de BO*.

Scott's team had convened around the large oval table. Raj and Mike had both loosened their top buttons and their ties and rolled up their sleeves. Mike seemed to be suffering the most, his face a tomato red with beads of sweat on his forehead.

Raj had brought in a packet of chocolate Bourbon biscuits, which were welcomed by all.

"Okay, the victim is a Christopher Johnson, age forty-five." Scott pinned a picture of Johnson to the briefing board, adding his name, age and title alongside it. "He was the assistant head at Edmunston-Hunt boarding school for five years. You've hopefully all seen the body cam images Abby relayed back to the office?"

Scott waited for a collective agreement from those around the table. Whether it was the heat causing the lethargy or the time of day, his team appeared a little flat and unengaged. He took their lack of response as a general agreement and pushed on.

"Did you glean anything from the school?" enquired Mike.

"Not as much as we would have liked, Mike. We spoke to Mr Collier, the head, and he wasn't able to shed much light on Johnson. Sorry, let me rephrase that, he either wasn't able to shed much light or wasn't willing to, in my opinion. I got the impression he was being economical with the truth. That's my hunch anyway," Scott added, "According to Mr Collier, Johnson didn't have any pressing worries or concerns around his job, money or relationships. His mental health appeared good. He was a grafter and a well-trusted member of staff, so it's a bit of a mystery."

"I've checked his history, guv," Raj added. "He had been with the school for five years. Promoted after one year to assistant head whilst also being the housemaster for Ditchling. I'm still doing a bit more digging around on him."

Scott wrote the extra information on the whiteboard. "Abby and I will speak to the other teachers at the school to find out a bit more about our man. I've also got a few more questions to ask the head. Sian and Mike, as we left, the head gave us permission to speak to the pupils in Ditchling House. Find out what type of man Johnson was. Kids have a habit of saying more than they are supposed to."

Scott crossed his arms and looked at the picture of Johnson staring back at him. It was a formal photograph taken as part of the staff photos. He was standing side-on, head to the camera, against a backdrop of an external brick wall. The formality of his grey suit, light blue shirt, and yellow tie were offset by a slight, but friendly smile. He still had a full head of dark hair, but it was receding with age.

What was so bad in your life that you needed to do this?

"The forensics team found a piece of paper with Latin words on it as well as a white feather in his pocket," Scott continued. "Raj, can you translate it for me? Try Google to begin with. Latin can be interpreted in different ways, and considering that it's evidential material, I'd also suggest touching base with someone at Sussex University. Start with the languages department. We need someone who can decipher this for us accurately."

Raj nodded and brushed biscuit crumbs off his notepad before writing down Scott's instructions.

The low vibration of Abby's phone on the table interrupted Scott's train of thought. The interruption and subsequent attention caused her cheeks to redden. She looked at him apologetically, fumbling with her phone.

Before she had time to do that, the phone signalled the arrival of another message. Scott raised an eyebrow at her, passing on an *I expect better of you* look.

She mouthed *sorry*.

Scott turned to Raj. "Check in with the high-tech unit. We need to pull all phone records from Johnson's phone and identify multiple callers. My guess is someone called S will be one of his most frequent callers. I found several messages in his wallet, and they weren't any old messages. They appeared to be love notes, which were pretty racy in places."

Mike wolf-whistled. Those around the table smiled.

"Mike, grow up, will you?" Scott said sharply. Mike sat up straighter, having been put back in his place. "As much as you'd like the goings-on between Johnson and this mysterious person to descend to a laddish level, they could be vital to our investigation. Given that this seems to have tickled you the most, find out what you can about this mysterious S. See if there are any other teachers with a name beginning with S."

"I presume that could be male or female?" Mike replied.

"That's a fair assumption, but in this case it's likely female, unless you know of a man who likes to wear heels and stockings? See what you can dig up from Johnson's past. We know he was probably seeing someone, but what about past relationships? Was he married at one time? Any acrimonious splits?"

Sian raised her pen, a look of concentration on her face. "What did the pathologist and forensic team conclude at the scene regarding the method of death?"

"We won't know until the post-mortem is over tomorrow morning. At the moment, we believe it was strangulation by hanging. The loose end of the rope had been tied around the base of the tree. Its position seems to suggest he went to great lengths to ensure that when he jumped off the branch, he would hang just a few inches above the ground."

Sian grimaced. "You'd have to be pretty determined to go through with something like that." "You'd have to have some pretty heavy shit going on in your life to string yourself up."

It was a thought that had crossed Scott's mind too.

"That's what we need to find out. He could have had money worries, personal relationship issues, a terminal illness or even a mental health illness." That last point brought Scott to another avenue of research. "Sian, get banking details, a full job history and medical records. His doctor's records could help us eliminate or determine if terminal illness or depression had a part to play in his death."

"Aren't we going into a lot of detail for what could be a straightforward suicide?" Sian asked.

"We have to cover every possibility here, Sian. We don't know enough yet to conclude that he took his own life. We didn't find a suicide note."

Scott mulled over another theory as his eyes flitted around the room, processing what he'd seen at the crime scene plus subsequent conversations.

"Care to share what's on your mind, guv?" Abby prompted.

Scott thought for a moment, biting his bottom lip and tapping his temple with two fingers. "The scene that we saw this morning was perfectly plausible, but...there was something about the way the rope was positioned that didn't sit right with me. Call it a gut feeling."

The vagueness of his reply only seemed to stir up more curiosity.

"Okay, let's get to work first thing tomorrow," Scott said. "Get home and get an early night. I'm stopping in to brief DCI Harvey now."

ABBY SWITCHED her phone on once they were back in the corridor. She hissed as her beeping phone signalled the arrival of one message after another. She began scrolling through them, not paying much attention to where she was going. Her concentration was interrupted when she collided with another officer coming out of an office.

Her phone flew out of her hand. "I'm so sorry," she said, smiling and blushing.

Scott picked up her phone and handed it to her. "Seriously, what is it with you and your phone? You're up to something, I can tell."

She couldn't hide it from Scott. He'd find out sooner or later.

"Don't laugh, but I took your advice. I joined Match.com. Now my phone won't stop. The amount of email alerts I'm getting from guys on there is crazy."

Scott raised a brow. "Welcome to the twenty-first century. You've finally taken the plunge into the whole internet dating thing?"

"Yeah. I've not met anyone yet, but I've been chatting to a few guys online. Just as I thought, I'm getting lots of pictures of knobs. Don't get me wrong, some guys have been really nice to chat with, but for some reason a percentage of males seem to think that the way to open a conversation with someone is to send them a picture of their cock." She rolled her eyes. "No wonder they're bloody single."

Scott grimaced. "Seriously, blokes do that?"

"Yep. I'll show you if you want?"

Scott turned and walked in the opposite direction, raising his hand in the air. "Erm...I'll pass on that. I'll leave you with that pleasure."

As Scott ducked through the back door, headed for his car, his phone pinged. It was Abby.

I've got a date tonight with Phil. He's an electrician. What happens if he doesn't like me? Wish me luck!

Scott shook his head. *Glass half-empty, Abby.*

———————

7

Sounds of nocturnal life broke the silence of the night. The eerie and distinctive sound of an owl perched high up in the trees was sending a wave of panic through the small rodents in the forest. The predator watched and observed, on high alert for any movement that could suggest a possible meal.

In the Stanmer House dormitory, eight boys slept. The only sound to break the stillness was the occasional creak of a bed as someone turned to get more comfortable, or a fart under the covers.

The dormitory door opened, and three boys entered. Just like the owl, three sets of eyes locked onto their prey. They too preferred to hunt at night, taking their victim by surprise, using stealth to attack.

They circled the bed of Matthew Edrington, waiting for the right moment to attack. He was fast asleep, his bedding pulled tight up around his neck, cocooned to keep him warm and cosy. A luxury that would soon be shattered.

James Rollings gave the other two a nod. Tobias Ford ripped the bedcovers away and Stephen Hunter gripped

Matthew's neck, pinning the boy to the bed. He jolted awake in terror, but Hunter's grip muted any noise from his mouth.

Fear gripped Matthew's body; his heart threatened to explode as he gasped for breath. He thrashed and fought, trying to dislodge the strong, powerful hands from his neck. Despite his bravest efforts, he couldn't free himself. He was weak; he'd always known that. His mind spun out of control as a lack of air blurred his vision and muddied his thoughts.

As his hopes of surviving slipped away, the crushing weight on his windpipe eased. Hunter and Ford dragged Matthew out of bed, each grabbing an arm, and dumped him face first on the floor. Matthew lay in shock, not quite comprehending what had just happened. His conscious mind fought hard to make sense of everything.

Hunter ground Matthew's face into the floor and sat hard on the boy's back, expelling the air from his lungs. He pinned Matthew down with a knee to his spine. Lightning bolts of pain raced up and down his back, causing Matthew to wince.

Ford threw a pillowcase over Matthew's face, robbing him of what little sight he had in the dark, and turned him over. Rollings, who up until this point had been directing the assault, kicked Matthew in the stomach. The pain erupted through Matthew's entire body. He drew his legs up into a foetal position, hoping they would offer some degree of protection.

His assailants said nothing as their punches and kicks rained down on his body. Matthew winced and threw his arms up around his head to shield himself. He pulled his body as tight as he could into a protective ball, but he wasn't strong enough to repel his attackers.

The attack only lasted a few seconds but felt like minutes. His body ached. Rollings knelt over Matthew, who was face down again, and pinned Matthew's neck to the floor.

He leant in close. "You lost our house the race...you

pussy," he hissed. "You're a waste of space. There's no room here for weak, pathetic girls like you. Man up or else..." He slapped the back of Matthew's head.

Matthew fought the bile that crawled up into his throat, his mouth filled with saliva, and his jaw ached from clenching it too tight. Now his cheek stung, burning red hot.

There was a dead silence around him. The boys had released him, but had not left – of that he was sure. *But what now?* Dread filled his racing mind when he heard trouser zips being undone.

His pyjamas, wet from the three assailants urinating on him, clung to his skin. They laughed. The ammonia smell invaded his nostrils, and he gagged.

Underneath their hostile gazes, his fragile confidence and self-esteem ebbed away even more.

THE MAN PACED NERVOUSLY in the dark, waiting for the others to turn up. The gravel beneath his feet felt firm and uncomfortable. The ornamental gardens, the product of many years of dedicated care and attention from resident gardeners and groundsmen, were a place that offered him quiet and solitude. It was a sanctuary he escaped to often.

The light from the moon allowed him to see what surrounded him. The rusty creaking wrought-iron gates opening drew his attention, followed by the sound of people walking. Three men came into view.

"You took your bloody time, didn't you?" he barked at them. "I know one or two of you are concerned by what happened to Johnson." He stared at one particular man who seemed slightly inebriated. The smell of whiskey hung in the air. He glanced at each man in turn. "But we have remained steadfast and resolute for many years. We all swore to keep this buried and keep our mouths shut. At the moment, we have no evidence to suggest it was anything more than Johnson bottling out and taking the easy route."

The men mumbled amongst themselves, shifting nervously, staring at the ground, and kicking at the gravel.

The drunken one, perhaps buoyed by the alcohol in his system, chose to speak out. "I don't like this. I don't like this one bit. You made it very clear that this problem would go away."

How dare he challenge my authority?

The man stepped forward and came nose to nose with the drunken visitor.

His jaw clenched, and he seethed. "Let me make it very clear to you. I will not tolerate dissent in the ranks. You listen to me and no one else. Do I make myself clear?"

The drunken visitor trembled. He clenched his fists and breathed in and out rapidly. "Okay, I admit it. I admit I'm scared. What happens if someone's found out?"

"No one is going to find out. No one is going to open their mouths. We are all going to act normal," he said, looking at the three men in turn. "And you are going to stop drinking." He poked the chest of the inebriated man. "Your tongue is far too loose, especially when you've had a drink. I will not tolerate that. If anyone steps out of line, they could wind up like Johnson. Do I make myself clear?"

The threat hung like a heavy rain cloud overhead. The men nodded, turned and headed off in different directions. The three visitors knew that it wasn't a veiled threat but a consequence. And they'd do well to remember it.

8

Laurence Goddard unlocked his front door before stumbling in and resting against the wall in his hallway. His head was pounding and spinning wildly.

He fought hard to focus, but his eyes wouldn't let him. Everything appeared blurred, hazy, and off-balance. The sidelamp seemed to defy gravity as it tilted to one side, and the banister newel post lurched as he reached for it to steady himself. He needed another drink. Whether his body could tolerate another was a different matter.

He walked slowly, dragging his feet on the floor, as if they were weighed down. The drinks cabinet came into view. He jerked his head back in surprise when he saw two cabinets.

"I'm sure I didn't have two before," he said as he grabbed a bottle of Jack Daniel's and ripped the stopper from its neck.

A hefty glug of whiskey shocked his taste buds and set his mouth alight. The harsh liquid burned a fire trail down to his empty stomach.

He couldn't remember the last time he'd eaten, breakfast maybe?

Goddard scrunched up his face as his throat continued to

burn. He squeezed his eyes shut as he waited for the usual soothing sensation to replace the gritty feeling he felt inside. He ran a hand through his brown, receding hair.

The warmth of the alcohol built from deep within, a burning ember that rippled out from his core, leaving a sensation that soothed him.

Damn bitch.

His moment of contentment was short-lived as his thoughts turned to *her*.

He despised her. Hated the sight of her face.

Goddard looked at the ceiling, his bedroom directly above. He wasn't even sure she'd heard him come in, her sleeping pills no doubt taking her to a land of bliss and ignorance. His eyes narrowed, and his jaw clenched tight. His breaths came short and sharp. He took one more gulp of whiskey before slamming the bottle down hard on the dining table.

The house was quiet, but his mind throbbed and ached as if the London Philharmonic Orchestra played Mahler Symphony No. 5 at maximum volume to annoy him. He groaned as he took one stair at a time, ascending into the darkness of the upstairs landing.

His bedroom door was closed.

Fucking bitch, you fat fucking bitch.

Goddard staggered into the room, his eyes searching out the figure that lay under the duvet and in *his* bed. Anger seeped from every pore; his teeth ground together as his temper reached fever pitch.

He tumbled onto the bed, grabbing his wife's hair. The assault shocked her awake.

"Get up, you silly bitch!" he yelled, his eyes wide with aggression.

"Please stop!"

Samantha Goddard's pleas fell on deaf ears.

"Shut the fuck up. You make me want to puke. You don't think I know what you're up to."

He sneered as he cupped her neck and pulled her face within inches of his. His alcohol-infused breath forced her to look away. "Don't turn your face when I'm talking to you. You whore. Look at you, dressing up in short skirts, tight tops, flaunting yourself. You make me sick. Do you hear me?... Sick!" He slapped her across her face, sending her crashing to the floor.

He glared at his wife, her arm protecting her head as Goddard stood over her.

"You're not my wife, do you hear me? You never have been," he replied, punching her in the face. "It was the biggest mistake I ever made marrying you. I can't cope with you and that stuff. It's killing me!"

He gripped his head. Anger seethed, and he hit her again.

The blow sent her sprawling across the bedroom floor. He watched as she dragged herself to the corner of her bedroom and wedged herself between the bed and wall, cowering as tears turned to a whimpering cry.

He sneered at her in disgust before he turned and stormed out of the bedroom.

Goddard returned to the lounge and collapsed into the armchair.

His hand stung; his knuckles and ego were bruised.

He eyed the bottle of Jack Daniel's.

Jack was his friend. Jack was whom he turned to when darkness closed in. Knowing what he knew felt like a life sentence – an imaginary weight around his neck dragging him down. Frustrated, he repeatedly banged his head into the cushioned back of the armchair.

I can't do this anymore, I can't.

He silently screamed deep inside his dark, distorted mind.

Jack would know what to do; Jack *always* knew how to take his pain away.

He took another large mouthful and let it burn a trail through him. He closed his eyes and leant back. Jack took over, taking him to a place where no one could hurt or blame him.

9

A bby pulled up alongside Scott's car in the mortuary car park. He greeted her with an exaggerated grin as he stepped out. The early morning sun was bright and warm, causing him to squint.

"Morning, how was Phil? Did sparks fly between you?" He winked, looking pleased with his attempt at humour.

Abby shot him a glance. "Really? Is that the best you can do?"

"Well, come on, spill the beans. Did he manage to thaw the ice maiden?"

"You make me sound like some frigid old woman," she replied, playfully punching him on the arm. She wagged a finger at him. "Choose your next words carefully, sonny Jim."

"Seriously, how did it go?"

Abby shrugged. "It was okay. A bit awkward to start but a pleasant enough evening."

"Your *excitement* is bubbling out of every pore, Abby." He laughed. "I used to date a female electrician; she was shocking in bed." Scott roared with laughter.

Abby groaned. "Oh my word, they get worse. Don't give up the day job."

"Why did Mr Ohm marry Mrs Ohm?" Scott asked, desperate to crack another joke. Not waiting for an answer, he continued, "Because he couldn't resistor. Get it? Resist her?" Scott rocked his head back, chuffed with his latest jokes, his shoulders shaking.

"So pathetic, so, so pathetic," Abby replied, shaking her head in disbelief.

THE OFFICERS KITTED up in face masks before joining Cara, the pathologist, who was well advanced with the post-mortem examination of Christopher Johnson. Scott had only seen Cara a few hours ago after she'd spent the night at his, but he was pleased to see her once again.

She was definitely having a positive effect on his life. The grief he'd experienced, the loss of his family, had taken him to dark places; he'd sunk to new lows and contemplated his own existence. Much of this he'd kept buried from others. It had been a lonely and desolate journey that appeared to have no final destination.

Cara had brought light back into his life. He welcomed her balancing influence; he cherished her support and energy that had rescued him from the precipice.

A sharp cold enveloped the examination room. The faint whirring of the air conditioning slowed down body decomposition. That in itself sent cold shivers down Scott's back, and the hairs on his neck stood up. The white and cream tiled floor and walls added to the blandness and lack of warmth that made the room so unwelcoming.

Johnson's body looked like a pasty off-white rubber

mannequin that the medical students used to practise their dissection skills.

The cadaver lay on the first of three tables in the mortuary. Scott recognised Cara's assistant Neil from his last visit. Neil stood on one side of the table, peering over the cadaver, holding a silver specimen tray, whilst Cara undertook her detailed examination opposite him.

Neil looked up as Scott and Abby approached, pushing his thick-framed glasses back up the bridge of his nose and acknowledging them with a friendly nod and smile.

Cara glanced up, offering them a small smile, which lingered on Scott for a few moments. "Morning... You got here a little late, unfortunately. I've got a lot on today, so started on Johnson earlier than I anticipated."

"That's not a problem. We've got a lot on too. We just need the summary points so far," Scott replied as he visually inspected the cadaver.

Johnson's body had been opened up in the formal Y formation. His internal organs had been removed for sizing, weighing and analysis, and some were sitting on the metal bench at the back of the examination room, ready for closer inspection. His face was a shade of blotchy red from where blood had become trapped and tiny blood capillaries had burst. His face was slightly swollen, with thick puckering of the skin beneath his jaw.

"Well, at first I thought this was a straightforward suicide when I inspected the body at the scene, but there were a few discrepancies that concerned me."

"Really?" Abby asked.

"Yes." Cara moved back to the neck region. "Let me give you a bit of background to cases like this. When a body is suspended, like a short-drop death in this case, the weight of the body tightens the rope around the trachea and neck structure. The person experiences some degree of struggle before they go limp and reach an unconscious state, because their jugular vein and carotid arteries are blocked and blood flow to the brain is reduced. However, the person dies slowly of strangulation, usually over the course of several minutes, and in some cases up to fifteen minutes."

Cara continued with her feedback. "This results in a considerably longer and more painful death compared to what we call a long-drop hanging, which is intended to kill by using the shock of the initial drop to fracture the spinal column at the neck. Normally in long drops, there'd be evidence of a dislocation of the C_2 and C_3 vertebrae that crushes the spinal cord and/or disrupts the vertebral arteries. There's no evidence of dislocation in this instance.

"If the airway is constricted and full suspension achieved, by that I mean their feet are fully off the floor, this method, at least initially, is likely to be very painful. The person struggles for air against the compression of the noose and against the weight of their own body being supported entirely by the neck and jaw. It's a pretty horrible way to go, to be honest."

"You said you felt there were discrepancies in this case?" Scott reminded her.

"Erm...yes. I'll get on to that in a bit. Let me finish my lesson, Scottie."

Abby bowed her head to stifle her laugh.

Scott held up his hands in mock surrender.

"The neck of a hanging victim is usually marked with furrows where the ligature has constricted the neck. An inverted V mark is also often seen. And we have both in this case." Cara confirmed by pointing to the thick red line beneath the jaw. "There's also some evidence of petechiae, which is purple spotting. This is clearly seen in places on his face due to broken or burst capillary blood vessels." She pointed that out with a thin metal spike that resembled a metal toothpick.

"Coming back to your question, Scott, yes, we have ligature marks under the larynx and the presence of significant injury to the skin of the neck. But my suspicions grew when I noticed under a magnifier, scratch marks on the ligature, and lots of scratch marks on the skin either side of the ligature mark in various places around the neck."

"What does that mean?" asked Scott.

"If I had to make a more concrete assessment, it looks like he was frantically trying to pull the rope away from his neck."

"Do you reckon he started to go through with it and then changed his mind?" Scott suggested.

Cara nodded. "That's plausible. He may have intended to go through with it and then tried to stop, but it was too late."

"You said at first, Cara...?" Abby interrupted. "You found something else, didn't you?"

"Yes. My suspicions grew because I also found bruising to the skin on his face, stomach, and knees," Cara replied, looking at Abby.

"Recent?"

"Yes. And something else I spotted whilst at the scene. There were distinct, long scuff marks on the ground beneath the victim. I asked forensics to look a bit closer at that. And there was a second disturbed area of ground a few feet away that Matt pointed out to me. The foliage had been scraped away, exposing the earth beneath it."

"What do you think caused that? Foxes?" Scott suggested. "Like they were scratching on the forest floor?"

"Perhaps. Or scuff marks from shoes trying to touch the floor? Just a thought."

Scott and Abby shot a glance at each other. There was a new angle to the case now.

10

Scott ordered the eggs royale, and Abby ordered a coffee. Moksha Caffé was another favourite haunt of Scott's. He enjoyed going there on a Sunday morning and tucking into a cooked breakfast whilst leisurely enjoying a cup of their fresh, locally sourced filter coffee.

He'd spent many hours people watching there. He was fascinated by human interaction and would try to figure out people's personalities and character traits simply by watching from a distance. Often, he'd smile to himself as he determined who was the extrovert or introvert amongst couples, who was visual or kinaesthetic, or who was confident or not.

Abby turned her nose up when Scott's food arrived. "How can you eat after a PM? You astound me every time. I can just about stomach the coffee." She sipped from her cup.

"As I said, a man's gotta eat," he replied, shovelling in a large mouthful.

Abby looked away. "Cara's findings put the death in a new light, eh? More questions than answers?"

Wiping his mouth with a napkin, Scott replied, "Mmm, yes, it does. We need to look into Johnson's background in a bit more detail. We need to find out what was going on in his life, personally and professionally. I definitely think Collier knows more than he's letting on. As each minute passes, it becomes more of a suspicious death."

Abby nodded, cupping her coffee and pulling it close to her body.

"So, sparky...you going to see him again?" Scott teased.

Abby smiled. "I'm not sure. He texted me this morning to say he'd had a nice time. He's got a son aged fourteen, so between his job and seeing his son, he doesn't have much free time. Besides, it's early days. I might be brave enough to face a few more first dates if some of the other profiles look good." She shrugged. "Their pictures and what they look like in reality are two completely different things."

"They might be thinking the same about you." He winked.

"You cheeky git." Abby threw her scrunched-up napkin at him.

THE TOURIST CROWD was already starting to pack out the seafront. The roads around the Old Steine were coming to a standstill as parking spaces became rarer than shit from a rocking horse. Thankfully for Scott and Abby, they were able to circumnavigate the tourist traffic by taking the back roads to the office.

On returning to the office, they made a detour via the canteen to grab an extra couple of bottles of water. It had been a warm morning. Despite the mortuary offering a coolness and respite from the heat, the short journey back to the office had left them feeling decidedly hot and bothered.

As they queued up now, Abby nudged Scott in the ribs and pointed over her shoulder. Scott turned to look.

Tucked away in the corner of the canteen, he spotted Mike in deep conversation with a female officer. Scott could tell by his body language that Mike was either more than friends with her or wanted to be more than friends. He had his jacket slung over the back of the chair, his tie undone, his sleeves rolled up. He was clearly on a charm offensive. The female officer rocked back in her chair, laughing, covering her mouth in embarrassment.

"Looks like Mike is eyeing up his next unsuspecting victim," Abby said, rolling her eyes. "He really does have his brains in his pants. He's such a lech. When you're in the middle of a conversation with him, he can't help looking at the backside of every woman who walks past, *even* if you're looking him right in the eye. Worst still, he always talks to your boobs, especially if he's interested in you. And to top it off, if he's walking behind a woman, he's always staring at her arse."

On this occasion he agreed with Abby. As far as he could recall, just in the past six months alone Mike had dated – if they could be called dates – two female officers and a civilian support officer. For some reason, they always fell for his charms. However, the novelty usually faded within a few weeks. It wasn't long before they got to see the real Mike.

"Poor cow, you'll have to try to warn her," Scott said with a laugh.

Abby was just about to reply when Scott's phone rang. He grabbed the phone from his pocket and smiled when he saw Cara's number.

"Hey there, what's up?" His face became serious for a moment as he listened to Cara. "Listen, listen, calm down. Did you see or hear anything?" he asked before falling silent again.

Abby had an inquisitive look on her face.

Scott raised a hand to ask Abby to wait a minute.

"Just stay put. I'll pop back over. See you in a bit." Scott hung up. "Listen, Abby, can you hold the fort for half an hour? I just need to pop back to the mortuary."

"What's up? Development in the case?"

"No, Cara's car has been vandalised in the mortuary car park. She's in a right state."

11

Giles Rochester was home alone, quietly working through some new course notes. He'd had a usual run-of-the-mill day at school. Students had been a tad unruly for his liking, and staff members had huddled in their small groups in the staff common room, talking about England's result in the test series against their formidable enemy Australia. From his recollection, it had certainly provoked a heated debate about the whys and wherefores of the England team's tactics.

Despite being in close proximity around his colleagues most days, he preferred his own company whilst in the staffroom. He'd sit in a solitary chair in the corner of the room closest to the ornate bookshelves that were set into the walls at right angles. Whilst his colleagues often sat in a circle on low, high-back chairs, the fabric of which had been worn away many years ago to leave a dull shine and imprints of various sizes.

While Rochester was lost in thoughts, the intruder entered through the back of the house via the kitchen. He left a length of rope on the kitchen table. At the same time he picked up Rochester's car keys, knowing that they would come in handy later. Slowly, he made his way through the house, careful to avoid any creaking floorboards.

Upstairs in the study, he peered in and saw Rochester, his next target, quietly sitting at his desk. But he was sitting side-on to him, which meant he couldn't creep up from behind as he had done with his first victim. He'd have to rush this one, hoping the element of surprise would give him the upper hand.

The intruder burst through the door, rushing towards his intended target. His action jolted Rochester out of his semi-daydream. He reeled back in his chair as the masked intruder bore down on him. The intruder pinned him back by his throat.

The intruder's fingers felt like steel clasps as they gripped Rochester's neck, closing off his windpipe.

Gasps of breath mixed with spittle exploded from his mouth. Rochester's face reddened, the veins in his neck bulging as the tourniquet-like grip tightened.

His mind swirled in confusion in his fight to comprehend what was happening. His eyes widened in fear. The bala-clava-covered face of his assailant came closer to his own. Dark brown, angry eyes glared at him through a slit in the fabric.

Rochester caught a glint of a steel blade. If his assailant was trying to terrify him, then he had achieved his goal.

His stomach knotted in fear, and his eyes bulged as the pressure built in his head, drowning out any noise around him.

"I...I...c-can't b-breathe," he managed to squeeze out as he pulled hard on his assailant in a desperate attempt to fight him off.

The intruder loosened his grip slightly as he inched

closer to his victim. "I've been waiting for this for a long time," he said in a slow, deliberate voice.

"I...d-don't know w-what you mean?" Rochester stuttered in reply. "Waiting for what? Who are you? P-please...Please don't h-hurt me."

"It's too late for that. You're coming with me." He grabbed Rochester by the arm and jabbed the tip of his blade into the man's jaw, careful not to pierce the skin.

Rochester demanded, finding his voice, "Now listen here, I'm not going anywhere with you. I don't know what you think I've done. This has to stop right now."

Enraged by Rochester's demand, the intruder said, "I'm not looking to hurt you. I just want a friendly chat. That's all."

You've got a cheek to think we will play by your rules.

Rochester paused for a second; he stared at the hooded assailant, confusion in his eyes.

"Hold on a moment. I'm sure I recognise that voice." His mind raced, desperate to make the connection and join the dots. His eyes widened once more as he stared into the eyes of his assailant. "Yes...Yes, it's you. But why –"

Before he had time to finish the sentence, his assailant pushed him violently through the doorway of the study. The knife was firmly pressed between his shoulders. As Rochester was marched down the stairs, he struggled to keep his balance. The intruder shoved him through the house and out the kitchen door, into the semi-darkness.

"Don't mutter a word, or I'll slice your innards out here on the grass," the assailant whispered, being careful not to attract unwanted attention.

He threw Rochester up against the silver VW Golf, continuing to pin him in place with the knife whilst reaching in his pocket for the car keys. Throwing the keys on the roof of the car, he demanded that Rochester drive.

"This isn't my car," he tried to bluff.

"Don't take me for an idiot... I want you to get in the car. I'm going to sit right behind you in the back seat, and you are going to do everything I say – understand?"

Giles Rochester nodded slowly as his shaking hand grabbed the car keys. His thumb trembled as he tried to unlock the car in the dark. He finally pressed the button, two pulses of orange lights confirming his success.

Rochester was forcibly pushed into the driver's seat, and the assailant quickly slid into the back. In a split second, he wrapped white plastic packaging tape around Rochester's neck. He pulled it tight, startling Rochester and forcing the man's head back into the headrest, pinning him in position.

"Drive to Teville Gate car park in Worthing," the assailant instructed.

Rochester hesitated for a moment. "What...? Why?"

The assailant tugged a little harder on the plastic tape as a warning. The sharp edges of the tape cut into Rochester's skin, creating a sharp stinging pain.

"Shut up and drive."

12

They travelled in silence as they made their way to Worthing. Giles nervously glanced in his rear-view mirror, but at this time of night there were very few cars on the road. His grip on the steering tightened as fear churned inside him, turning his knuckles so white.

His eyes darted left and right, hoping he might see a police car. But what good would that do? Short of driving straight into them, he had no other way of attracting attention. Each time he tried to drive erratically to attract attention, the assailant had tightened the plastic tape around his neck as a warning.

Teville Gate car park was an isolated spot close to Worthing rail station. Set behind industrial offices and nondescript small factory buildings, it was the last place Giles wanted to end up.

It was an urban, grey concrete monument empty at night. Giles was forced to drive to the third level. He passed by graffiti tags on the walls.

On the third level, he stopped. The assailant dragged him from the car and pushed him hard against the white railings.

Giles avoided the discarded needles and condoms scattered on the ground. The stomping ground for teenagers and drug addicts, who left regular calling cards. He tried not to breathe in the overpowering smell of urine.

His ribs stung as the metal rail dug into his back. The tip of a knife was positioned beneath his jaw, ensuring he remained firmly rooted to the spot. Giles reached out and grabbed the cold steel of the railing. His eyes were fixed wide in terror. His body shook violently beneath the eerie, bright glow of the strip lights.

"I've waited a long time for this," the hooded man said in a slow drawl. "I've counted down the days, just waiting to finally say what I wanted to say."

The smell of the man's stale breath assaulted Giles's nostrils; his chest heaved.

He shook his head in bewilderment. "I don't understand. What have I done wrong?"

"Everything. You let it happen. You knew about it for all these years, but you've remained silent. You're nothing more than a coward." The man hissed and grabbed Giles by the throat, then leaned him over the railing.

Giles shook his head violently, still unable to comprehend. His eyes bulged as the man's grip pressed down hard on his windpipe.

"Nancy boy," he uttered. "Remember that?"

It took Giles a few moments to process the words as his mind raked over the years, recalling all the times, places, and situations in his life.

And then somewhere deep within the recesses of his dark mind, he latched onto the elusive memory. He brought his gaze slowly to the hooded assailant. Their eyes connected, and in the silence that prevailed, silent words were shared.

That was all the hooded man needed, and with a final push, he shoved Giles over the railings.

Giles grappled for the edge in a vain attempt to save himself. His chilling screams echoed around the quiet car park as he fell to the ground. His guttural scream was soon silenced by the concrete.

The hooded assailant didn't bother looking over the edge. He turned and walked towards the stairwell, taking his time to reach the lower level. The adrenaline coursed heavily through his veins as sweat beaded on his forehead. He was pleased with his work.

He stood over the mangled body of Giles Rochester. The man's arms and legs were contorted in a gruesome manner. A shiny pall of liquid darkness grew around his head. It glinted in the moonlit night sky.

He felt no remorse; he felt no anger. *This fucker got what was coming to him.*

He crouched next to the twisted body with a morbid curiosity, his eyes assessing the mangled mess. In silence he gave an assured nod, pleased with his end result.

Before leaving, he placed a small scrap of paper and a white feather in the man's trouser pocket.

Then his footsteps faded into silence in the dark night.

13

S cott groaned as he was awakened by his phone rattling and vibrating on his bedside cabinet. Today for some reason he was feeling tired. Yesterday, everyone seemed to want a piece of his time. He'd spent several hours in the afternoon trying to reassure Cara that all would be fine after her Ford Focus had been vandalised.

Although the nature of the damage had raised some suspicion in Scott's mind, he hadn't shared his thoughts with Cara. The last thing he wanted was her freaking out even more. Both her windscreen and driver's window had been smashed.

What surprised Scott was that nothing had been taken. Her satnav was still stuck to the windscreen; several pounds in loose change were still in the pocket in the centre console; her pink CD case was still on the passenger seat. In the majority of car vandalism incidents, these were typical items that opportunists would have stolen.

DCI Harvey had also been on his case for most of yesterday evening. She had wanted a progress report on their latest murder at a time when the team didn't have much to go on. Even though it was just the beginning of the investigation and only three days since the discovery of Christopher Johnson's body, the DCI was demanding answers. It wasn't the way the DCI usually operated. Something or someone was causing Harvey to be short with him. That alone was enough to stress him out.

Scott returned his head to the pillow as he held his phone above his face, allowing the screen to come into focus. "DI Baker..." he said in a coarse, gravelly voice.

"Sorry to disturb you, sir, Sergeant Trillo here. The DCI asked me to contact you immediately. Got a possible suspicious death." The sergeant paused.

"Go on..." Scott cleared his throat and rubbed his eyes in an effort to shake off his sleepiness. Cara rolled over, her ample, warm breasts pressing into his left arm. She moaned lightly, and her hand snaked down his chest. He tried to concentrate on the call.

The sergeant continued, "We've got what looks like a jumper at the Teville Gate car park in Worthing. We've got uniform in attendance."

Scott paused for a moment, allowing his brain time to catch up. Cara had already kept him up for most of the night and was clearly hungry for more. But that warm fuzzy feeling of the night before was fast fading with the prospect of attending a messy incident.

"Why is it *potentially* suspicious and not a straightforward jumper?"

"A vehicle was discovered in the car park with the driver door open and the keys in the ignition."

"Sergeant, that still doesn't make it suspicious. Get to the point." Scott sighed in frustration. He never understood why people waffled. And at that precise moment he had the patience of a gnat.

"The vehicle is registered to a Giles Rochester, sir. The

address of the registered keeper is...Edmunston-Hunt boarding school. He's a teacher there."

Scott's eyes widened. His mind furiously processed the information.

Was it stolen? Was the deceased the registered owner?

This was more than a coincidence. He had no proof as yet but more a hunch.

"Okay, I'll be there in forty-five minutes; make sure the scene is secure," he barked.

"Yes, that's all in hand. Shall I alert the rest of your team?"

"Yes, contact DS Trent and DC Wilson. Inform SOCO. We need the scene documented and photographed. Oh, and contact the pathologist."

"I'll do that right away, sir. We have tried to contact the pathologist a couple of times already, but she's not answering her phone, so we left a few messages for her to contact us immediately."

After hanging up, Scott stroked Cara's dark hair that was spread across his chest. "Wake up, trouble," he said, kissing the top of her head. "We've got a job on. Check your phone. You're needed too. We've got forty-five minutes to get to Worthing."

Scott wriggled out from underneath Cara.

"Oh, can't we just have five more minutes in bed? I'll make it worth your while," she said in a seductive, sleepy voice.

"Nope, so get your lazy ass out of bed."

"You're such a spoilsport, Scottie."

14

A group of curious onlookers were on the scene by
the time Scott arrived. He pushed his way through
the growing crowd. The white forensic tent was out
of view around the back of the car park, so the scene offered
little to see for those milling around.

Well, at least that's something. He hoped to keep the scene
as obscured as possible from this lot.

Scott signed in to the scene log and paused to scan the
surroundings, looking at entrances, exits, the type of buildings in the locality, their uses and CCTV, before proceeding
around the back towards the tent. He hated jumpers, not
because of what they did – they all had their own reasons –
but because of how it left their bodies. It wouldn't be long
before a council-approved cleaning company would be on
scene, washing away the remnants of someone's life.

Scott glanced back at the crowd beyond the cordon.
Various onlookers were recording images on their phones.
Scott picked out two individuals who stood out from the
crowd with their DSLRs and long lenses.

Bloody press.

The car park was L-shaped in structure, which afforded some degree of concealment. The incident had taken place at the inner corner of where the two sides of the car park met. The area looked out over a secondary open-air car park. A solitary scene-of-crime officer was finalising their work outside the tent as Scott walked up.

Scott acknowledged the SOCO with a nod before he peered in through the side flap. He saw the twisted body of a man, one leg projected forward, the second bent at the knee and flexed backwards. He was lying on his side, a dark, dried pool of blood framing his head. From this angle, Scott could clearly make out the large depression in the side of the man's head that had flattened the shape of his face.

"I've got this for you, sir," the SOCO offered Scott, holding out a clear evidence bag. "This was the only evidence we found on him."

Inside the bag were a white feather and a piece of paper with Latin words written on it.

Scott knew the incident involving the jumper was connected to his ongoing murder investigation.

He scanned the scene once again. The weeds breaking through the stones in the pavement and the rusty railings indicated years of neglect. He glanced up at the side of the car park and the path that the body had followed. From where he was standing, it was a significant drop. Scott hoped that the man had died on impact.

"Guv, up here." Mike was leaning over the railings on the third floor. "His car is up here."

Scott took the stairwell and instantly scrunched up his nose. The smell of urine was overpowering on certain floors. He trod carefully where there were dark stains from those who'd relieved themselves, and possibly worse. As he stepped out from the stairwell, he glanced around the deserted floor. The only car visible was behind a police cordon. Scott ducked under the tape and walked over to the car. The door of the silver Golf was still open, the keys in the ignition.

Scott peered in. "We'll get SOCO to do a sweep of the car and see if they can grab some prints."

He walked over to the rusted railings and glanced over the edge. He wasn't a great one for heights, and from where he stood, it looked like a long way down. From this height, though, he could get a much clearer view of the surrounding area.

There wasn't a lot to see except the back of low-rise office blocks. Some had their windows boarded up. Others still in business had had various windows broken, no doubt by stone-throwing youths who had little else to do in what was a run-down area.

He imagined that at night very few people had a reason to be in this area. It was a cold and soulless location. There were no local eateries, cinemas, or shops other than a local Morrisons supermarket off to his left and over the flyover. The fact that the location was not overlooked or busy at night made it the ideal spot for drug takers, vandalism and a few courting couples who could pull up for a quick bunk-up without being spotted or disturbed.

He saw Cara and Abby approaching the tent.

"Who found him, Mike?" Scott turned and leant back against the railings. Exhaling deeply.

"It was a council worker who was coming to do a sweep of the car park. Frightened the living daylights out of him, poor old sod. He's been with the council nearly forty years and due to retire next year. Said he's never seen anything like it in his life."

"Did you get a statement from him?"

"Yes, guv. Uniform has done that already."

"Mike, I want you to check for CCTV."

"Do we need to? He's clearly a jumper."

"Yes. They found evidence on the body, a white feather and a note with Latin words. Our murder and this event are connected."

Mike raised a brow. "I'll have a scan around and check with uniform to see if anyone in the crowd spotted anything."

"Okay, you do that. There's not much else for me to do around here. I think it's time I paid the head another visit."

Abby was lurking around outside the tent when Scott returned to it. Cara had also completed her brief examination and was jotting a few notes whilst sitting on her silver medical examination case.

"Great way to start the morning off, guv," Abby said.

"The body looks to be that of a teacher at Edmunston-Hunt if the car reg is anything to go by."

Abby crossed her arms and pursed her lips. "Coincidence?" she suggested.

Scott shook his head. "No, I don't believe in coincidences. We need to have another word with Collier. There's more going on at that school than he is letting on, and he's trying my patience now. Cara, is there anything you saw that looks suspicious?"

"Can't be a hundred per cent certain, because it's a bit of a mess. I could definitely make out some type of red banding around the deceased's neck."

Scott nodded. That extra bit of evidence, if true, would lend even more weight to his theory that the two incidents were connected.

The question was how and why.

15

In the space of three days, Scott found himself back at Edmunston-Hunt boarding school once again. On any other day, driving up to the school – with the smell of freshly cut grass wafting in through his car window, and the sound of birdsong reverberating around the grounds – would offer a peaceful and tranquil escape from the hustle and bustle of Brighton life. However, the death of a second teacher meant his visit had a more sombre reason.

As Abby got out of the car, she put on her scary face. "You ready for Cruella de Vil again?"

Scott smiled as they walked through the main doorway. He'd forgotten about the icy charms of Mrs Hilary.

Their favourite secretary was busily tapping away on a keyboard whilst wearing a set of headphones. They were the old-style ones that sat over the ears and drowned out most of the surrounding noise. He doubted she was listening to anything vaguely resembling music and was probably typing from dictation. She cast a brief look in their direction and carried on typing.

Scott leant over the reception desk.

"Mrs Hilary, we need to see Mr Collier," he asked, putting on his politest voice.

His enquiry was met by a wall of silence as she continued typing. Anyone would think that Scott and Abby were both invisible. Scott clenched his jaw and shot Abby a glance. Abby rolled her eyes in disbelief.

Scott cleared his throat loudly and knocked firmly on the countertop. Mrs Hilary stopped typing and paused for a moment, briefly staring at her screen, before slowly raising her eyes in Scott's direction. She clearly wasn't pleased at the interruption.

"Mrs Hilary," he repeated, his voice heavy with sarcasm, "we are here to see Mr Collier immediately."

"Mr Collier is busy. One moment, please. I'll just finish this and get you booked in for an appointment," she replied, adding a long-suffering sigh.

With Scott's patience both tested and exhausted, he placed his hands on the desk and leant in closer. "I'm not asking you, I'm telling you. We'd like to see Mr Collier *now*."

The woman's hard attitude remained steadfast. This was turning into a battle of wills, and Scott was in no mood to come off second best.

"What is it regarding?" she asked.

Scott lifted an eyebrow to suggest *really?* They were hardly popping in for a cuppa. "It's regarding the ongoing investigation and a new development," he snapped. "Would you like me to draw you a diagram?"

But Scott's sarcasm was lost on Mrs Hilary, who continued to throw a disapproving look in his direction. She picked up the phone.

"What does she think we're here for? A bloody parking fine? To swap knitting patterns?" murmured Abby as she stuffed her hands in her pockets. Scott smiled. Abby didn't suffer fools gladly either.

Mrs Hilary replaced the phone receiver. "Mr Collier will be out in a moment. You can wait over there," she said, nodding at a cluster of low-level leather chairs by the front door. She crossed her arms.

"Thank you, but no. We will wait here," Scott replied, knowing full well that invading her space would only rile the woman up more.

Mr Collier, impeccably dressed in a dark navy suit, crisp white shirt, and pale blue tie, arrived a few moments later. As he strode towards them, his gait reminded Scott of how army personnel marched: shoulders back, chest out, straight arms synchronised in a rhythmic swing. Collier looked concerned and frustrated; his eyes had narrowed and deep furrows lined his forehead.

"Inspector, Sergeant." His tone was strong. "How can I help? Is this to do with Mr Johnson?"

"I'm afraid not. Is there somewhere we can go that's a little more private?" Scott asked, glancing briefly at Mrs Hilary.

"Of course. Yes, come to my office." He turned on his heel and strode off just as quickly as he had arrived.

Abby followed quickly behind him.

Scott trailed a little farther behind, slowing to look at the portrait photos that lined one wall of the corridor. Each photo depicted a teacher at the school. It was a collection of teachers both past and present, judging from the dates. Many of the former teachers stared into the camera lens with sombre, serious looks. Grey backgrounds blanched their photos further. The most recent colour photos portrayed teachers in relaxed, side-on poses, with slight smiles. The new colour portraits had been taken in a different location to the black-and-white ones. They were taken outdoors on the main lawn, with the school as an elegant backdrop.

Scott entered Adrian Collier's room. On this occasion he didn't offer them a seat. The head chose to stand behind the closed door, his arms straight by his sides. "What is this all about?" His words were short, sharp, and deliberate.

Scott asked, "Have you seen Giles Rochester this morning?"

"No, I'm afraid not. I was made aware that he didn't turn up for classes this morning. I sent a member of staff over to his cottage to see if he is unwell, but he didn't appear to be in. His car was not there either."

"What car does he drive?" Abby asked,

Collier looked in the direction of Scott and ignored Abby. "He drives a silver VW Golf. Can I ask the nature of your enquiry?"

"Do you have the registration number for that car?"

Adrian Collier looked perplexed as he scanned the officers. "Not to hand, and I'm not sure why you need it."

"Mr Rochester may have come to some harm, so we are trying to establish some facts. It would be really helpful if you could provide us with his registration number."

Collier turned to his desk and dialled through to Mrs Hilary. "Could you give me the registration number for Giles Rochester's car?" He paused for a moment, listening to the woman's response. He looked up in frustration. "Just get me the details...now."

There was a long pause whilst he waited for the details. Then he replaced the handset.

Collier said, "It's FG15 FKL, Inspector."

Scott and Abby exchanged glances. It confirmed what Scott had suspected.

"Mr Collier, a body was found this morning in Worthing. We believe it's Giles Rochester."

Collier fell silent. He stared at the floor before looking at the officers again. "I'm sorry to hear that. It's tragic news. Are you sure it's Giles?"

Scott nodded. "We believe so, but we'll need to formally

identify the body. His car was found close by. Did he have any issues or problems that you were aware of?"

"I'm afraid I don't know of any."

Scott didn't want to release too many details at this stage or share his suspicions about the two deaths being connected.

"Mr Collier, what concerns me is that in the space of three days two members of your staff have been found dead. Do you not find that strange or disturbing? Are you not concerned about the welfare *and* safety of your staff and pupils?" he asked, staring at Collier.

Collier shrugged. "I admit, it's highly unusual. My job here is to run a school, provide an excellent teaching environment and deliver outstanding results. It's not my place to delve into the private lives of my staff. As long as they do what they're employed to and get the results, then I'm satisfied. Of course, the happiness and welfare of my pupils is important too, but we're not a kindergarten. We turn out a certain type of young man." The head puffed his chest out in military fashion.

"And what might that be?" Abby asked directly.

Collier glowered at her. "We turn out fearless young men, the future captains, majors, brigadiers of the British Army, the leaders of FTSE 500 companies, the entrepreneurs who shape our world, world-class sportsmen and our future politicians. We have no room for weak-mindedness." He walked over to the window that looked out over the magnificent striped lawns. "In battle, it's the cowards who are the instigators of defeat; bravery is a rampart of defence."

"So you'd agree with the quote, 'Weakness of attitude becomes weakness of character'?"

The head turned and wryly smiled at Scott. "Ah, Inspector. Touché. Albert Einstein certainly had a point."

Scott let Collier's reply hang for a moment even though

he disagreed. He was beginning to think that the man hadn't really moved on from his days in the army.

"Did he have any next of kin?" Scott asked.

Collier thought for a moment as he rubbed his chin. "I believe he had a sister, but she's in New Zealand."

"No one else in the UK?"

"Not that I'm aware of."

Abby asked, "Are you sure that he doesn't have any family in the UK?"

"Is it necessary that he does, Inspector?" he asked, ignoring her.

Scott was surprised by Collier's snub of Abby. The head clearly had an issue responding to her questions. Whether it was Abby herself or the fact she was a female was hard to tell. Scott suspected the latter. Collier was no doubt used to commanding the superior high ground, and with his military background, he probably wasn't used to being challenged by a woman.

"Mr Collier?" Abby pushed again.

Collier sighed in protest. "As I said to the inspector, not that I'm aware of, Sergeant," he replied, looking down his nose at Abby.

Abby straightened her grey suit jacket and reached for her phone, then stepped away to call the office.

Scott said to Collier, "We'll need to search his cottage, so can you arrange for us to gain access now, please?"

GILES ROCHESTER'S cottage was much the same in size and sparseness as Christopher Johnson's. Scott and Abby looked around and searched for evidence to explain the last few hours of his life.

Whilst Abby searched upstairs, Scott looked around the

ground floor. The lounge had a large flat-screen TV mounted above the fireplace. A stack of country living magazines sat beside a leather armchair.

As he wandered through to the kitchen, he stopped in his tracks. There on the table sat a large length of thick boundary rope. Scott examined it in closer detail, leaning over the table without touching it. Despite it being wrapped in a series of loops, he could clearly make out that one end had been tied off to form a possible noose. Scott's mind whirled as he thought about why it was there.

Is it linked to the first incident?

He was distracted by Abby's voice as she came downstairs. "Nothing in the bedrooms or bathroom. No signs of anything being disturbed or a struggle. How about you?"

"We've got a rope similar in thickness and look to the one used in the first case," he said. "Abby, the chances of him having next of kin in the UK appear slim. Grab his toothbrush, that mug on his desk, and see if you can pull some hair fibres off his bed pillow. We can give them to forensics to do a DNA match with our victim."

Scott was perplexed. Two bodies in three days. The same evidence found on both victims.

16

Scott and Abby arrived at the office not long after lunch. Heads buried deep in work on their PCs, the team hardly glanced up as they walked through the office. When the smell of freshly brewed Costa Coffee filled the floor, they lifted their heads.

"Grab yourselves a cuppa and a cake," said Scott.

They had also brought back a selection of cakes, including millionaire's shortbread, teacakes, lemon tarts and chocolate tiffin.

Big Mike moved first, as Scott had expected. His large beer belly hung over his trouser belt; the shirt buttons on his grey shirt fought a valiant battle to stay closed. A fine specimen of a man he was no longer. Scott had seen pictures of Mike from his army days. Back then, he'd been a fit, large, well-built trained sniper who had seen two difficult tours of Afghanistan and spent time based in Germany and Africa. His active lifestyle had ensured he'd remained a healthy weight and size.

But since becoming a civilian, he'd let it go. His hair had started to thin and grey. His trim, muscular frame had given way to an ever-expanding waistline, the consequence of a diet that gravitated towards convenience meals, Oreo biscuits and sampling craft beers.

Raj and Sian dived in, too. Sian, ever careful of her figure, tiptoed around the food. She tucked her dark brown hair behind her ears as she peered at the goodies. Her tortoise-shell-framed glasses slipped down the bridge of her pixie nose; she pushed them back up. She gleefully glanced over the selection before opting for a teacake.

DCI Harvey marched into the office.

"Scott, a word, please," she hollered, causing everyone to spin round in her direction. She turned and headed back out into the corridor.

Scott followed her to find Harvey pacing up and down the corridor. She looked concerned as she checked out her feet, her arms tapping each thigh.

"Yes, ma'am?"

She looked at him. "What's the latest on the jumper this morning?"

"Well, initially it appeared to be a suicide. However, I'm fairly certain it's not."

"Go on."

"The victim appears to be a Giles Rochester, a teacher at Edmunston-Hunt School. DNA evidence should confirm that, but he carries a resemblance to his driver's ID and school photo anyway. Secondly, a note with Latin words and a white feather were found in one of his pockets. Exactly the same as in Johnson's case."

This wasn't the news the DCI was hoping for. If anything, it would heap more pressure on her shoulders. Her forehead furrowed.

Scott sensed that Harvey was mulling it over. "What's on your mind, ma'am? I think I know you well enough to know when something's bothering you."

Harvey hesitated for a moment. "You need to get a result on this one, Scott, and you need to get it fast," she said firmly.

"With all due respect, ma'am, we are still very early into our investigation. I can't pull a rabbit out of a hat with the click of my fingers."

"Scott, you have to appreciate that *sometimes* our job becomes a little political, and more importantly, people up there," she said, pointing at the ceiling, "have a vested interest in this, and significant clout."

"What are you getting at, ma'am?"

"Superintendent Meadows is on my arse. He's just had a call from Chief Constable Lennon. CC Lennon moves in the same circles as several of the governors on the board of Edmunston-Hunt. I'll go as far as to say that they are members of the same Masonic lodge. The governors were a little *concerned* about the negative publicity that Johnson's death would have on the reputation of the school. That's something they want to guard fiercely. The last thing they want are parents – and I hasten to add very *influential* parents – pulling their kids out of Edmunston-Hunt. At forty-five thousand pounds a year per pupil, they have a lot to lose. If the second victim turns out to be Giles Rochester, then Lennon is going to be under pressure to deal with this matter quietly and swiftly, with the least amount of fuss."

If there was one thing Scott hated, it was him and his team being used as a political football.

"I'm not going to brush it under the carpet, ma'am, or hope that the file disappears under the other dozens of cases that we're dealing with."

"I'm not asking you to do anything of the sort," Harvey replied, a hint of anger in her voice. "Just be wary, and more importantly bear in mind who you and I report to." She shook her head furiously. "Sometimes you can't ignore *that* *we* are part of a team whether we like it or not."

Harvey looked at Scott, her fierce glare conveying the delicate nature of this matter as well as the ramifications if he didn't toe the line.

She turned and headed back to her office.

Scott's mind turned over Harvey's parting words as he leant on the stair rail. If he did his job, he'd be making trouble for himself, but his conscience would be clean. If he toed the line, his career would be safe, but he'd be going against every reason he'd joined the force.

Sian pushed through the doors, and his attention snapped back to the present.

"Guv, there's a call for Raj, but he's not around, can you take it?" she said. "It's Simon Barrett. He's a lecturer in modern languages at Sussex University."

Scott returned to his office and picked up the phone.

"Simon, this is Detective Inspector Baker from Brighton CID. Thank you for coming back to us regarding our enquiry," he said, sitting down.

"My pleasure, Inspector. How can I help?"

"I hope you've had enough time to review the information we've sent over to you. For our own clarity, we're hoping you can interpret the Latin?"

"Most certainly. But I have to admit, it's not the usual type of request I receive," he replied, with a deep belly laugh. "Usually, it's feedback on Latin in books or photos, and even the odd artefact."

"That makes sense. Can you tell me what it means?"

"*Ignavus iners timidius tu mori debes* essentially means 'You, a coward, deserve to die.' It's pretty much self-explanatory."

Scott thanked the lecturer and hung up. He tapped his pen slowly as he leant back in his chair. The sharp sound was loud in the quiet of his office.

You, a coward, deserve to die ran on repeat in his mind. But how did that relate to Johnson and Rochester? That was what he needed to find out and fast, as the conversation with DCI Harvey entered his thoughts again.

He glanced at his watch. The PM on the jumper would be taking place now; he'd call Cara later for her results.

First, he needed a team update.

17

A bby made her way to the drinks machine to grab a bottle of water before the briefing. Mike, chatting with the same female officer he'd been talking to in the canteen, blocked her access to it. He was so engrossed in conversation that he didn't see Abby approach.

"Ahem," Abby said, clearing her throat loudly to catch Mike's attention.

He turned and gave Abby the cheesiest of grins. "Hiya, Sarge, how's it hanging?"

Abby stared at him, her mouth open, her eyes wide with incredulity.

"If you know what's good for you, Constable, you'll get up to the briefing room now. The boss is about to start." She shook her head and grabbed a bottle before heading off.

Behind her, she heard Mike throwing out more one-liners to the poor girl. "Catch you later, sweet."

"Hey, wait!" he shouted to Abby. He trotted up alongside Abby, a satisfied grin on his face. "See that smile she gave me? I reckon I'm well in there."

"She's either got a screw loose, or she's taking pity on you," Abby said with another shake of her head. "I mean, do yourself a favour and get some new chat-up lines. Anyone would think you're still at school and about half your age." She punched him playfully in the arm. "'Catch you later, sweet'? Really? This isn't *High School Musical*, and you're certainly not Troy Bolton. She looks ten years younger than you, and that's being generous, but lines like that aren't you."

Mike shot her a quizzical look. He had no kids, so the reference about *High School Musical* and Troy Bolton was clearly lost on him.

"Well, she seems to like me," he said. "I make her laugh, which is more than I do with you."

"You sure she's not laughing *at* you?" she teased.

"Yeah, whatever."

Abby paused for a moment by the door to the briefing room. "Oh, and one last thing. If you ever say 'how's it hanging?' to your skip again, I'll cut your nuts off. Then you definitely won't have anything hanging. Get my drift?"

———

RAJ and Sian were already seated when Mike and Abby entered. Scott was busily scribbling a few notes on the whiteboard. He glanced over his shoulder to see them enter.

"Okay, team, we've got another case that I now believe is linked to our first victim, Johnson. Initially, it was thought that the jumper from Teville Gate car park was unconnected and nothing more than a suicide. Evidence has now come to light that suggests both cases are connected. In particular, both victims were found with a note and white feather in their pockets. According to our Latin scholar, the words translate to, 'You, a coward, deserve to die.' In my opinion, these deaths were murders, and the victims were killed for a particular reason.

"Hopefully, DNA evidence will confirm that the second victim is Giles Rochester, a teacher at Edmunston-Hunt, but it's safe to assume it will. There are similarities between these two cases, one that I've already highlighted, I don't believe in coincidences, so we need to look for motive, and the Latin words are key to that."

As Scott looked around, he could see that the others were making the connections in their minds. His thoughts were met with nods of understanding.

Scott continued, "Sian, I want you to widen the search and look for anything on CCTV. Check all the roads leading into the area and to the multistorey car park. It's not the busiest of areas, but there are office buildings in the vicinity, and there's Worthing station. There is a chance something may have been picked up. Second, get on with the high-tech unit. I want the phone records downloaded from his phone as fast as possible. If they haven't got time to do it, let's find a designated officer who can."

Sian agreed and wrote down her instructions.

Scott carried on. "The thick boundary rope that Abby and I recovered from the second property resembles the same type of rope that was used in our first case. Hopefully, forensics can confirm that through fibre-type analysis. What I can confirm, however, is the rest of forensics' feedback so far.

"Johnson had a significant amount of alcohol in his bloodstream that had been consumed over several hours. The pathologist estimates something in the region of half a bottle to a full bottle of red wine. The prints on the glass belong to Johnson. The forensics team were able to lift some clear impressions off the love notes from S. There's nothing showing on the database against those prints, so that person is still unknown to us. Forensics found two sets of prints in his room, one belonging to him, the other matching mystery person S. This person certainly visited Johnson in the past."

"Start with the usual stuff, guv?" Mike asked.

"Yep, friends, relatives, relationships, and social media profiles. Let's see if he had fallen out with anyone. Find out his movements over the last twenty-four hours and see if anyone spotted anything unusual either in his behaviour or around the grounds of the school."

"How have we got on with building a victimology on Johnson?" asked Abby, addressing the others around the table.

"He seemed to be a well-liked character," said Sian. "He was the housemaster for Ditchling House. I spoke to the pupils there. The consensus was he was firm but fair. He wasn't the type of guy to take any crap and said it as it was. I got the phone records for Johnson. He didn't make a lot of phone calls, to be honest. I guess he didn't need to. There's quite a lot of phone traffic between him and another number, though. I checked the number, but it's a pay-as-you-go number, and it's not registered."

Scott thanked Sian. "I've spoken to DCI Harvey, and because of the continued threat at the school, we're assigning some uniformed resources as a visible deterrent and for reassurance. Although I'm not sure how effective a panda car with a PCSO parked by the main entrance is going to be, but that's all we can allocate at the moment. The school is not in lockdown, so we need to remain vigilant there. We recommended that the school close for the time being. However, the school and board of governors felt it would send out the wrong message to the pupils and parents, many of whom are not in the UK and who wouldn't be too pleased with the decision."

Raj shifted around in his seat. Remarkably, he hadn't come bearing gifts today. Normally, there'd be some biscuits or cakes from him; without the offering, the briefing didn't feel the same.

The heat of the day appeared to be bothering Raj. He was wearing a grey shirt with his black trousers. In this heat and without the air conditioning. Two wet patches were clearly visible under each armpit. His hair looked decidedly more ruffled than usual, and his clean-shaven face now had short, designer stubble that reminded Scott of the unshaven villains in the old spaghetti westerns.

"Guv, what I find strange is the lack of reaction from the people running the school," Raj said. "Their assistant head is dead, and now it looks like a second teacher has died under suspicious circumstances. In any normal school, you'd have the usual mix of human emotions: panic, fear, outrage, sadness. But there doesn't seem to be anything like that. And now with a second teacher, you'd think the school would go into overdrive. I'd expect to see parents pulling their kids out and teachers panicking. There's none of that." He shook his head.

"I'm with you there, Raj," said Scott. "It was a very surreal atmosphere on both occasions that Abby and I were up there. The head had an almost nonchalant, cavalier attitude. There's definitely more going on at that school than we have been led to believe. We need to find out what. I want you and Mike to look into the backgrounds of all the pupils. Look for any disgruntled parents who perhaps have a grudge against the school. And, Sian, I want you to pull the records of all teachers past and present and review them. Does anything stand out? Were there any past convictions? Any disciplinary issues? Was there anything going on in their personal lives that could have some bearing on this case?"

AFTER WRAPPING UP THE MEETING, Scott briefed the DCI. Her mood hadn't really changed much since the last time he'd spoken to her. A knot had lodged in the pit of his stomach as he'd tried to explain to Harvey all the different avenues that they were exploring, in the hope that she'd be satisfied. He'd left the meeting decidedly uncomfortable, feeling that everything he had said had fallen on deaf ears.

Whilst the team busied themselves, Scott retreated to the sanctuary of his office. The emails had been piling up in his inbox. With the case taking up most of his time, he hadn't had the opportunity to sift through them.

Now, he groaned at the prospect of going through one hundred and twenty-four emails, most of which he knew would be internal memos and circulars.

He glanced up from his PC monitor to look at his in tray. He had another eleven case files to review. With the current case taking up much of the team's resources and time, it was easy for other case files to slip to the back of the queue. Rape, burglary, aggravated burglary, an armed robbery in a small off-licence in Hove, and a team of professional shoplifters working their way through stores in The Lanes were all on his review list.

It would have been easy for Scott to simply type up brief review comments before handing the files back to his officers. He'd come across other DIs who very rarely examined case files in detail. Typing the proverbial "I agree with the current approach and suggestions offered" seemed to be their preferred option. Anything for an easy life.

Scott didn't work like that. He trusted his officers, and in return they trusted him. A good team surrounded him, but at the end of the day, the buck stopped with him. If it meant reviewing every single case line by line, then that was what he would do. No stone left unturned.

His body ached, and his shoulders were tight.

Bursts of throbbing pain radiated through his muscles, and his eyes felt heavy.

Maybe he'd leave the case files until tomorrow when he could look at them with fresh eyes.

Now, he had somewhere else he needed to be.

18

The heat of the late afternoon sun beamed down on Scott's shoulders. The warmth penetrated deep, relieving the tension that had built up during the day. He stretched his arms out to the sides and pulled his shoulders back, in the hope of relieving the nagging pain between his shoulder blades.

He loosened his top button and pulled his tie off, rolling it into a neat ball. He finally removed his jacket as he walked through the cemetery, casually throwing it over one shoulder.

As the sun began its downward journey towards the horizon, the shadows of the trees and headstones began to lengthen. Scott never understood why cemeteries spooked some people out. To him it was a place of solitude and reflection. It offered a real connection with loved ones.

In the distance to his right, he saw a couple huddled around a grave. The woman gently wiped her eyes with a tissue; the man supported her and pulled her tight into him. Farther past them he saw a man, probably in his late sixties judging by his grey hair. He stood solemnly in front of a grave with his hands deep in the pockets of his trousers, gently rocking back and forth as he stared down at the newly laid flowers.

A sense of stillness surrounded him. Birdsong echoed through the trees. The odd bumblebee buzzed as it hopped from flower to flower.

He arrived at Becky's grave. He stared for a moment at his daughter's beautiful picture set in a heart-shaped, black marble headstone. His shoulders slumped as a dark and heavy sadness pulled them down, along with his broken heart. His eyes grew heavy with tears. He missed his family so much.

Scott's jaw clenched tight as he fought back tears that threatened to break free. That beautiful smile that greeted him every morning was nothing more than a precious memory. That very same smile looked up at him now.

"I brought you a present, little one. I promised to bring you your favourite toy." His bottom lip trembled. "Remember when we used to watch it together, and I'd make the piggy *oink, oink* noises, and you'd laugh. You would always say, 'Again, Daddy, again'...I loved being silly with you." He knelt down and placed a small, pink, Peppa Pig cuddly toy by her headstone.

Minutes elapsed as he stared at Becky's picture. Sobs ripped through his body, releasing the pain and sadness that continued to fester and build up inside him every day. Moments like this gave him the opportunity to let go.

"I hope you're resting in peace. I'd do anything to see your little chubby smile now."

The sounds of daily life faded into background noise. An inner quietness surrounded him. This sanctuary protected him from the tribulations of daily life. If he could, he'd spend every day here. His mind needed it. His body craved it, and his sanity depended on it.

Scott finally stood and straightened up. "Love you lots, my

little lady," he whispered as he kissed two fingers and touched Becky's picture. "I'll stop by real soon."

He left Angel's Corner and walked through the small meadow towards Tina's plot. A lot of care had been taken to create a cemetery that was both aesthetically pleasing and respectful. The meadow was a nice touch, a space for local flora and fauna to flourish, and a place for visitors to wander and be with their thoughts.

Visiting his wife's grave always filled him with mixed emotions. Part of him ached for her, his mind full of memories and pictures. Every time he thought of his wonderful Tina, those precious moments were invaded by the last image of her on the ground – her body twisted, and a narrow blood trail seeping from a head trauma. It was an image that always sent waves of repulsion through his body. His stomach flipped over again, forcing his breath out.

With a shake of his head, he pushed that image back to the darkest recesses of his mind, until it returned to haunt him again.

Another part of him felt guilty for not being able to protect his family. That sense of failure clung to him. During this visit, however, the guilt felt worse.

Cara, a wonderful woman he'd met, was helping him to heal the wounds of the past. She'd brought happiness back into his life.

Looking at Tina's picture wasn't helping to ease his guilt. He hoped that some divine or cosmic intervention would tell him what to say or how to feel, but the right words failed him.

"I'm sorry I let you down, babes. You're always in my thoughts. I'll always be with you. There are days I question if I can live without you and Becky, but I have to move on. I know you would want me to. I have to let you go at some point. I have to keep going. The only way I can cope is to keep working, keep busy and keep living my life. I have to remind myself what I'm here for...to make a difference to the world.

"I've met someone new. Her name's Cara. I think you'd like her; you'd approve. I can imagine you right now telling me to stop being a silly sod, to get on with my life and not to dwell on the past." He sighed as he plucked out the weeds around her headstone.

As Scott walked away, he felt a strange sense of remorse tinged with relief. It wasn't a feeling that he'd experienced before in all his visits.

Perhaps the tide was changing. Perhaps he was easing into the present rather than reversing into the past.

THE DOUBLE RING on his doorbell signalled Cara's arrival. Scott got up from watching the news about the latest crisis in Syria.

He opened the door. She had come straight from work, her hair in a ponytail. A simple pair of black trousers, a white sleeveless vest and dainty black patent ballerina pumps provided her with a simple yet stylish attire.

"Hey, handsome," she said, greeting him with a lingering kiss on the doorstep. Scott pulled away first.

She held up a white paper bag with a picture of a fishing trawler on it. "Dinner."

The familiar smell of fish and chips set off a rumble in his stomach.

They made their way through to the kitchen. As Scott grabbed some plates, Cara placed a hand on his arm.

"Scottie, you okay? You seem a little distant. Something happen? Have I done something to upset or hurt you?"

He shook his head as he turned to face her. Her deep brown eyes were soft, alluring and inviting. How could she possibly hurt him? Her loving nature was one of the qualities he loved the most. He needed to tell her.

"I went to visit their graves this afternoon."

Cara gave his arm a gentle and reassuring squeeze. "I'm sorry."

"I know you'll think this sounds silly, me talking to them and all that, but I told Tina about us. Well, you in particular. I know she's gone, but I still think she's around. Daft, I know." He paused. "I needed to tell her. I felt like I was betraying her...betraying her memory. I...I can't really explain it, but I needed to tell her so I could move on and not feel guilty all the bloody time."

"Guilty about us?" Cara asked.

"I guess..." He shrugged.

Cara pulled her hand away, and an awkward silence followed.

After a moment, she said softly, "Would it be easier for you if we didn't see each other?"

Scott studied Cara and her flawless complexion, high cheekbones and full lips. She was mesmerising. He was afraid to admit just how much she meant to him.

She tilted her head to one side. "Speak to me, Scott." Her words held sincerity and meaning. Her chest heaved as if this was difficult. On the outside she was trying to act cool and collected.

He held her by her arms. "Cara, I need to move on with my life. I've been through hell and back. Sometimes I feel like I'm in quicksand and I'm paralysed, and the harder I try to fight it, the stronger the pull is to a place I don't want to go."

Cara offered the smallest of smiles, her vulnerability apparent as she wrapped her arms around herself.

"Okay, I understand..."

He needed to explain. "No, you don't... I've no intention of letting you go, Cara."

19

Scott left Cara putting on her make-up, and he threw his jacket on to leave. He felt good this morning and put that down to an evening of closeness and affection with Cara. She had an easy knack of blending love with laughter to lighten the mood.

He opened the front door whilst pressing the unlock button on his car fob. Brilliant sunshine and its warmth bathed his face. He walked to his car.

Horror fast replaced his enjoyment as he paused mid-step and looked down. Staring up at him with black, lifeless eyes was a pig's head – a fresh pig's head.

Alarm bells rang in his mind. His pulse quickened as he stepped over the head and ran down his path to the front gate. He looked up and down the road to see if anyone was lurking about.

As a police officer, he'd been called many names, but the undesirable elements of society often referred to them as pigs. And he had been referred to as one on several occasions. A part of him thought that maybe the severed head was perhaps a prank. But another part of him took it seriously.

He paused and scanned every single car he could see. If the perpetrators were around, they could be parked up and watching. From where he stood, he saw neither someone hanging around in the street nor anyone sitting in a car observing him.

"Cara, you'd better get down here!" he shouted upon returning to the house.

"I'm nearly finished, hon."

"No, I mean get down here now."

The severity in his tone had Cara rushing downstairs moments later. "What's the matter?"

Scott stood to one side so that Cara could see behind him and to the porch.

Her eyes widened in shock. She covered her mouth with her hand.

"Shit almighty...What?...Oh my God." Her gaze darted between the pig's head and Scott, searching for answers. "That's just disgusting. What's it doing here?"

"I don't know." Scott shook his head. "It could just be a prank, but in my line of work, it's often something more sinister."

Cara looped her arm in his, her gaze fixed on the head. "What are you going to do?"

"I'm going to bag it up, take it to the office and report it. I'll have to inform the DCI and get an officer to phone around all the butchers, to see if any sold a pig's head recently. You get yourself off to work, and I'll sort this out."

Scott's mind whirled. He played it calm in front of Cara, brushing off his worry. The last thing he wanted to do was alarm her. In his line of work, he couldn't be too careful about his personal safety as an officer. He'd heard of officers' personal cars being vandalised by suspects who had been arrested or charged. But two random events in the space of just a few days seemed odd to him.

First Cara's car is vandalised at work, and then I get a pig's head on my doorstep.

As he drove off, he scanned the area, hoping he'd see a couple of teenagers on bikes giggling to themselves.

He passed a parked black BMW, its windows blacked out. Scott didn't see the man in dark clothing hunkered down low in the driver's seat.

ABBY WAS STRUMMING AWAY RHYTHMICALLY on her steering wheel to the sound of Coldplay as Scott pulled up.

"Where have you been?" she asked, tapping her watch as she stepped from her car.

"You wouldn't even believe me if I told you."

"There's the caretaker again? He looks odd to me," Abby said, nodding at the man they'd seen on their earlier visits.

The caretaker wearing grey overalls slowly swept the flagstones that skirted the school. The slow sweeps of his broom accompanied his long, narrowed-eyed look at them. His mouth was downturned, his chin was jutted forward, and his forehead creased as he continued to stare.

"Odd perhaps, but he's no bother to us."

"He reminds me of old man Smithers the creepy janitor from *Scooby-Doo*, but with hair."

Scott didn't reply. He didn't have a clue what Abby was on about.

"Let me guess, another late night with Cara and she's worn you out?" Abby elbowed him as they walked to the main door of Edmunston-Hunt School.

"Well, that's partly right, but as I was leaving this morning, I found a bloody pig's head on my doorstep – a *proper* pig's head."

Abby looked at him, her eyes narrowing with suspicion. "You're joshing me...right?"

Scott shook his head. "Nope. I'll show you if you want. It's in the boot," he said, nodding at his car.

"Kids playing a prank?"

Scott shrugged. "I'd love to say yes; I can't be certain. How many times have you been called a pig in your career?"

"Um...I couldn't even put a figure on it, but a fair few times."

"Exactly, and I bet at least half of those slurs involved someone that we apprehended or charged. How many scrotes have said they'd get us back?"

"What are you going to do?"

"Report it, make a few enquiries and just remain vigilant." Scott sighed.

His mood didn't lighten as he stood in front of his favourite receptionist, Mrs Hilary, waiting for her to finish her current phone call. She neither looked up nor acknowledged them.

Scott rapped his knuckles once on the desk before walking off in the direction of the head's office. Abby looked at Mrs Hilary and then chased after Scott.

Behind them, Mrs Hilary abruptly told the caller, "One moment, please, one moment," before she began to shout after them.

Scott heard the sound of rapid footsteps as she quickly tried to intercept them.

He reached the head's office before she did and opened the door.

"Welcome, Inspector," greeted Collier, his back to Scott and Abby as he looked out the window.

He turned with a tight-lipped smile, his shoulders pulled back, the thumb of each hand hooked into the pockets of his waistcoat. "How can I help?"

Collier was either calculated and cunning or plain ignorant of the situation that the school faced. Scott's guess was that he was a bit of all three.

"Mr Collier, I believe that you're not being entirely forthcoming with the goings-on at the school. Two members of staff have been confirmed dead in the space of four days, and you really don't seem to be alarmed or concerned in any way."

The head cleared his throat and levelled his gaze with Scott's. "I'm not entirely sure what you're insinuating, *Inspector,* but I'd be careful about throwing around assumptions."

"Oh, I think you do, Mr Collier. I think you know exactly what I'm talking about. And I don't take too kindly to being threatened."

Collier shrugged and turned to face the window again.

Scott continued, "Both of the deceased had identical evidence placed on them, which is why we believe the two events are connected. What does the phrase 'You, a coward, deserve to die' mean to you, or a white feather?"

The man bowed his head. With Scott's knowledge of patterns in human behaviour, the silence and turning away were classic ploys that people employed when they wanted to avoid giving anything away, especially in their eyes. He knew from experience that the eyes were the window to the soul, the mouth the door.

Collier shook his head as he turned. He walked towards Abby, giving her a derogatory glance. "I'm afraid I haven't got a clue. All sounds rather sinister if you ask me, straight out of a *Poirot* episode."

"Mind if we have a look around the school?" Scott asked.

"Of course, be my guest. I'm here if you need me."

Scott nodded. "By the way, who's the chap in the overalls sweeping up outside?"

"That's Alan Bennett, our caretaker."

"Been with you long?"

"As a matter of fact, yes. Seven years. Keeps himself to himself. A bit of a loner but gets the job done."

"And before that?"

Collier paused for a moment, looking unsure whether to divulge Bennett's prior history. "He's an ex-prisoner. Came to us via a charity and Jobcentre Plus."

"Do you know the nature of his offences?" Scott enquired, knowing full well that he could check once back at the office.

"Some type of violent assault or fracas outside a pub in Soho, London...but I can assure you that he's a reformed character now. He's given me no cause for concern and is of no threat to our pupils – or staff."

"Where does he live? I assume he has accommodation on-site like most school caretakers?"

Collier stiffened, jutting out his jaw and turning the edges of his mouth down. "Yes, he does. He has small lodgings around the back, behind the row of cottages designated for teachers."

Scott nodded as he studied Collier for a moment before heading off with Abby to take a look around the school.

20

M atthew Edrington was trapped. The other boys had caught up with him whilst he was on his way to the music room. The first shove he received, thrusting him against the dark oak-panelled walls of the corridor, had startled him. The unevenness of the surface had rubbed against his thin shoulder blades. The back of his head ached from where they'd slapped him hard.

If only I'd run, he thought, feeling angry with himself.

It would have been easy to say that he was getting used to being singled out, but the truth of the matter wouldn't bear the lie. The attacks, the verbal abuse and the intimidation had broken him further.

"You never learn your lesson, do you, Edrington?" the lead bully, Hunter, said.

"Please, please leave me alone. I don't understand what I've done for you to keep hurting me like this."

"You...you just being you is what you've done to deserve this. You're a liability, the weak link. *Everyone* is expected to give a hundred per cent to the house; we're lucky if we get fifty per cent from you!" Hunter yelled and delivered another slap to the side of Edrington's head. The sting spread through Matthew's scalp.

James Rollings pushed the other two boys aside and stepped in between. He grabbed Matthew by the throat, pushing him hard into the wall. "You don't belong here. I think you'd be better suited at Roedean, where all the girls go." He sniggered, then released Matthew with a step backwards.

Ford and Hunter stepped forward again. They crowded Matthew, their faces just a few inches away from his. Matthew could smell their stale, hot breath. He gritted his teeth and clenched his jaw tight. He needed to be strong even though all he wanted to do was cry. He couldn't handle this anymore. He hated being here, hated the way they treated him.

"Enough!" boomed a voice from behind them. It startled the boys, and all three spun round.

Timothy Saunders, the catering manager, strode towards them. "What do you think you are doing?" he demanded, shooting each of them a glance.

A wall of silence met Saunders's question.

Rollings stood there, his hands buried deep in his pockets. His long fringe partially covered his eyes. The corner of his mouth was turned up in a slight smile.

Ford remained impassive. His light brown eyes appeared to be glazed over as if affected by illegal substances, which, knowing Ford, might have been true. His eyebrows seem to be permanently raised as if a brow lift had gone horribly wrong, and together with his pale complexion, he looked like a macabre ghost.

It was Hunter who was the aggressor in the pack. He had tight cropped hair and a thin face. Hunter had a penetrative menacing stare that was at odds with his boyish looks. With his head slightly bowed, he stared at Saunders, his fists clenched tight by his sides.

"Hunter, Rollings, Ford, I've seen enough of your bullying to last me a lifetime. Leave the boy alone. If I see you three at this again, I'll frogmarch you to the head's office. Do I make myself clear?"

"Yes, Mr Saunders."

Abby and Scott overheard the altercation whilst they were wandering through the school.

"Everything all right in here?" Scott asked, observing the tense icy stand-off.

He could see the terror in Matthew Edrington's eyes as they flicked nervously between Scott, Saunders and the boys. His hands were clenched tight in a ball under his chin, his arms shielding his chest.

"Nothing I can't handle," Saunders said in frustration.

"You okay, Matthew?" Scott asked.

"I *said,* nothing I can't handle," Saunders insisted.

Matthew opened his mouth to speak but immediately decided against it when one of the bullies turned and shot him a threatening glare. Matthew shot Scott a quick look and gave a tremulous nod.

"Get on your way now, the lot of you...go!" Saunders shouted before he too turned and hurried away.

One of the boys shoulder-charged Matthew as they walked off. "We'll see you *later*..."

Scott watched as they sauntered off, nudging one another and laughing.

Edrington headed in a different direction.

"Matthew, wait..." Scott said.

Matthew paused mid-step and slowly turned to face Scott. With one eye on his aggressors, he clutched the rucksack on his shoulder while his other hand was buried deep in his trouser pocket.

Scott walked over to him and placed one hand on his shoulder in support. "Are they always picking on you?"

Silence met his question.

Matthew simply stared at the ground.

Scott decided to change tack. "Do those boys pick on other kids?"

Matthew shrugged his shoulders, not answering.

Scott could feel the bones in the boy's shoulders through his blazer. Scott gave him a reassuring pat on the back. "Listen, if there's anything you want to talk about, here's my card. Give me a call." Scott pulled out his card from the inside of the suit jacket.

Matthew scurried off, keen to put some distance between him and the others.

"The poor boy looks terrified." Abby tutted. "Kids can be so cruel."

Scott paused for a moment. Bullying was something he knew happened in every school. Whether it was a state comprehensive or an elite boarding school, boys or girls, it happened. Schools would try their hardest to stamp it out, but in his experience as soon as a victim sought help from the teaching staff, it inevitably led to further victimisation from the aggressor.

For that very reason, so many victims chose to remain silent. They would endure years of torment, looking forward to the day they could finally leave school. Their lasting impression of school wasn't one of carefree fun and learning. It was of fear and sadness.

"What makes you think that Matthew's been singled out?" asked Abby.

Scott stared down the corridor as Matthew disappeared from view. "When we first turned up here, do you remember how he was talking about how he had let his house down and they were going to be angry with him?"

"Yes."

"Well, it looks like his fears were true. They're getting him back because the house lost out in the run."

21

L aurence Goddard attempted to put his key in the lock for the third time, leaning against the frame for support. Each time he tried, the key either slipped or refused to slide into the keyhole.

He cursed, "Useless piece of shit."

To him, the task was as impossible as threading a needle. He finally drove the key home with a satisfied grunt and pushed the door open before stumbling in. Another day of dealing with illiterate adults and snotty-nosed kids had left him with little patience. He had decided to seek solace at a pub around the corner. The last thing he wanted to do was come home.

That evening, he found solace with his favourite friend, Jack. Several rounds later, the tension eased from his shoulders, so much so that the world around him began to spin. He'd not eaten anything since breakfast.

Glancing at his watch, he realised he'd gone more than twelve hours without food. Goddard's mouth was tinderbox dry, yet his throat was still parched.

He looked down at his bruised hands. His knuckles were red and purple. As he rubbed them, the anger once again bubbled up inside. His stomach tightened, causing his body to shiver.

She did this to me. She forced me to hit her. She never listens. That filthy slut of a wife of mine.

In the pub earlier, his eyes had fought hard to focus on the other punters. A mixture of old, sad, and lonely men like him had co-existed with young city types and their floozies.

"Women, bloody women," he snarled through clenched teeth.

He hated the way they had this Amazonian ability to twist any man around their little finger. The short skirts, high heels and big breasts were all that any hot-blooded man needed to fall under their hypnotic charm.

How can men be so weak?

But he was just as weak.

A common saying rolled around inside his head: Women, can't live with them, can't live without them.

He was guilty of thinking it. Believing it. Living it.

He'd been staring at the creamy flesh of those floozies all night, dulling his raging desires with booze. But it hadn't worked. Their slender thighs and tight calves – oh, how he'd wanted to touch them. God, how they turned him on. His heart pounded. His head spun...

He needed sex. Now.

Back home, the floozies became a distant memory as Goddard hauled himself slowly up the stairs. The quiet of the night was broken only by the sound of his laboured breathing. The drink hadn't dulled the cacophony of voices inside his head. They were banging off the walls of his skull like a pinball machine. A heavy throbbing in his neck kept him company more and more these days.

A thin crack of orange light seeped from underneath the bedroom door and pierced the darkness of the landing. He paused for a moment as his mind took a few seconds to catch up with what he was seeing. His wife was never one to go to sleep with the bedside lamp on.

This confused him as he swayed back and forth.

Goddard pushed open the bedroom door, expecting his wife to be fast asleep – wife...That was a joke – only to find her sitting on the end of the bed, fully dressed.

He glared at her, bewildered. Samantha Goddard was fiddling with her wedding band and engagement ring that rested in the palm of one hand. He steadied himself against the doorframe with one hand as his eyes caught a small suitcase by her feet. She looked up at him nervously, neither of them speaking first.

Goddard did. "Wha...What da fuck 'r you doing?" he slurred.

"I-I'm leaving you, Laurence. I can't s-stay here anymore. I need to leave now."

Goddard glanced around the room, his head bobbing like a nodding toy dog. His jaw dropped as he realised what she was saying.

Thick crease lines ploughed his forehead. "You're not going anywhere!"

"You can't stop me, Laurence. The only person you're interested in is yourself. You never confide in me, and yet keep telling me that you can't cope anymore. You drink too much and then come home and beat the shit out of me...I'm not going to be your punch bag anymore."

"Do you think I don't know what you been up to?" he slurred, jabbing a finger at her. "The way you dress up...you're inviting it. How many has it been, one, two – ten men? You're a disgrace, you filthy whore."

"No, Laurence," she said. "You're the bloody disgrace. Look at you. I don't even know who you are these days. You're drunk all the time. Overweight, losing your hair and obsessive and secretive. You're not the same person I married."

Goddard hated being challenged. The kids at the school challenged him daily. Their parents argued with him, and now his wife dared to speak to him in this way. He was fed up with being taken for granted.

He clumsily launched himself in the direction of the bed, his forward momentum carrying him as he part walked and part stumbled. He rushed his wife and gripped her by the throat, pinning her to the bed.

Her legs flailed as she thrashed around. Drool escaped from her shocked open mouth and ran down both cheeks.

Goddard leant into her, his face just inches away. He tried to kiss her, but with each attempt she'd thrash her head from left to right. Her resistance was rewarded with a heavy slap to her face. The sound of skin hitting skin echoed off the walls. Vibrations from his punishment ran through his palm, but the pain was numbed by the drink. The redness in his hand matched the redness on her cheek.

Goddard unzipped his trousers and dropped them to his ankles. He scratched and clawed at his wife's skirt, pushing it up to her waist. She kicked out furiously. Her attempt to escape was soon crushed when he punched her hard in the stomach. Samantha bent over, winded.

"Stop fighting, you silly bitch," he hissed at her. "You're mine...do you hear me? You're mine!"

He tore at her underwear, snapping the elastic and tearing the fabric in the process before tossing them away. He fell on top on her, then thrust into her with an aggressive grunt as he grabbed her hair and pulled with each movement.

Goddard let out a final grunt and shudder before rolling off and on to his back. He lay there a moment, his breath laboured and erratic.

His wife didn't move beside him, her body limp, her eyes clamped shut.

22

Matthew had spent the best part of an hour cowering under his duvet. He gripped the top of his bedding and pulled it tight under his chin. He looked fearfully into the darkness. His body craved sleep, but his mind raced in fear. He couldn't win either way. If he fell asleep, he knew the nightmares would wake him, as they had done so often. If he stayed awake, the waves of anxiety that racked his body would only intensify.

He finally succumbed and drifted off into a deep sleep. His subconscious mind replayed the events of the day as he tossed and turned, beads of sweat covering his forehead. His body jerked as he remembered the assault from earlier.

The door to the dormitory opened quietly, and Hunter, Rollings and Ford silently made their way to his bed. They glanced around at the other boys, deep in sleep and blissfully unaware of the fate that awaited one of their roommates. The odd groan and snort punctured the silence.

The three gathered around Edrington's bed, their eyes fixed on him. Rollings gave the other two a nod to proceed.

Hunter pressed a length of duct tape over Matthew's mouth whilst Ford held the boy down by his shoulders.

Hunter's eyes drilled into Matthew, who was still asleep, menace pouring from them for the ginger-haired boy. He smiled a sadistic smile.

Many students privately thought that Stephen Hunter was unhinged and a complete nutter. He had a reputation around school, a reputation that was fully justified. Several months earlier students had witnessed him capture a bird and break its neck as it thrashed around in his hands. He'd laughed as the bones cracked. He couldn't explain it, but he relished the act. He'd enjoyed seeing those around him wince in disgust and horror as he threw the lifeless body of the bird in nearby bushes.

The year before, another pupil had burnt his arm in a chemistry class after someone splashed bleach on it. Despite an internal school investigation, the perpetrator of the crime had never been officially identified. It was widely accepted by his peers that Hunter had been the instigator, but a wall of silence fuelled by fear meant that no one would come forward.

Rollings stepped forward as the other two boys dragged Matthew out of bed. The poor boy's eyes popped open as his arms were forcibly held behind his back. When a black hood was dropped over Matthew's head, Matthew let out a faint squeal. Hunter punched him hard in the kidneys, silencing him.

The trio forcibly pushed Matthew towards the door. Rollings peered out into the dark, cold corridor to check the coast was clear before nodding at them to follow. Hunter and Ford held Matthew tight as he stumbled blindly. His bare feet shuffled on the hard, cold parquet floor.

Matthew was led from Stanmer House, through the winding historic corridors that, over the years, had been graced by future politicians, CEOs, army generals and doctors. At night, these corridors took on a different meaning to Matthew. They were his hell.

He'd rather face a night on his own in the middle of the forest than endure the fear, humiliation, and degradation that he faced every day.

They walked Matthew through a much older part of the school, long consigned for redevelopment and no longer fit for purpose. Through a lack of maintenance and upkeep, it had fallen victim to ongoing disputes between the school and the planning department at Brighton and Hove Council over proposed plans for expansion. It was out of bounds to all students.

Plaster crumbled from the walls; damp crept up from the floor, destroying everything in its path. The parquet floor had long been removed to reveal a dusty, uneven concrete underneath that felt as rough as sandpaper on Matthew's bare feet. A lack of ventilation made the room feel claustrophobic with a stench like a mouldy damp cellar.

Matthew heard a door creak open, the swollen timber dragging on the uneven floor. He was thrust into a new room before coming to a stop.

The hood was yanked from his head. Matthew blinked furiously as he tried to adjust to the semi-darkness. The dirt and dust from years of neglect gathered on the boarded windowsills. Cobwebs draped from the ceiling, and dust particles drifted in the still air. Small candles placed around the room flickered, their ghostly shadows dancing on the walls. The faint trace of heat from the fireplace warmed his face, the orange and yellow glow illuminating the features of those gathered.

"I told you we'd see you later. The weakest amongst us need to be weeded out," Rollings said as he circled Matthew.

"You faggot. Now for your punishment...You'll take this like a man."

Without another word, Ford and Hunter secured ropes to Matthew's ankles and wrists before pulling them tight through iron fixtures in the wall. Strung up like a starfish, his shoulder blades and hips ached from the stressful position. Confusion clouded Matthew's senses. He pulled and thrashed in the vain attempt to free himself, but the harder he toiled, the more the rope cut into his skin. The stinging sensation burnt as red welts formed.

His eyes widened in shock as Rollings bent next to the fire and retrieved a small tin of black shoe polish. Matthew struggled, his breathing fast and heavy as panic consumed him. Ford grabbed Matthew's face, firmly gripping his chin and forcing him to look forward. Tears streamed from Matthew's eyes as he shook his head violently, trying to free himself. High-pitched, muffled cries indicated the terror that engulfed Matthew.

He became increasingly frantic, his head turning left and right as he tugged on the ropes that secured his arms. His body twisted and contorted as if possessed; beads of sweat raced down his face with his efforts.

Rollings walked slowly towards Matthew with a glint in his eyes. One gloved hand carried the warm tin; the other held a thick paintbrush. He nodded at Hunter, who pulled down Matthew's pyjama bottoms and underwear. He sniggered as he relished the opportunity to break the boy's fragile confidence and self-esteem even further. Matthew stood trembling, naked from the waist down. Cold, sweaty, and humiliated, his fate was in their hands. He had nowhere to go and no way of releasing himself. Tired, exhausted, and dazed, the last shred of fight drained from his small body.

Rollings stood before Matthew, his face expressionless, a cold stare fixed on the boy. He knelt down and smothered

Matthew's testicles with warm, black liquid shoe polish. Black-balling was the ultimate punishment and a long-standing ritual in boarding schools up and down the country. Once cooled and dried, the polish would be hard to remove. Matthew's screams intensified as they echoed around the room; each piercing cry bounced off the walls. He writhed in pain as he bucked in an attempt to escape the heat that scorched him. Tears streamed from his eyes. His cheeks reddened as each stroke of the polish-laden brush left him clenching his fists and curling up his toes.

Rollings ripped the duct tape from Matthew's mouth. His skin stung as the firmly fixed tape tugged at his wet skin. He screamed in agony through bleeding lips.

Another stroke of the brush prompted a haunting shrill of a scream that filled the room. His raw and hoarse throat burnt. The blood-curdling screams were in vain because no one would hear him. The old room had been the former music room. Despite its state of disrepair, the walls were still soundproofed.

He prayed for this to stop. He pleaded silently, unable to speak. His ginger hair, now heavily matted with sweat, clung to his face and shielded his view.

Matthew went limp, his body spent.

———————

23

S cott's thoughts still troubled him as he made his way into work the next morning. The intimidation he'd witnessed of Matthew had distressed and concerned him. Three against one meant the odds were heavily stacked in favour of the bullies who'd been harassing Matthew. An early morning run along the seafront hadn't helped to shake off the nagging feeling that clung to him.

On this running occasion, Abby had joined him. She was a far more competent runner than Scott. He saw it as a way to stay fit and get in a bit of cardio. Abby, on the other hand, always saw it as a competition – something he had noticed in her a while ago. She would strive to be the best in everything she applied herself to. She was a good mum to her kids and a top-class copper. She hated failure, and that was the catalyst that spurred her on. It was a quality he admired in her.

His gentle jog along the seafront had become yet another challenge for Abby. She'd left him for dust at the 3K mark when he'd chosen to head back. Abby ran an extra 5K, which was closer to her preferred distance of between eight and eleven kilometres. She had wanted to shake off a mild hangover after her date the night before with Jonathon, an optician.

Scott had teased her as they ran together, questioning whether Jonathon had forgotten his glasses at the office. She replied by saying that she'd quite enjoyed this whole dating lark, but found it stressful with the whole dressing-up thing and sorting out childminding.

It was typical Abby, the pessimist.

At the station, the duty sergeant buzzed Scott in, acknowledging him with a nod.

Scott could hear Mike's voice echoing from the floor above as he made his way up the stairwell. He found Mike outside the CID office in deep conversation with the same female police officer from previous occasions. They were talking in hushed tones; their conversation came to an abrupt halt when Scott got nearer. Mike had a pathetic grin on his face that suggested things were going well. The female officer looked rather more sheepish as she made her excuses and scuttled off down the stairs, casting a brief, embarrassed sideward glance at Scott as she brushed past him.

"Don't tell me you..." Scott said, pointing over his shoulder and shaking his head.

"Oh, yeah...Well, worth a round of drinks and curry last night."

"One day all these women are going to gang up on you, strip you naked and tie you to a lamp post as revenge."

Mike didn't have an answer as he followed his boss through the double swing doors leading to the main floor.

Scott headed over to the incident board to see if anything new had been added. The before and after photos of the two deceased men stared back at him. The images of victim two were disturbing to look at, his face half the size of what it was prior to the fall.

"Okay, team, let's get an update going. What've we got?" Scott perched on the edge of a desk.

Raj threw his pen on the table. "I've been talking to the other teachers and Mary Harrison. They couldn't shed any new light on the situation. Some seemed devastated at recent events, and others appeared unaffected, which seemed odd to me."

He continued, "Mary Harrison has been signed off work with stress, so I went to see her at her home. Apparently, the whole situation is getting too much for her. She seemed at odds with the head. I got the impression they didn't see eye to eye on how the school should be run or Mary's views on modernising the curriculum."

"Did Collier overrule her?"

"Not sure, to be exact, guv. I pushed her a bit and concluded that Collier wants things done in a strict, traditional way, and Mary Harrison wants to inject more variety into the school and make it more appealing and modern."

Abby chipped in, "The pathologist's report on Giles Rochester is in the system now, guv. We know he died because of the fall. He had multiple fractures to both arms, his hips, several broken ribs and severe trauma to the head. However, Dr Hall also identified a red band of bruising around the victim's neck. It's about an inch wide."

Abby continued flicking through the notes online. "The red banding was only around the front of the victim's neck. There's some localised bleeding where it cut into the skin. She believes the tiny lacerations are from applied force."

"Could he have been strangled and then thrown over?" asked Raj.

"Possibly, but I doubt it. You'd have to be pretty strong to lift a dead weight and throw it over a barrier," Scott replied.

He turned to the incident board and put a question mark by the word suicide. This was potentially looking like a second murder investigation. He made a mental note to talk to forensics about it. The victim's car needed to be examined in closer detail.

"Sian, what have you got for us?" he asked.

"I'm still working through the phone numbers and contacts, guv," she said, resting her elbows on the desk, her hands clasped together.

"How about CCTV?" Scott enquired.

"There isn't a lot of CCTV coverage by the car park or in the surrounding streets. However, we picked up the silver VW Golf driving past Worthing rail station in the direction of the car park. It's a bit of a grainy image because it was dark, but from the stills I pulled off, there only appears to be one person in the car, the driver." Sian passed round a few copies.

Scott tapped his whiteboard marker next to the images of victim two before pinning one of the still images beside Giles's case details. "So he went alone. Who did he meet there?" he asked quietly, staring at the grainy image depicting a lone figure in the driving seat of the VW Golf.

"Guv, he may have gone alone to meet someone, but there's nothing on CCTV. There's no one walking towards the car park, and no one walking away either," Sian said, scratching her head.

Scott stared at the grainy image for a few moments. "Sian, if you look at the image closely, something looks odd. I can't tell if it's a street light reflection distorting the image or something else. I'd get it checked out anyway."

Scott's observation caused the others to examine their copies in closer detail. Mike squinted as he strained to see the finer detail, and Sian rested her glasses on her head to get a closer look.

"Well, even though he hasn't been formally identified yet, we're working with the assumption that the victim from the car park is Giles Rochester. Forensics will no doubt confirm that with DNA sampling taken from the items we recovered from his property."

"Sian, what happened with the background search of staff members?" Scott asked.

"One name has come up, guv. John Morecombe. He was sacked about a year ago after confronting Collier about bullying of both staff members and pupils. He wasn't there long, one academic year. Last known whereabouts, according to the electoral register, has him living in Crediton in Devon."

"Did you follow up?"

"Yes, guv. I spoke to our colleagues down there. Crediton is a bit of a backwater, to be honest. They had less than fifty crimes reported in the previous twelve months, and the local police station is just a neighbourhood unit mainly manned with PCSOs. They checked his last known address, and he's since moved on. He's not known to them. I checked with DVLA and the Motor Insurers' Bureau, and there isn't a car registered in his name. He's disappeared off the radar. I'll check with DWP in case he's been drawing benefits somewhere. There's also the local authority and local education authority in case he's been working in schools, and I've still to do financial checks with Equifax."

Scott shifted as she settled on the edge of her desk. "Good job, Sian. Circulate his details locally and with the Devon lot. Check neighbouring counties too. We need to find him if for nothing more than to eliminate him from our enquiries. He may have an axe to grind..."

"Enough to kill?" Sian asked.

Scott shrugged in reply. "If so, then why not go after Collier? Find out if Morecombe had any issues with our two victims."

The team headed back to their desks in a flurry of activity.

SCOTT PUSHED OPEN the door to digital forensics and was greeted by the consistent sound of officers tapping keyboard keys. This office was where the magic happened. Highly trained specialists partnered with forensics and outsourced specialists to scrutinise evidence that, in his experience, made the difference between a conviction and a crime going unsolved. He thought of them as techies and geeks, but in reality, they were talented, calculated individuals with naturally curious minds. A team trained in forensic video and image analysis.

Scott wasn't technically versed in the finer points of their role; he just needed them to deliver results. They'd be called upon to assist with tasks like transcoding, image enhancing, slowing and enlarging video footage, right through to more complex tasks such as reverse projection and reconstructions, height calculation and comparative analysis. Whatever they did always left Scott in awe.

Martin Jones was a thin, middle-aged man with bony fingers that moved with grace and speed over his keyboard.

"Hi, Martin. Good to see you. Everything okay?" Scott asked.

"Yep, all good on the Western Front. Hear you've got a tricky case running. What do you need?"

"I need the image on this video still enhanced, if you can." Scott handed Martin a memory stick.

Martin plugged the stick in and opened its directory. The still image of Giles Rochester behind the wheel of his car filled the screen. "Any part in particular?"

"Yes, the driver portion."

Martin opened up another application on his screen and then dragged the image into it. A few clicks isolated the area in question, and then he scrolled on the wheel of his mouse. Each click sharpened the image a fraction until it was clearer.

"That's the best I can get it," Martin said.

They both peered closely at the highlighted section. Rochester had a distressed expression on his face. His head was firmly pulled back into his headrest, and his teeth were clenched with his lips pulled back in a snarl.

"Looks like he's got some sort of restraint around his neck. See that faint white line?" Martin pointed out.

"Looks like he's being held in place?" Scott offered.

"Looks like that to me, too. You've got someone else in the car with him."

24

M atthew Edrington paused for a moment, his hand just an inch from the door. He licked his dry sticky lips; his jangled nerves stopped him from catching his breath. He stared at the oak panelled door, in two minds as to whether to knock at all. He knew that once he walked through the door, there would be no turning back. He just wasn't sure if he had the courage to follow through.

He'd already attempted to knock once, pulling away as his hand twitched. With a deep breath he finally knocked again. He waited for what seemed an eternity, and when no response came, he knocked again, his knuckles smarting from the extra force. The noise echoed up and down the corridor. It was sharp and short like a cricket ball striking willow.

"Enter," came a firm, booming voice from behind the door. It made Matthew jump.

He tentatively turned the handle and took half a step in, peering around the door.

"Come in, Edrington...don't just stand there," said

Edward Chapman, the housemaster for Stanmer House.
"Take a seat."

He motioned to a metal-framed leather seat that sat to the
side of his bureau desk. He swivelled around in his chair,
smoothing out the creases in his grey corduroy trousers as he
did. He was a rotund man with a rosy face and double chin.
He had an unusual-looking face, small eyes closely set
together with a pointed, thin, Roman nose.

Matthew took a seat and nervously wrung his hands in
his lap, his jaw on the verge of chattering with nerves.

Chapman placed his hands on his thighs as he leant back
in his chair. "How can I help, Edrington?"

Matthew looked around the room. His nerves were
paralysing him, threatening to engulf him in a dark whirl-
wind of fear and panic. He still had an opportunity to make
his excuses and leave, his mind a mix of confusion and fear.

Should I? Shouldn't I?

His stomach flipped, and he couldn't tell if he was going
to throw up or shit himself. And all this time Chapman stared
at him with a raised eyebrow.

"Well?" A sense of annoyance in Chapman's tone
suggested frustration with Matthew's silence.

"S-sir," he stammered, his mouth parched, making it difficult to say anything. "Sir...I'm...being bullied..."

There, he'd said it. There was no turning back now. He
thought he'd feel a sense of relief for sharing his burdens, but
he didn't. He felt as if he'd just opened up a huge chasm in
the side of Vesuvius, and now all hell would break loose. The
secret that he'd carried for such a long time was now
exposed. He started to doubt whether this had been a good
idea.

Chapman raised a brow again and cocked his head to one
side. He studied the boy for a few moments as though unsure
as to how genuine the claim was.

"Can you tell me *exactly* what you mean by being bullied?" he asked slowly, resting his hands on his thighs and leaning in towards Matthew.

Matthew clenched his hands tighter as they glistened with sweat. He shifted nervously in the chair; every ounce of his courage was being drawn upon to reveal more of his treatment.

"Some boys have been hitting me. They corner me in the corridors and push me around. Sometimes they punch me. They've attacked me in the dorm at night and done other things to me..." His gaze dropped to the floor, his voice nothing more than a whisper.

"You do realise that allegations of this nature are not to be taken lightly?"

Matthew nodded slowly but didn't look up, a mixture of embarrassment and fear paralysing him.

"Listen, young Edrington, are you sure about this? There's plenty of argy-bargy in every school up and down the country. A bit of tomfoolery comes with the territory, I'm afraid. It's part of the toughening-up process. You know sometimes it can get a bit out of hand, but there's no malice ever intended."

"But...sir..." Matthew fell silent, unable to find the right words to explain his plight.

Chapman raised his palm to stop Matthew. "Here's what I suggest. Why don't you start by having a chat with the house prefects. They lead by example, and it's their job to support boys like you in tough times. They have been chosen for their exemplary record, their leadership, confidence, and initiative. And I hasten to add, their job is to create an atmosphere of friendly cooperation, peace, discipline, and unity in the school. Prefects should serve as counsellors to junior students like yourself." He drew in a deep breath and puffed out his chest.

"But, sir –"

"Yes, I know, lad," he interrupted. "It can be a daunting thing to talk about, but you've done the right thing. The prefects are there to maintain the front line of discipline; we want the pupils to sort out their differences. If they can't, then we step in as housemasters." He gave an exaggerated shrug, holding his hands out in front.

"Yes...sir," Matthew replied. His shoulders drooped as the dejection played heavily on his mind. Resignation washed over him.

"Good man, now why don't you go and find them? Have a little chat and see how you get on, hmm?"

Matthew swallowed hard as he stood and made his way out. The fear rose in him, bile burning the back of his throat. How could he? He couldn't turn to them. His prefects were Rollings, Ford and Hunter. Would anyone even believe him? Maybe the police would. Mr Saunders would.

AT FIRST, the man stood alone, looking around. It was a room that brought back a multitude of memories. Back then, he'd visited it once a week for his guitar lessons as he was growing up. A wry smile broke across his face as he recalled his attempts at learning his chords, scales, and progressions, much to the dissatisfaction of his teacher. Back then, opting in for music lessons meant an easy way out from attending other timetabled lessons.

The room had seen better days, now just a former shell in comparison. Crumbling plaster lay scattered on the dusty, uneven concrete. Dampness hung in the air, and dust gathered on the boarded windowsills.

Old traditions die hard, he thought as he noticed the

small candles dotted around the room. A sombre cloak of melancholy replaced his smile.

His moment of reflection was disturbed by the arrival of two others. One stood holding the door frame for support, his face pale and hollow with prominent cheekbones. His effort to climb a few flights of steps and navigate empty, dark hallways was clearly evident from the tiny droplets of sweat in his tightly cropped hair. A walking stick helped with balance. Sharp, heavy intakes of breath were equally matched in length by long whistling exhales.

The other man shifted on the spot, undecided whether to leave his hands in the pockets of his bomber jacket or jeans. He clearly felt uncomfortable meeting with the others. Their numbers were fast shrinking, which increased the apprehensive churning he felt. His dry mouth screamed for a drink from the nearest pub.

"We...we can't go on like this," said the first man as he caught his breath.

A slight whistle and crackle in his breath indicated asthma and COPD. Years of a twenty-a-day smoking habit had left him with chronic obstructive pulmonary disease. He'd been warned about it on many occasions, but he'd never managed to give up his Marlboros. The deadly weed had finally claimed his health and his job, forcing him to retire early.

The second man nodded in agreement but was too wary to speak up. He was scared of himself and what rubbish might tumble out of his mouth. His head felt like it had been hit with a sledgehammer, a thumping headache eating away inside him. The culprits: a lack of sleep and dehydration. He couldn't think straight. A dull fog clouded his thinking on a daily basis.

"The other two brought it on themselves," one said. "They weren't careful enough. For all we know, they may have blabbed to some fool and, well...who knows? I want you both to keep your mouths shut and remain vigilant at all times – understood?"

The two men nodded quickly in unison and glanced at each other, both lacking the backbone to challenge the leader.

"If anyone asks, you stick to the story. You didn't know the others particularly well, and you can't explain why anyone would wish to harm them. Now return home and wait for further instructions and updates from me. Carry on as normal. Don't do *anything* that might attract attention." The leader turned to face the fireplace, placing his thumbs in the pockets of his waistcoat.

The other two men stood there for a few moments, exchanging awkward glances in the dark, unsure what to do.

They turned and left, one scurrying away, his rapid footsteps echoing in the corridor. The other, a slow steady tapping from the walking stick as it signalled his slow departure.

25

His drive home had been filled with a swirling mass of confusion. His chest burnt, his lungs felt tight, and saliva kept pooling in his mouth. In recent years, he'd noticed the COPD worsening. The reality dawned on him that in the near future he'd be reliant on an oxygen bottle in order to survive. The thought of dragging a bottle around on a trolley grated his nerves. He looked like a man twenty years his senior, already consigned to the pipe and slippers brigade. He walked with a slight hunch, deeply set lines prematurely aged his face, and he rarely smiled through tobacco-stained teeth.

Under his breath, he cursed his misfortune.

It's just my luck; bad luck seems to follow me around like a bad smell.

How can they be so blasé about this? People are dying.

He thumped the steering wheel every few minutes. "What's the point in keeping my mouth shut and remaining vigilant at all times? Are you having a laugh?" he shouted. "When will this all end?" he mumbled through a raspy cough that rattled his chest.

Slow deep breaths in and out helped. He had to be careful of his hypertension. The last thing he needed was more health complications. On numerous occasions the doctor's advice had been to take it easy. It was advice he'd heeded by tending to his potted plants in his small greenhouse and chatting to the neighbours. Many of them were retired and relished any opportunity to fill the massive hours of loneliness that now filled their lives.

Turning into his road, he reflected on how much he enjoyed where he lived. For as far as the eye could see, bungalows surrounded him. It was a safe neighbourhood, a place where he looked forward to seeing out the rest of his retirement. He'd deliberately chosen this property, a corner plot that added generous dimensions to his property. An L-shaped front lawn wrapped around two sides of his house. To the right was a small cul-de-sac, something that meant less traffic noise. He was grateful for the quiet to enjoy the serene moments in his garden.

He carefully turned into his driveway, craning his neck get a better view as he navigated the narrow lane. The darkness of the night played tricks on his eyes. He crept slowly up the drive, careful not to damage the assortment of plants and shrubs that provided a natural border.

He remained in the car for a few moments, tiredness consuming him. Devoid of all energy, the prospect of walking just a few yards to his front door seemed like a Herculean task.

A dark-clothed figure leaning up against a wall on the other side of the road observed his every movement. His patience had been rewarded. When the car door opened, it flooded the inside cabin with light and showed him his target. Beads of sweat chased down his back; his heart pounded like a drum. His next victim was in sight.

He watched as the interior light was extinguished, and a

car door slamming shut echoed in the street. The target shuffled slowly around to the front of his house, a methodical scraping noise puncturing the silence.

The man dragged his feet, each step heavier than the last. His breathing was laboured; a fast, shallow wheeze signalled the need for his medication.

The small wrought-iron gate creaked eerily from its rusty hinges. He took the final few steps to his white front door. His laboured breaths drowned out the light footsteps that had followed him for the last few feet.

Without a moment's hesitation, the assailant looped a length of thin white plastic tape around the man's neck, cutting into his skin. The man staggered backwards, his jaw clenched, his eyes wide with fear. He pulled frantically at the tape that was fast blocking off his airway. He wanted to shout, but all he could manage was a faint hiss. His body was unable to either support him or fight off the attacker, who was now pulling him backwards down to the ground.

He fell back hard on his elbows. The sound of bone cracking caused him to cry out in pain. A deep throbbing pain radiated up his arm and into his shoulder. His mind whirled.

His assailant flipped him over onto his front and knelt on his back, forcing the air out of his weak lungs. The plastic tape did its job. The veins throbbed in his neck, and black spots appeared in his vision. Darkness took over, and his life ebbed away. He gurgled one final breath, the mucus in his throat finding no place to escape.

The assailant looked around to see if he had attracted any attention. He'd done what he needed to do. Standing over the lifeless body, he waited for the adrenaline rush to die down.

26

Hangleton Valley Drive was the last place Scott expected to be called out for a suspicious death. Situated on the northern-west fringe of Brighton, it was skirted by the Benfield Valley Golf Course and the A27, which was conveniently hidden behind dense woodland. The low drone of traffic thundering along the Shoreham bypass could nevertheless be heard on the golf course.

A safe, quiet neighbourhood sprang to mind as he made his way along the wide road. It was the type of place that families and downsizers moved to when they wanted a better balance between quiet and the buzz of Brighton. He figured it was a place for retirees who wanted a more laid-back, community feel.

On either side of him were clean, well-maintained, deep driveways proudly sporting well-tended lawns and shrubs. Bungalows stretched out in front of him as far as the eye could see. There was no evidence of litter, or loitering youths and boy racers who annoyed residents in other parts of the town.

Scott took an instant shine to the area. It wasn't a place

he'd usually have cause to visit in the line of duty – until now. That thought dulled the pleasant thoughts that ran through his mind. The area had a close-knit feel, and he could imagine living around here himself one day, a thought that made him smile.

Look at me. I'm already planning my retirement, picking my house and choosing the right lawnmower...just need to find out where the nearest lawn bowls club is.

Scott shook his head in light-hearted disbelief.

The cordon was well established by the time he'd arrived. Having signed in with the scene guard, WPC Willits, and put on a paper forensic suit, he headed over to the white tent that was positioned over the front door of the property.

Matt Allan, the crime scene manager, packed away his notepad when he saw Scott approaching.

"Morning, Scott. We've got another one for you, same MO from the looks of it," he said, holding up two clear plastic evidence bags.

Scott made out a white feather in one and a small piece of white paper in the other. He grimaced and sighed as he leant in for a closer inspection. "Strangled?"

"Yep, looks like it... How did you guess?"

Scott didn't reply, offering a shrug instead. He crossed his arms in frustration and glanced around the plot. "The pathologist here yet?"

Matt looked at Scott, a small knowing smile curling the edges of his mouth. "You should know that, mate..."

Scott stared at the ground, unsure of a response. "I don't get your drift."

"Mate, you and the *path* are the worst-kept secret in the nick... Everyone knows you two are an item." He laughed.

"Erm, really?" he asked, shaking his head in embarrassment. "So much for keeping it quiet."

"No chance, mate...You're front-page news, and I have to

say that a few of our female colleagues are a tad upset that you're off the market."

"That's all I need...more gossip."

Keen to change the subject, he turned towards the tent and peeked in. Another crime scene officer was crouched down, taking close-up photos of the victim's neck. He had been turned onto his back for closer examination.

"He's got ligature marks around his neck, but no other signs of assault or bruising," Matt said over Scott's shoulder. "We did find some plastic tape still wrapped around his neck. We'll get that analysed to see if we can get anything from it."

Scott spun around. "Seriously?" He hadn't been expecting that. They hadn't found similar evidence on the last victim, so either the killer was getting sloppy, or they weren't bothered about it being found. "Okay, Matt. Keep me informed."

Scott made his way towards the cordon tape where Abby and Raj were talking to neighbours and bystanders watching the macabre scene. Cara had turned up moments earlier and was already making her way to the tent. She and Scott had agreed to travel in separate cars and stagger their journeys to avoid the awkward moment of them both arriving in one car. The intention behind that master plan had clearly backfired on them.

"What do we know about the victim?" Scott asked the pair.

"Guv, residents have confirmed that an Alex Winterbottom lived here. The car over there" – Raj waved to the side of the house – "is registered in the same name, and the contents of the wallet found on the deceased match up too."

Scott ingested the information as he glanced around at the surrounding properties. He hoped that someone might have CCTV set up on the front of their house, but his optimism was short-lived. It didn't call for such measures around here, he figured. Nevertheless, he saw the familiar yellow sticker of the neighbourhood watch scheme in all the windows and made a mental note to get Raj to contact the coordinator to build up a picture of the area.

His thoughts were interrupted by Abby continuing with a review of her notes. Something she said made him backtrack.

"What was that?" he asked quickly.

"He's an ex-teacher... Edmunston-Hunt boarding school. Neighbours said he'd been retired a few years now due to ill health."

"Anyone see or hear anything last night?"

"Nope, a neighbour who lives a few doors down in The Meadows walked past about nine thirty p.m. last night after walking the dog and swears that he looked in the direction of Winterbottom's house and saw nothing out of the ordinary."

Scott's phone vibrated in his pocket. Pulling it out, he saw Mike's number flashing up on the screen.

"Yes, Mike..."

Scott listened intently, throwing in the odd "hmm," "yes," and "okay" before hanging up.

"Abby, can you take over here? Liaise with the pathologist when she's out? I need to head over to Edmunston-Hunt. Mike has just had a call from your *creepy* caretaker. He's found something and alerted the police."

27

The case played on Scott's mind as he headed out of Brighton towards Ditchling. *Three deaths in under a week.*

At first his thoughts centred on a problem with the school and the current teaching staff. *A disgruntled member of staff perhaps?*

But most of the staff had been interviewed; background checks had nearly been completed with a few outstanding. Nothing stood out that rang alarm bells, not even a bloody parking ticket.

He pondered the prospect of the murderer being a disgruntled parent, but that was highly unlikely. The majority of parents held important positions, had wealth and status. Murder wasn't on their agenda. *Would they risk losing all of that?*

He tapped his thumb on the wheel in time with a random song on the radio.

As he made his way down the long access road towards the school, a lone figure stood by the main entrance. As Scott neared, a man in blue overalls came into focus.

There's your creepy caretaker, Abby.

The man shuffled slowly towards Scott as he got out of the car, his steps small and quick. The oversized overalls hanging low between his legs hindered his stride length.

"Alan Bennett?" Scott asked.

The man nodded once.

"I'm Detective Inspector Baker. You've probably seen me around here a few times. I understand you called my team because you've found something?"

"Erm, yes, I did."

Scott wasn't sure which part Bennett agreed with, seeing him before or finding something, but nevertheless carried on. "Do you want to lead the way?"

Bennett looked sullen as he turned, his head a little bowed, and made his way around to the side of the building. As Scott followed, his feet scuffed over the large gravel area that skirted the front of the school. The crunching sound amplified in the quiet between them. He was led through a smaller side door that took them through to an older part of the school.

From the looks of it, the old section hadn't been used for many years. The dusty floors and musty smell that hit his nostrils confirmed it. A dull light streamed in through the old, dirty steel Crittall windows.

Bennett walked through the winding corridors, barely stopping to check if the detective was still with him. He stopped outside a room and pointed at a padlock and shackle that had been forcibly broken. Thin marks etched in the wood hinted at a blunt instrument being used.

Scott glanced at the door before looking at Bennett. The lack of explanation for being brought here perplexed him. He shrugged, waiting for more from the caretaker.

Bennet said, "I locked the door myself many years ago,

not been in this part of the building for just as long. But I found this damage last night on my rounds."

"Who has access to this part of the school?" Scott enquired as he leant in to take a closer look.

"No one. I have the only keys; someone's broken in..."

Bennett's powers of deduction were remarkable.

"Is the route we took the only means of access to this room?" Scott asked, looking along the abandoned corridor.

"No..." Bennett replied slowly, scratching his temple. "It can be accessed from an old storeroom in the main building. The lock to the door in the storeroom has been broken too."

"Have you been inside?"

"Yeah, someone's been here."

Bennett opened the large, heavy door. It had dropped from its hinges over the years and now scraped across the floor as it was being opened. He looked at Scott, stone-faced, telepathically inviting him to take a look inside.

Scott stepped into the room. It was dark but not so much that he couldn't see the footprints that criss-crossed in random directions. Recent activity had disturbed the grey carpet of dust that had built up over the years.

An acrid smell hung in the air. Half-burnt tea lights lay scattered around the floor, the window ledge to his left, and on the old, dark oak mantelpiece around a small fireplace and hearth.

Scott walked over and knelt beside the fireplace, his footsteps softened by the bed of dust. He picked up a shard of scorched kindling next to the base of the fire. He sniffed one end and immediately caught the distinct smell of an accelerant – perhaps lighter fuel.

The remnants of a singed newspaper lay scattered around the hearth. He combed his fingers through several pieces before picking up a small fragment, scalded brown and blackened around the edges. As he scanned the words, he noticed it was the header of a newspaper dated two weeks prior.

Scott rose and continued to look around the darkened room, no doubt used by persons unknown, and recently enough.

Thoughts turned over in his mind. Was this connected in some way to his current investigation, or were the pupils using it as some sort of den?

Then something caught his attention. It was hanging from a silver hook screwed into the wall by the window. Not wanting to disturb the scene any further, he stayed where he was. From his position he observed a length of rope, about four feet in length. Curious enough, but what sparked Scott's curiosity further was the loop that had been tied in the end. As he looked to the opposite wall, he saw a similar hook and rope attachment.

Some sort of improvised bindings.

"Mr Bennett, I'm going to arrange for some officers to come down here to take a closer look at this room. No one is allowed in, and nothing must be touched – understand?" Scott instructed.

Bennett nodded once.

Scott stood outside the entrance to the old school section that he and Bennett had used. As he paced around, he placed a call to the station to send uniformed officers and SOCO to the scene. Ordinarily he would dismiss such flimsy evidence, but with three deaths in six days and rope being used in at least one of those cases, he needed to cover all bases. With DCI Harvey on his back for a speedy result, and Chief Constable Lennon taking a personal interest in this case, Scott had little margin for error. Every lead, every piece of evidence and every hunch needed to be thoroughly investigated.

From his location, he could see a small cottage different to the ones for teachers, sitting close to the edge of the forest, that could be responsible for the noise.

As far as he recalled, Bennett's small lodging was behind the main cottages for teachers. Scott walked over to it. The dwelling was small, possibly just a single bedroom and what he'd call a two-up two-down compact des res. A dull white pebble-dashed exterior in need of some TLC was in marked contrast to the chocolate-box cottages offered to teaching staff.

Scott strolled around the back of the cottage, only to discover the source of the noise. A purpose-built aviary held an assortment of birds that were fluttering from one stand to another. His arrival only intensified their chirping and cooing. Scott leant on the wire mesh of the cage. This only agitated the birds further, as they flew in his direction.

He couldn't pick out the breeds of the smaller birds, but what had spiked his interest was the presence of several white pigeons. The same colour feathers as was found on the victims.

As he walked away, he also noticed boundary rope stored neatly by the back door of the cottage.

Scott pulled a number on his phone and waited for it to connect. "Matt, can DNA analysis be done on a pigeon feather?"

Matt replied, "I would imagine so, but it's not really my field of expertise. Considering you can do DNA analysis, DNA screening and profiling of animals, and pretty much everything else, I can't see any reason why you couldn't. I'd imagine there are specialist companies for that. Any reason you're asking?"

"Just something I'm playing around with." Scott hung up, then picked up a few feathers from the ground and placed them in a clear evidence bag for analysis.

28

S cott left the room in the derelict part of the school in the hands of SOCO after their arrival. None of the pupils had noticed the activity, and school life carried on around them. That in itself worried Scott, that illegal activities could be happening there without anyone's knowledge.

There was a sense of suspended reality to this place. The school carried on as if nothing bad had happened. Teachers delivered classes, pupils appeared unfazed, and the atmosphere had a controlled and clinical feel to it. It certainly wasn't what Scott had expected, but then again, this wasn't a *normal* school.

When Scott arrived at the head's office, Collier was seated in his red leather wingback chair. He sat facing the large leaded window overlooking the front of the school. For a man in charge of a school embroiled in a series of murder investigations, he seemed unfazed by it. That should have surprised Scott, but having witnessed the man's demeanour on several occasions and the general atmosphere around the school and staff, nothing surprised him now.

"Mr Collier, you and I need a chat," Scott said firmly as he walked in.

Collier replied with nothing more than a nod.

Scott placed himself between Collier and the window and crossed his arms. "I've just come from the old music room, and it appears that despite it being out of bounds, it was accessed recently. I need answers, Mr Collier, and I need them now."

Scott's firm tone left Collier with little doubt as to the gravity of the situation the school faced.

Collier had his elbows resting on the armrests, his fingers joined in a steeple that supported his chin. His eyes were fixed in a vacant stare that ignored Scott and looked out at the gardens. He looked weary. The events of the past week had clearly taken their toll on him.

With a heavy sigh, Collier's shoulders dropped, and he lifted his gaze to meet with Scott's. Pulling himself up straight, he stood up, resignation etched into the creases on his forehead and around his eyes.

"Walk with me, Inspector?" he asked as he trudged towards the door.

An eerie silence followed the pair as they made their way back out through reception past Mrs Hilary, who watched open-mouthed, unsure as to what was happening. She'd already locked horns with Scott earlier as he'd breezed past her, ignoring her demands that he wait.

Stepping out into the sunshine, Scott squinted. The heavy mood didn't change as they walked slowly around the grounds of the school, their footsteps muffled by the closely cropped lawns.

"So much has changed since I was a pupil here from age eleven until I joined the army at eighteen." Melancholy tinged Collier's voice. "It was a good school, the best. It's why I came back here after my twenty-two years of military service to begin my teaching career. It was in my blood, you see. I couldn't imagine doing anything else. I taught for two years before progressing to housemaster, deputy head and finally becoming the head at the age of fifty-six. That was twelve years ago.

"My experience of being a student here will remain with me forever. It was a fair but well-oiled machine. Discipline was key," he remarked as he cleared his throat. "We were the future leaders of industry, the future of the British Army – the future ambassadors and attachés of the British government in far-flung countries. This establishment comes with a strong, proud history. More than one hundred years, Inspector, a strong pedigree, you see. Did you know that it was set up by Brigadier General Edmunston of the Queen's Royal Artillery and the Reverend Christopher Hunt, a chaplain to the forces who held the rank of major?"

He carried on without waiting for an answer from Scott.

"Then she came along..."

"Who?"

"That Harrison woman. That wretched woman... She wanted to modernise the school, make it co-ed. Many objected – me included. All the traditions we valued and lived by have been replaced by modern-day thinking. The prospect of co-ed education. Whatever next, eh?"

"Hmm," Scott replied.

"The board of governors, well, the majority, agreed with the changes," Collier continued through gritted teeth. "She convinced them. Batted her eyelids and had them eating out of her hand. The modernisation programme included knocking down the older parts of the school, including the music room, and replacing it with dance studios, a small theatre, a drama room. There was even talk of selling off some of our land to build an elite finishing school for girls. Some bloody joint venture with the Roedean crowd." Collier dropped his head, worry lines creasing his forehead. Sadness and anger were clearly eating away at him. He had his hands tightly locked behind his back.

"So what can you tell me about the music room?" Scott asked.

"Ah, the music room. I never really had a reason to go there as a teacher. I taught history and politics – my forte. To be honest, I didn't even know it was being used now." He shrugged weakly.

Scott felt a degree of remorse for the man. He was well and truly attached to the past, a past that had shaped and guided him, but nevertheless, Collier knew more than he was letting on. Scott was sure of that.

Collier continued, "I knew that things went on in there. They happened even when I was a lad here, but it was just how the school was run. Of course, there was a bit of argybargy, and the proverbial initiation ceremonies before acceptance into a house by the senior pupils. The prefects got a bit heavy-handed, but it was boisterous more than anything else. If you can't take a bit of aggro, it's unlikely that you'll survive in the real world."

The pair came to an uncomfortable pause on the lawns as Collier glanced around to survey his domain.

Scott said, "Obstruction or withholding information that could help my investigation is a criminal offence. I hope you realise that, Mr Collier."

"I've nothing to hide, Inspector. We live by the sword; we die by the sword."

An odd and perhaps extreme ideology.

"Mr Collier, let me remind you that two members of your current teaching staff are dead; a former member of staff is dead too. This is a multiple murder investigation, and this school, *your* school," Scott said, sweeping his arm at the main building, "is at the centre of it. My team is currently poring over every detail of this school, its history and its staff. We will find out who's committing these crimes. It's only a matter of time, and I hope for your sake – and for your career – that you're not tied up in this."

Collier faced the school. He paused for a moment as he stood alongside Scott.

Then he turned his head slightly, his eyes heavy with resignation. "My career is already over, Inspector."

29

Any hope of Scott slipping in to work without being seen by DCI Harvey evaporated when the desk sergeant pointed out that the DCI had been asking for him. She was clearly tracking him down because several other officers stopped to also mention it on his way to his office.

He breathed a sigh of relief when he made it without seeing her, only to jump when he saw DCI Harvey sitting in his chair. Her hands were clasped together on the desk, fingers interlocked. She raised a brow at him.

He'd seen that look many times on her face. She was pissed off.

"Ma'am?"

"Scott, CC Lennon is...shall we say, a little *concerned* at the lack of progress, and frankly, I don't take kindly to getting a barrow full of elephant shit down the phone first thing in the morning. I've got three deaths in under a week on my watch, no evidence of substance, no witnesses, sketchy CCTV, and more importantly, no one sitting in a bloody cell downstairs. Have I missed anything, Inspector?"

Scott had hoped to correct her on some of those facts, but she wasn't far from the truth. It looked just as grim for her as it did for Scott and the team. They'd made little progress, and a week on, questions were being raised from management, questions he didn't have answers for.

"Ma'am, I know it doesn't look great, but we're dealing with a bit of an unusual case here and –"

"There's nothing unusual about it, Scott," she interrupted. "We've got three suspicious deaths. They appear to be connected. Statements need to be taken and reviewed again. Forensics need to be re-examined, and questions need to be asked." She paused for a moment. "What's difficult about that? You're a *detective*. You lead a team of *detectives*. Do what you're supposed to do, or do I need to find someone else to take over the investigation?"

Scott had never seen Harvey come on so strong. She was enraged and frustrated, and her words were sharp and precise. In all the time he'd worked for her, she'd never questioned his authority, management of his team or his capability. If he felt pressure, then she was likely getting it tenfold from CC Lennon.

"It's not as clear-cut as that, ma'am."

"Don't mug me off, Scott," she said, thumping a fist on the desk.

Scott blew out his cheeks as he collapsed in a chair opposite Harvey.

Any investigation involving a suspicious death could take weeks and sometimes months to solve. He had a stack of files somewhere on the floor filled with unsolved deaths, cases dating back months and years that without new evidence, new breakthroughs in forensic science or witnesses, would likely languish away in a brown box.

Occasionally, he would pull them out and have a flick through. He would cast a fresh look over them in case something had been missed on previous case reviews. Invariably, nothing changed. They were statistics, nothing more than case file numbers.

"Ma'am, as I was about to say" – Scott glared at DCI Harvey – "we are making inroads. The plastic tape that we believe was used to kill victim three this morning was still wrapped around the deceased's neck. Forensics have that now. I've just come back from the school after being called out there by the caretaker. A derelict room in the old part of the school has been used recently. Now it may or may not be connected, but we're following up. And I'm sure that the head knows more than he's letting on."

"So why isn't he in here being interviewed?" Harvey snapped back.

"I'm planning to, ma'am..."

"Planning isn't good enough, Scott," she barked, rising to her feet. "I want a progress report from you first thing, understood?"

Scott nodded as she made for the door.

"First thing," she repeated and left.

Some would have questioned their ability after DCI Harvey's verbal attack. Others would have walked around like a bear with a sore head all day, but Scott had been on the receiving end of worse. Whilst in training as a rookie, he was forever saying the wrong things to defuse confrontational situations. This had led to several of his trainers pulling him up on his communication style. It's one of the reasons that he'd gone on to learn neurolinguistic programming. He saw NLP as a way to better his ability to read others, understand human behavioural patterns, as well as improve his own depth of communication.

Scott took a deep breath and slowly released it, to refocus his thoughts.

After straightening his Thomas Pink deep navy tie and fixing his suit jacket, he headed off to grab a coffee.

On the way he shouted to his team, "Quick catch-up in five minutes!"

30

L eaning on the edge of Abby's desk, Scott sipped on the tepid, bitter coffee as he stared at the incident board that now had pictures of victim number three pinned to it. Three middle-aged men, all teachers, all dead.

"Listen up, team. I spoke with Matt Allan earlier. It's taken some time, but we can confirm that the rope found at Giles Rochester's property had the same fibre composition as the rope used on Johnson. I had a look around the school lawns to see if there was any missing from the boundary rope, but that's all intact. But I'll come back to that in a moment. Remind me if I forget, Abby."

An officer from the back spoke up. "Guv, there's been a sighting of John Morecombe, the missing teacher. Hampshire police got back to me. Morecombe was nicked for speeding on the A31 east near Winchester. He was driving a hire car, heading east."

"Towards Sussex?"

"Possible, guv. That was two weeks ago. A week before that, he was arrested and bailed for being drunken and disorderly. He assaulted the door staff trying to throw him out. He threw a chair at them. Spent the night in the cells, sleeping it off."

"Where's the car and Morecombe now?"

"Not been seen since the speeding offence. The car was never returned. I've circulated the car details to uniform here so they can keep a lookout just in case he's coming back to Brighton."

Raj waved a sheet of paper. "DNA analysis, using the hair fibres and toothbrush from Rochester's property, confirm that vic two is Giles Rochester, but we knew that anyway. Also, there were tiny fibres found on the compression marks on both Johnson and Rochester. In Johnson's case, two different sets of fibres were found under magnification. Fibres matching the boundary rope were present, however..." Raj paused as he referred to his sheet. "A second set of fibres were found on Johnson that matched those found on Rochester's neck."

All eyes were on Raj as he revealed more. It was during moments like this that Raj lapped up the attention. More often than not, he was given menial information-gathering tasks that kept him occupied, and more importantly silent – much to the relief of the team. The thirty-one-year-old officer played the practical joker card a little too often, which meant Raj wasn't taken seriously as an officer or someone looking to push on in their career.

"The fibres are PP or polypropylene – as you'd find in plastic strapping tape."

"Okay, that's helpful. Thanks, Raj," said Scott.

"What's PP?" Sian asked.

"It's a type of plastic, Sian," Scott replied. "In this case and judging from the width of the depressions left in the skin and how clear and sharp the edges are on the skin" – Scott pointed out the impressions identified in the close-up post-mortem pictures – "I'd say its PP straps similar to those used as bindings around cartons and boxes."

He continued, "Unfortunately for us, it's a common packaging tape used around the globe, so not easy for us to follow up on. You can buy it anywhere. I guess there's the option to do a chemical composition analysis on it."

The news left the team with mixed feelings. It appeared to be another dead end.

Scott said, "The DCI is really pushing for some results, so we need to pull out all the stops. There's more to this case than meets the eye. The head is without a doubt hiding something, so, Mike, I want you to bring him in. Tell him he's helping us with our enquiries. I've just come from the school, and he's a little too laid-back for my liking. He seems angry about all the proposed changes put forward for the school. Our first two vics seemed to approve and side with Mary Harrison about future proposals. It's clear the school means a lot to Collier, and he'd do anything to keep the status quo."

"Enough to commit murder?" Raj asked. Scott didn't have an answer.

Scott's phone vibrated in his trouser pocket. Ignoring it, he continued.

"Sounds like it, guv," Mike said.

"Guv, you said to remind you," Abby said.

"Yes, cheers, Abby. Two things. After I left Bennett, I came across an aviary of some sort...behind Bennett's cottage. Amongst the birds were a few white pigeons. Could be completely random, and they're freely found in any park, but the fact that we have white feathers left with the victims is suspicious. I thought that they could have come from there. There was also more boundary rope behind his house. Now purely circumstantial again, but we still need to follow it up."

"Are you suggesting that Bennett may be involved?" Raj asked.

"I won't rule him out as a suspect, but he doesn't seem capable of planning something like this. I can't think of a motive. Collier, after all, gave him a break with a job. We know criminals are less likely to reoffend if they have a job, but we keep Bennett on our radar for the moment. The cage isn't locked, so anyone could have had access to the birds. I've given Matt some feather samples," he said. "There are firms doing DNA profiling for animals, but results take five to seven working days. Clearly we haven't got that long, so he's going to try to push them to prioritise our analysis."

"Who would have thought you could do that," Raj remarked.

Scott said, "Apparently, it's very common in racing pigeon circles because birds are so precious. They do all sorts of testing and screening like DNA parentage, genetic disorders and infectious diseases like cryptosporidium and pigeon circovirus. And before you ask, no I haven't got a sodding clue what they are, nor do I wish to know."

A light ripple of laughter spread through the team.

"The other point I wanted to bring to your attention was the CCTV still image we've got of Rochester. I've had the image enhanced," he said, pinning a fresh, blown-up image to the incident board.

He had their full attention now. The team straightened up in their seats and took in the new image with a mixture of nodding heads and the odd raised brow.

Scott took his pen and used it as a pointer. "As you can see, Giles Rochester appears to be in a state of distress, but what you can see clearly now is a white line of some sort around his neck. We can assume that he was driven to the car park under duress and that the line is some sort of ligature. From the way the ligature is placed and secured, it looks tight, and that suggests someone was in the back holding it."

"So the persons unknown were hunched down in the rear passenger well to avoid detection?"

"Correct, Abby. They wanted to avoid being caught on camera. Unfortunately, there's no evidence or indication of who it is, but at least we can assume that Giles Rochester went to the car park with the person who most likely killed him."

Scott's phone bleeped again in his pocket. Pulling it out, he realised he'd missed a call and now a text from Cara. She could wait.

"Also, Bennett, the caretaker, showed me an abandoned room in the old part of the school. It's certainly been used recently, and there's evidence of something going on that I'm not comfortable with. I've got SOCO down there now. Sian, can you check with the council to see what objections have been raised, if any, towards the new development?"

Scott locked his fingers behind his neck and stretched his back. The vertebrae cracked and released the stiffness that had been building for days.

He continued, "This whole white-feather thing has been playing on my mind. If we explore that a white feather represents cowardice, then something may have happened in the army. A triggering event. I've checked the backgrounds of the deceased. They all had backgrounds in the army, including our victim from this morning. Collier was a prefect when he left Edmunston to join the army. All the deceased were recruited by Collier into the army after their days as school prefects, and then from the army back to Edmunston as teachers when Collier returned to Edmunston as deputy head. They basically followed him."

The information raised a few eyebrows as the possibility of a new line of investigation opened up.

Scott added, "Mike, with your military background and understanding, get working on that the moment you get back here with Collier. Did anything happen in the military? I need some answers by first thing tomorrow when I need to update the DCI. Abby and I will interview Collier."

Mike nodded as he rose, pulling his suit jacket off the back of his chair before tucking in the bottom of his shirt.

The team turned back to their desks, busy with a fresh to-do list.

Scott headed back to his office to call Cara. He smiled and unlocked his phone, looking forward to a nice message from her. His moment of excitement fast evaporated.

Cara's panicked voice faltered. "Someone's outside the mortuary...They've been banging on the windows. I can't see who it is. I've called the police."

31

Scott sped the short distance from the police station to Brighton and Hove mortuary on the Lewes Road. He'd left Abby to deal with the imminent arrival of Collier, assuring her that he'd be back in time for the start of the interview.

There'd been too many strange occurrences recently for Scott not to take Cara's call seriously. What he couldn't figure out was whether the perpetrator had it in for him and was using Cara as bait. Just as likely was the theory that a disgruntled family member had a grievance with Cara over a case she'd dealt with.

As he pulled in through the gates of the cemetery where the mortuary was located, he couldn't see evidence of anyone acting suspiciously in the grounds.

Scott pulled up to the mortuary behind an area car that had arrived moments earlier. Cara was standing with two officers by the front door, pointing towards the side of the building. He watched as one officer set off on foot to walk the perimeter of the building.

"Hey, you okay? What's happened?" Scott asked as he made his way over to Cara and the remaining officer.

"Guv," the officer said, with a slight nod of acknowledgement.

"Someone spooked me," Cara replied. Her face flushed red with embarrassment. "I could hear someone banging at the main entrance. I came down, and there was no one there. I thought it was kids. I went back to the office and carried on. Then it happened again, but when I went to the door, no one was there, but the bushes over there were moving," she said, pointing at the hedge line close to the building. "I still thought it was kids."

Cara cursed under her breath.

"Then someone banged loudly on the frosted glass around the side of the building. I went to have a look, hoping if I saw kids, I could shout at them and threaten them with the police." Drawing in deep breaths, she continued, "But it was a man. I could see his outline, a man, thumping on the windows with both hands. I shouted at him to stop, but he didn't. The banging got louder and heavier. Then he let out a loud scream...and that's when I got a bit worried and headed to the office to call you and the police. He then moved to other windows and banged on them too. I felt trapped," she said.

Scott glanced around. He saw nothing that was concerning him now. "Did you see anything on CCTV?"

"No...that's the worrying thing. The screen is blank, like something was sprayed over it."

Scott had heard enough. This appeared to be a deliberate act of intimidation for some reason unknown to him. "Have you had any run-ins recently, whilst driving, with family members here, anything at all?"

She thought hard, searching her mind for anything,

anything at all. Cara rubbed her eyes and shook her head slowly.

"Let's head back to my place. It's safer there."

"Can we go via my place to pick up a few things?"

Scott nodded and turned towards the officer standing beside them. "Can you do a sweep of the area, including those bushes. See if there's anyone hanging around and then check all the windows and doors."

"Will do, guv. I'll get control to report back to you once we're done here."

"Thanks, that would be helpful."

THE DRIVE to Cara's apartment in Montpelier Crescent was in silence for the most part, with Scott glancing across every so often.

Cara was still insistent that she had no idea as to the identity of the person, and more importantly, why the attack. In her mind, she was hopeful that it was an isolated incident involving someone who at best was doing it for a prank or wind-up, or at worse, someone who was less then mentally balanced. It was something Scott couldn't agree with, especially after what appeared to be a deliberate act of obscuring the CCTV lens.

His suspicions grew not long after they'd parked in an available parking space close to Cara's apartment.

Montpelier Crescent was a sweeping arch of mid-nineteenth-century grade-two-listed buildings set back from a small, grass parkland opposite. Imposing three- and four-storey white structures commanded attention. Regency styling blended with Victorian grace, creating a desirable location. A mixture of cast-iron first-floor balconies with ornate stone cornices and large sash windows only added to the grandeur of the street.

Cara led the way through the communal front door, but froze within feet of her door. It was open. Wood splinters were scattered over the hallway carpet.

She turned to Scott, her eyes wide in fear.

Scott raised a finger to his lips as he took slow, light steps past her. He turned and mouthed *stay here* to her.

He slowly pushed the door open and peered inside. There were no sounds of movement. He took one step at a time as he made his way down the hallway, taking a moment to peer into every room.

Once sure the apartment was clear, he gave Cara a shout to come in.

She took tentative steps forward, one hand covering her mouth in disbelief. Her concern turned to confusion as she realised that nothing had been disturbed – that was until she got to her bedroom, where Scott waited at the doorway.

Her eyes went to the top drawer of a small four-drawer chest that sat in an alcove. It was half pulled out, the contents in disarray.

"That's my underwear. It's on the floor," she said, looking at the assortment that lay scattered on the carpet.

Cara was about to step forward when Scott put his arm out to stop her. She glanced at him in bewilderment, trying to make some sense of the events.

"From what you can see, Cara, has anything been taken?"

She hesitated for a moment as she ran her hand through her dark hair. "I don't think so. Why wasn't my TV taken or my iPad that I left on the sofa? My Kindle or the Michael Kors watch by my bed?" She pointed to her underwear. "But some perv has rummaged through my underwear drawer...I don't get it."

"Listen to me, Cara," Scott said, turning her to face him.

"This isn't your normal run-of-the-mill break-in. To me, this is getting personal. First your car, then the pig's head at my place, then the morgue and now this. This is personal."

"Scott, I don't know...I just don't understand," she said, her eyes darting left to right. "Is someone after me, or trying to frighten me?"

"I'm not suggesting that, but look at the events over the past week. Something is going on."

Cara wrapped her arms across her chest, scared to move. "I don't know what I've done... What do I do, Scott?"

"Well, you're coming back with me for a start anyway. Don't go in the bedroom; it's a crime scene. I'll get Matt from forensics to send someone over to do a sweep. It's a long shot but worth a try. If you need more clothes, we can stop at the shops on the way to mine."

Cara nodded, worry distorting her features.

The events were more than a coincidence. Someone was out to put the frighteners on Cara or him. The question was who.

32

Matthew Edrington felt tired and frail. Dark circles framed eyes that were on constant alert, scouring the corridor for any signs of danger. He blended in with the throng of pupils that snaked their way from the breakfast dining room back to their dorms. He was safe for now. Danger only came when he was alone, defenceless and weak. He was an easy target for the prefects.

Or so he thought.

Someone pulled him up by the collar, yanking him backwards. The force took him by surprise and tightened the fabric around his throat.

The prefects pushed him into the doorway of an empty classroom. It appeared that his confidential discussion with his housemaster, Edward Chapman, had been anything but.

The bullies reminded him in their own inimitable way that snitches were lower than pond scum. Rollings pursed his lips and struck Matthew across his face. The sharp crack of skin slapping skin echoed off the walls. Vibrations of pain exploded across Matthew's face. Rollings's palm was bright red, and the same red mark was visible on Matthew's face.

Matthew stared at Rollings, his eyes wide in fear, as he lifted his hand to protect his fire-red cheek from another attack.

Rollings flicked his shaggy hair back. There was no remorse in his expression; he stared at Matthew with anger in his eyes. A triumphant grin spread across his face.

"You pathetic, limp-wristed prick," Hunter said through clenched teeth. His usual impish boy looks were changed by a menacing stare. He locked his eyes on Matthew. "Not only do you let our house down, but you also let yourself down. You're supposed to take this like a man, but you're not. You're a waste of space. Do us all a favour and go hang yourself like Johnson," he said with a sneer.

A laughing Rollings repeatedly slapped Matthew around the head in a frenzied attack. After, Matthew's ears were hot, red, and stinging. He grappled with Ford next as the boy gripped his blazer. It was hard for Matthew to know where to focus his attention.

Rollings was incessantly taunting him whilst Ford was attempting to rip his blazer from his tight clutches. Other students walking past turned a blind eye, whilst others took alternate routes to avoid the drama.

There was an unspoken rule amongst pupils: avoid those prefects at all costs. They ruled the school through intimidation. Speaking out against them would only ensure that they too would be on the receiving end of their "personal attention".

Relief came in the form of Timothy Saunders, who showed up. This was the second occasion where he'd had to step in to break up an assault on the same pupil. As Saunders tried to step in between the two sides, the prefects laughed at him. They did not fear his authority. Bravado and adrenaline fuelled their determination to stand their ground.

"This is wrong. This is so wrong. I will not tolerate

behaviour like this," Saunders said. "Any form of bullying is not tolerated in the school, and those found to be doing it will be severely punished. Do I make myself clear?" he threatened the prefects. "I'm going to report the lot of you to the head."

His threat of disciplinary action was met with sniggers and further sarcastic taunts of "Oooh, you're really scaring us now!"

Saunders turned to face Matthew, glancing over his shoulder to make sure the prefects had left. "Are you okay, lad?"

Matthew stood there, nervously shifting his weight from one foot to another. He still had one hand covering his red, stinging cheek. He nodded once. His eyes welled with tears; a lump stuck in his throat, making it hard to swallow.

"I'm not going to tolerate this, lad," Saunders said. "Listen, I know how you must feel. It used to go on in my school as well. You must be strong. You must stand up to them, or they'll continue to keep picking on you." He placed one hand on Matthew's thin, bony shoulder. "Don't make the same mistakes I made. I let people walk over me."

"B-but, sir, I have no one else to turn to. I've already spoken to my housemaster. The prefects found out about it. If I tell anyone else, they'll..." Matthew trailed off as his chin dropped to his chest. He fixed his gaze on the black stone floor.

"Listen here, Edrington. I will speak to the head. I won't stand by and have another child's life ruined by bullies. Besides, I thought school was supposed to be the happiest days of your life. Unfortunately, they weren't for me. I've got nothing but bad memories. But we don't want that for you now, do we? Leave it with me. If those boys bother you again, I want you to come and find me. Understand?"

Matthew shrugged before picking up his blazer from the

floor and trudging off wearily, his shoulders slouched in defeat and resignation.

———

SAUNDERS WATCHED EDRINGTON SHUFFLE AWAY, his thin, bony frame dwarfed inside a school uniform that was a size too big. The months of mental, emotional, and physical torment were clearly evident. The next job on his list was to see Mr Collier.

Saunders stormed into Collier's office without the normal consideration of knocking first.

"A word, Mr Collier? I've just broken up yet another incident involving pupils of Stanmer House. How can you tolerate prefects picking on younger boys?" he asked, slapping an angry palm on Collier's desk.

Collier rose abruptly from his chair before striding around to Saunders.

"May I remind you, Mr Saunders, that the discipline within this school is my responsibility and that of the senior management team? I suggest you focus on what your role is: the catering manager of this institution," he replied in a firm, but measured tone.

Saunders pressed his fists into his sides, incensed that Collier was clearly more concerned with titles and the demarcation of jobs than the welfare of pupils.

"Are you not listening to me? A pupil was just being bullied out there," he said, pointing to the open door. "And you're more concerned with whether I'm doing my job."

"Mr Saunders, you're treading a fine line of insubordination –"

Saunders laughed. "Are you that detached from reality? You're happy to turn a blind eye to what I've just witnessed. It's not the first time I've seen this happen."

"There's no bullying in this school. What you have is conditioning –"

"Conditioning?" Saunders interrupted. "Are you for real? This isn't the army or some secret sect. This is a school!"

"These men need to be tough. They think it's tough in here? Hah! It's a ruthless world out there. They could be representing our nation on the battlefield, or our government in a far-flung country. Do you think there's room for weakness in combat?"

"They're boys," Saunders said. "Just boys learning about life and themselves. This should be a safe space, but what you're doing here is wrong. Do you hear me? It's wrong. You're ruining lives."

Collier erupted, his face reddening. He ripped off his glasses and went nose to nose with Saunders.

"Get...out...of...my...office now, before you find yourself unemployed. Consider that your first and final warning!" His jawbone tensed; his lips were pursed tight into a thin line.

Saunders shook his head in a mixture of frustration, anger and sadness. He had tried, Matthew had confided in him, and now he felt like he'd failed Edrington.

"I won't let this rest, Collier. I'll-I'll contact the governors. You can't keep ruining their lives." He stormed out of the room.

33

Scott had dropped Cara off early at the mortuary with strict instructions to dial 999 if anything concerning happened. She'd nodded slowly, her eyes glazed over and fixed on nothing. That morning, her usual exuberance and confidence had been replaced with a quiet, pensive, and guarded mood. The events of the past few days were clearly affecting her more than she was willing to admit. He felt for her.

They'd both had a restless night. Any chance of sleep had faded fast after Scott had bolted upright in bed, startling her awake. His eyes had widened after the usual nightmare of losing his family. It had left him exhausted and drenched in sweat.

She'd pulled his head tight to her warm chest, repeating a soft "ssssh" and "I know you're hurting". Cara hadn't seen this side of him much. The gentle, vulnerable side that he hid from friends and colleagues.

Despite his pain, his vulnerability brought them closer. Peeling back another layer brought her closer to the real

Scott. He remained nothing more than a child in her arms until he'd finally fallen asleep again.

SCOTT PUSHED through the double doors of the CID office, keen to get an update from Abby's interview with Collier. He'd told her to proceed alone, that he wouldn't be back in the office.

Abby at her desk flagged him down as he made his way to his office.

"Guv, Mike couldn't find Collier last night; he was nowhere to be found. He went back first thing this morning and managed to track him down. You've got one pissed-off head waiting downstairs in the interview suite," she said, leaning back in her chair and taking a sip from her mug of tea.

Scott paused for a moment. Interviewing Collier now would be a wise move considering the DCI wanted an update first thing. Perhaps he could squeeze something out of Collier that would get DCI Harvey off his back.

"Where's Mike now?" he asked.

"Where do you think?" she replied, rolling her eyes. "Filling his belly. He moaned about missing breakfast this morning. He's in the canteen, getting a sausage and bacon butty."

Scott sniffed the air, smelling perfume. "Did he get anywhere with the MOD enquiries?" he asked.

"Not yet, guv, getting through to the right department last night wasn't easy. The pen-pushers at the ministry have a unique technique of delay and distraction. They send you from one extension to another and keep you on hold whilst some garish music tests your patience. The hope is you eventually hang up. Our Mike isn't gifted with patience, as you know," she said with a shrug.

She carried on, "He did finally get through to the right department but ended up going round in circles with some AO, but the administrative officer didn't have the authority to release details of past service. He was going on about how only a grade six and seven had the authority to divulge such information."

Scott tutted and folded his arms.

"So, as you can guess, Mike didn't really get anywhere."

"Don't tell me...a senior manager wasn't available?"

Abby nodded. "We're expecting a call back this morning, guv."

"Not good, Abby. Get Mike to chase it as soon as he gets back. We could be waiting hours for a call – and that's being optimistic."

Scott looked at Abby, a small smile breaking on one side of his mouth. "Are you wearing perfume?"

Abby looked sheepish, looking at the tea in her mug rather than at Scott. Her cheeks flushed with embarrassment.

"You are, aren't you? You never wear perfume." Scott stroked his chin before wagging a finger in her direction. "Don't tell me. You're in *lurve*...with Jonathon. Things getting serious?"

Abby couldn't help but smile, a smile that said it all. "I'm not. We're just getting on well, that's all." She was clearly reluctant to admit that Scott might be right.

"Well enough to roll out the perfume, Miss Trent? You must be keen. Do I need to buy a hat?" he joked.

Abby was not one to publicise her private life. Her Facebook page only ever showed the occasional funny quote or pictures from the gym every few months. She certainly didn't fall into the prolific Facebooker category, and there was never any reference to her kids or personal life.

Looking a little uncomfortable, she cleared her throat and busied herself by staring at her PC monitor.

Scott was disappointed with the progress on chasing up information. He'd hoped to have had something to use during Collier's interview, and for Harvey. She'd be chasing him soon for a progress report. The last thing he wanted was to tell her that nothing new had been uncovered.

For the time being, he needed to stay off her radar.

34

C ollier sat impatiently with a hand wrapped around
a cup of tea while the fingers of his other hand
drummed on the table. He'd reluctantly agreed to
accompany Mike to the station and had waived his right to
have a solicitor present. Mike's imposing, heavy build and
weathered face often meant he got what he asked for, and
many dared not to question him.

Abby set the recorder up and covered the formalities as
Scott sifted through his file. He noticed that as Abby went
through the introductions for the tape, Collier didn't avert his
gaze from her.

The guy has a serious hang-up about listening to women.

"Mr Collier, did you enjoy your time in the armed
services?" Scott asked.

His question caused Collier to straighten up and puff out
his chest.

His training in neurolinguistic programming had taught
him to think of the brain as a computer, and the eyes the
filing system. It had helped him to understand that when

someone was asked a question or asked to recall a piece of data, the brain went on a search. A person's eyes would move in many directions depending upon the type of search and what they were thinking or recalling.

As an officer, it was essential to create an environment that would facilitate the extraction of information and evidence. Scott relished interviews more than most of his colleagues because of his fascination with human behaviour and the mind. He had found that using words more suited to a person's normal way of processing information often helped him to glean more. He had put it to the test on more than one occasion by asking questions in multiple ways to see which approach gave him the best results.

Collier was looking slightly up to the left, indicating that he was accessing his stored visual memories. He then looked down at the table. Scott picked up on this small movement.

He's having a chat with himself.

"Can I ask why you should need to know about my military service?" Collier asked. "I was led to believe that I was here to help you with enquiries to do with the murder of my teaching staff."

"You are, Mr Collier. I'm just trying to build a timeline of those involved."

"I see."

"Well?"

Collier cleared his throat. "I had an excellent career in the forces. I wouldn't swap it for anything. You learn a lot about yourself, what you can handle – and how far you can push yourself." He gave a measured nod as his confidence returned.

Abby watched the exchange, letting Scott lead.

"And did you see it as a hard thing to push yourself?" Scott asked.

"Not particularly," he replied, shaking his head.

"You led soldiers, if I'm not mistaken?"

"Yes, that's correct. Very well, I hasten to add."

"How did you find that part of it?"

"It was an honour and a privilege to command a troop. To turn boys into men – fighting men. We don't have room for whingers and cowards."

"Cowards?" Scott said with a raised brow.

Collier didn't answer.

"Cowards..." Scott repeated. "Did you come across any in your military career?"

Collier sat back in his chair, crossed one leg over the other. He locked his fingers together before resting them on his knee.

He casually looked upwards to his left, then right. "Not that I recall."

Scott leant back and mirrored Collier by crossing his legs and locking his fingers over his knee. "You see, Mr Collier, I have a dilemma. I'm dealing with a triple murder investigation. Two of your staff have been murdered, a third retired teacher, also from your school, has been murdered, and that's no coincidence. Don't you agree?"

Collier looked down to his left, deep in conversation with himself, before he looked at Scott. "It certainly looks that way."

"Is there anything that happened during their military careers that could be connected to their deaths, or even prior to their careers in the military?"

Collier's eyes darted everywhere. Scott had him scared.

Collier settled, then shook his head without a reply.

"For the tape, Mr Collier shook his head. Before their deaths, did you have any conversations with any of them? Did they say anything that may have suggested they were concerned, worried or fearful for their lives?"

Collier stared at a spot over Scott's shoulder. A slight

adjustment in his eyes from centre to top left and then right went unnoticed by Abby.

Another shake of his head followed.

"Mr Collier, for the tape, can you say your answers, please."

"Not that I recall."

Liar.

"What can you tell us about John Morecombe?" Scott asked next.

"Who?" Collier said in confusion.

Scott smiled and glanced at Abby. "Oh, I think you know exactly who we're talking about. Ex-teacher John Morecombe? You sacked him about a year ago after he stood up to you about the bullying culture."

Collier raised a brow. "Ah, yes, Morecombe. We had a clear difference of opinion. We concluded that it was in his best interest to seek a more appropriate position elsewhere."

"That's a diplomatic way of putting it," Abby said as she crossed her arms.

"Have you had any contact with him at all since his departure?" Scott asked.

Collier shook his head.

"No texts, phone calls, letters, nothing?"

Collier shook his head again, but then paused. "Actually, now you come to mention it, I did get a few letters of the hate mail variety."

"What did they say?"

Collier stared at the ceiling a moment, drumming his fingers on his kneecap. "I can't remember to be precise, something along the lines of *I won't get away with it.*" Collier chuckled. "It didn't bother me, frankly. I've been called worse and threatened far worse than that. Staring down the barrel of a gun whilst on a tour of duty gives you a bit of a tough skin, Inspector."

"Where are these letters?"

"I threw them away a long time ago. Whoever sent them doesn't scare me." Collier stiffened and pulled his shoulders back.

"We believe Morecombe may be heading back towards Sussex or may already be here. Is there any reason he may do that?"

"I have no idea, Inspector. Maybe he's missing us all," Collier said, with a smug smile.

Scott concluded the interview not long after and arranged for Collier to be taken back to Edmunston-Hunt.

"He was as tight as a duck's arse." Abby sighed as they made their way back to the CID office.

"Far from it, Abby, he was lying. The victims and Collier had had conversations recently. I'm certain of that."

Abby shot Scott a confused glance. "How do you know that?"

Scott paused in the corridor just outside the doors to the main office. "It's quite simple. When I was asking questions about cowards in the army and whether he'd had conversations with the deceased recently – if you'd watched his eye movements – he casually glanced up to the left and then right."

"I didn't see that, guv."

"That's because you weren't looking for the signs. When someone looks up to their left, they're remembering a picture or a scene. When they look to the right, they are trying to access a part of their brain to help them lie by making up the scene in their head."

Abby looked perplexed.

Scott added excitedly, "He lied about the cowards, and he

lied about not having conversations with the deceased men. He's connected to the three murders in some way, and he was running scared in there."

35

Т he morning was getting away from Scott. Even though the triple murder investigation was taking up much of his team's time, a bundle of other case files sat in his in tray, waiting for reviews and instructions. He had no choice but to prioritise the current workload, leaving many of the cases untouched. That was the problem with modern-day detective work: too much work and not enough time.

Each case file usually took him a few hours to review. He'd closely review the action steps that his officers had taken on that case and identify if they had missed anything before leaving instructions over what action to take next. With more than a dozen files on his desk, he just didn't have the time to review them all now.

The cases played on his mind. He felt personally responsible for the outcome of all his team handled. Budgetary cuts across the force meant overtime wasn't an option, so they had to make do with the resources they had available to them. Frustration tinged with guilt always accompanied him because there were victims and concerned loved ones waiting on any snippet of news. Their pain carried on every day. They couldn't walk away and close the door like Scott could at the end of his shift.

His stomach rumbled. He'd had nothing to eat since breakfast. A grated cheese and lettuce baguette from yesterday would have to do as he flicked through the current case file.

Mike had emailed him, having finally got past the guardians at the Ministry of Defence. Their service records had all come back clean: no misconduct, no issues with tours of duty – nothing. Scott had hoped that their enquiries might have thrown something up, but he'd hit yet another brick wall. The team was working on identifying all known colleagues, past and present, of the victims to find a break-through. The school itself was under guard to protect staff and pupils.

Scott stood and stretched. His shoulders cracked in approval.

He walked out and saw Abby on the main floor, the sole member of his team still around. She was typing up the notes from their interview with Collier.

"Where are the others?" Scott asked.

"Unfortunately, Mike and Raj have officer safety training for the rest of the day, and Sian's about somewhere."

"OST, really? We're in the middle of a triple murder case, and they've been told to do officer safety?"

Officer safety training was something that all officers went through annually, so there was little he could do about it. It was part of the force's policy to safeguard their officers, which he accepted was important. However, training on how to apprehend and secure suspects safely and quickly using handcuffs or batons, or how to handle public order incidents was something they all knew how to do competently. In his eyes, bureaucratic time-wasting like this was frustrating.

Matt Allan from forensics poked his head into the CID main office. His bright red chequered shirt stood out like a beacon against the blandness of the brown doors.

"Ah, Scott, thought I'd find you here, mate. Can I have a quick word?"

Scott nodded towards his office just as Sian appeared. It didn't matter what the time of day or what the weather was doing, she was always impeccably turned out. She wore a white, short-sleeved blouse and dark grey skirt, giving her a smart, professional appearance. Her look said a lot about her outlook and approach to work.

"Sian, do me a favour... Mike's not around, so can you look at the school records of our three victims? Mike's already looked at their time together in the army and turned up nothing. Let's go back even further. They all went through Edmunston-Hunt School, so have a look and see if anything else stands out. See if there's anyone else they had associations with. Maybe we missed something."

Sian nodded. "Yes, guv."

Scott closed his office door behind him and Matt. Matt sat and put his feet on the desk.

"Make yourself at home..." Scott said, pushing Matt's legs off.

"Oh, I was just getting comfortable."

"Not in here, you aren't, mate," Scott replied. He ran one hand down his face. "Tell me you've got some news – good news, any news."

"Er, well, now that you're unavailable, you're no longer the most eligible male in the station, so it means I can sidle into the top spot."

"I meant proper news." Scott rolled his eyes.

"Well, yes and no..."

Scott groaned. "Go on."

"Cara's flat..."

Scott leant forward, interested, but also alarmed as it dawned on him that he hadn't texted or called her today to make sure she was all right. *Shit.*

"We didn't pick up any identifiable prints from Cara's flat other than hers and yours, I'm afraid." Matt looked at the brown file on his lap. "But we did find traces of semen on her underwear...and the door handle of the bedroom."

Scott's eyes widened. "Don't look at me."

"Don't worry. I've checked your DNA profile already. It's not yours...Yours was only on her bed sheet."

Scott looked suitably embarrassed and cleared his throat.

Matt continued, "The door was levered open with a flat instrument, probably a crowbar, pry bar or something of that nature. That's all we've come up with so far." Matt got up from his chair and headed for the door. "We're running checks now on the semen sample. I'll give you a shout as soon as I know more."

"Okay, thanks for your swift attention and discreet feedback. Keep me posted."

Someone's got it in for her. He punched a quick text on his phone to her.

Hope you're okay. Sorry for not checking in sooner, bit manic here. Scott x

36

The day had dragged on for Laurence Goddard. Another mind-numbing day of teaching young adults had taken its toll. Over recent years, he found his patience being tested more frequently. In his eyes, getting delinquent adults in their twenties ready to sit their GCSE English exams was a thankless task. *Those idiots should have paid attention in school.* But then again, it paid his bills.

Goddard had lost count of the number of times he'd discussed the concept of themes in *Of Mice and Men* or *Pride and Prejudice.* The room felt stuffy. His small office was situated off the main teaching room, with no windows or natural light. The faded white walls seemed to close in on him, crushing him, squeezing his chest.

His mind spun; his eyes strained to focus on his best friend Jack. Tonight, it was just the pair of them. Jack helped to take away his pain, his fears, but they didn't stop the trembling in his fingers as he held his hand out in front of him. The trembling had worsened in recent months. He'd kept meaning to make an appointment with his GP, but fear stole his courage every time.

His chair squeaked as he leant forward. He pushed through the untidy mess of files across his desk, an attempt to create some space. It wasn't really space he needed on his desk but space in his mind. Space to contemplate and make some sense of the confusion around him.

Sweat beaded on his forehead, zigzagging down his temples before settling in his long sideburns. The clamminess of the office made the room feel like a sauna. His back felt as damp as his forehead. He was a mess, and he knew it, but there was nothing he could do – nothing anyone could do. They were all gone.

If he lay low, he might be okay. If he watched his back, he might live.

His eyelids fluttered closed, due to the combination of tiredness and his friend Jack, taking him to a place where he could escape his demons. His mouth was bone dry, and his breath reeked of alcohol. He'd had enough for today and didn't plan on staying much longer before heading home.

Home...Do I really have a home?

He'd already made the decision to go back and teach his wife another lesson. He'd enjoyed her futile attempts at fending him off before. A few slaps and punches would be enough to beat her into submission again. He felt manly, more in control when he pinned her down. At least she was one part of his life he could control. At least he didn't have to pay for it. *She would put out whether she liked it or not.*

The door flew open. There was a pause of a few seconds before his mind registered commotion behind him. He turned in his chair slowly, unable to comprehend exactly what was happening. It wasn't long before he realised it was his turn.

He stood up too fast; the room spun like a centrifugal force around him. He was defenceless; he was weak...too weak to even open his mouth. He lazily brought his arms up to his sides in surrender, in a comical way only seen in the old cops and robbers movies.

"Youuu fuckerrr," Goddard slurred as he desperately tried to focus on the intruder. "Who...do...you think...you...are?" His head dropped to one side.

The intruder, dressed in black from head to toe, stood there rigid and rippling with menace. His bravery had grown over the week. Fear had gripped him before, ruling his life in equal measures with anger, but not anymore.

"*Ignavus iners timidius tu mori debes.*"

"Come again?" Goddard replied as his eyes narrowed in confusion.

"Did you think you could get away with it? Surely, you must have realised that I would come looking for you."

Goddard sluggishly lunged at the intruder. His mind wanted to strike first, but his body was slow in getting the message. His fist lazily swung out, but he was too far off the mark. The momentum sent him off-balance.

It was all the attacker needed as he came up behind Goddard. The flash of white plastic tape caught the light, wound several times around each hand. He pinned Goddard down on the desk and wrapped the tape around Goddard's neck.

He pulled hard, the tape slowly cutting off Goddard's means of survival. Goddard attempted to steady himself with one hand while the other desperately grabbed and clawed at the tourniquet that slowly starved him of oxygen. He flailed his arms, pushing folders and files off his desk, scattering paper across the floor.

Goddard snarled as his lips pulled back. With his jaw clamped tight, spittle sprayed out from between his stained, rotten teeth. Red blotches tainted his skin; white spots filled his vision as the world around him started to darken.

Triumph came over the attacker as he let out a satisfied

sigh. This had been the easiest one so far. Goddard slumped, falling to the floor in a contorted ball.

37

S cott was about to start an evening briefing when the call came through that a body had been found in one of the serviced offices in the Knoll Business Centre in Hove. Scott, Abby and Sian raced over to Hove, gathering details en route about the incident. A cleaner had stumbled across the body, and paramedics had confirmed the victim was deceased on arrival but still warm.

The team was optimistic. The incident was fresh, and with SOCO and Cara en route, the first few hours after a body were found were critical in any investigation.

The scene had already been secured by the time Scott arrived, the familiar blue and white police tape cordoning off the entrance to the business park. Scott had called ahead to instruct uniformed officers to start searching the locality in case the perpetrator was still lurking. Scott had found that in some cases, a perpetrator would hang around the crime scene, watching from a distance with a macabre curiosity as the emergency services arrived on scene.

Knoll Business Centre, situated on the western outskirts

of Hove, didn't have the glamour of modern serviced units. It was housed in an old 1900s boys' primary school set behind tall railings just off the Old Shoreham Road. The drab and dreary external brown brick façade was in marked contrast to the modern bright, white interiors, polished wooden parquet floors and funky-coloured furniture.

Scott noticed as he pulled up outside the business centre that traffic had started to crawl along the busy dual carriageway as drivers rubbernecked. He'd need to get some traffic units to manage traffic flow if an accident was to be avoided.

Emily Bates, who had found the victim, sat in the back of a patrol car, visibly upset. She held a tissue to her mouth, her face puffy, her eyes red and swollen from her crying. Scott instructed Sian to take a statement from her, and Abby to talk to other business unit holders who might still be around. He also instructed Abby to get on to the caretaker of the centre to see if anything was captured on CCTV.

Local officers had directed Scott to Goddard's offices. Along the way, Scott took note of other businesses that occupied the centre. A cake-making business called *The Dough Knot* proudly showed off its name across its double doors. It made him smile. He wondered how some people had the ability to be so creative with business names.

Farther along the corridor was a room with desks and terminals. The sign on the outside of the door indicated it was a flexible co-working lounge where individuals could rent a desk. Other signs indicated meeting rooms, light industrial units and studios scattered amongst the two quadrangles that formed the centre.

An inner cordon of blue and white police tape signalled the location of Goddard's unit. There was urgency in Scott's steps as he peered into Goddard's office. With the death being so recent, the next few hours were crucial, and hopefully CCTV would be his saviour. Two SOCOs were already present and starting their preliminary analysis, painstakingly photographing the scene, the victim, and his surroundings.

Scott was hit with a warm blast of air from the stuffy room. High temperatures, sweat and the stench of alcohol caused him to pinch his nose. Cramped conditions meant the SOCOs had little space to move around the room, let alone around the body.

He could see the outline of a man slumped on the floor. The body was curled into a foetal position, his white shirt still damp from sweat. The end of a red tie poked out from beneath the body. Scott spotted a pair of thin-rimmed glasses that lay a few inches from the man's head.

Scott wouldn't be able to inspect the body for the time being, but he could live with that. Another officer had informed him that the pathologist was on her way but had been held up in the evening rush hour traffic. Cause of death would have to wait, but paramedics had confirmed evidence of a fresh ligature mark around the neck with localised minor bleeding.

"Guv," Abby said as she came up to him, "I've spoken to the caretaker. The unit was rented out to a Laurence Goddard. He ran a private tutoring business. He's been renting it for the past few years and paid his rent on time." She glanced at her notebook. "He's getting me a copy of the CCTV footage. Apparently, there are cameras at every entrance."

Scott nodded and cast an eye over the body. His thoughts over whether this suspicious death was connected to his ongoing investigation were soon confirmed as soon as he looked at the row of certificates and framed photos.

One photo caught his attention. A gold-framed photo

identical to the one he'd seen in Edmunston-Hunt of the current serving teachers. It was of a bespectacled man with a large forehead, caused by a receding hairline.

The gold inscription beneath the photo read "Laurence Goddard, English Teacher, Edmunston-Hunt School".

38

The scenes-of-crime officer had retrieved a wallet from a jacket that hung off the back of Goddard's chair. The photo ID on the driving licence appeared to match the victim. Scott's next task was to get the body formally identified.

He stood in a small close just off the Dyke Road. It was a street of modern town houses with bay-fronted windows and Juliet balconies on the first floor. Low-level laurel bushes framed the front of each house, neatly tucking in under the ground-floor window ledges.

Scott and Abby checked the address to confirm they were standing outside the correct property before Scott pressed the doorbell. They could hear footsteps in the hallway and then the flick of a switch.

A woman with brown, highlighted shoulder-length hair answered the door. She was wrapped in a pink, fluffy dressing gown, which had small red hearts dotted over it. Scott could see cream-coloured silk pyjamas beneath the gown. It wasn't what she was wearing that had caught his attention but what appeared to be heavy bruising on her chin, cheek and around her left eye. She shielded her face with a hand as she looked nervously between the two officers.

"I'm Detective Inspector Baker, and this is my colleague Detective Sergeant Trent. We are from Brighton CID," he said. Both officers held up their warrant cards for inspection.

The woman nervously looked between the warrant cards and the officers. "What's this about?" Her voice trembled. She wrapped her arms around her chest.

"Can you confirm your name for us, madam?" Abby asked.

She cleared her throat. "I'm...Samantha Goddard...Can I ask what this is about?"

Scott and Abby exchanged a glance. "May we come in for a moment?"

Samantha Goddard waved them into a modern but narrow hallway. Birch laminate flooring added a crisp, clean look to go with the light cream walls and white skirting and coving. She led them into a room on the left and offered them a seat. It was a warm comfortable lounge with modern contemporary low-back fabric sofas neatly angled, facing a large flat-screen TV fixed to the chimney breast.

Scott and Abby took the sofa whilst Samantha Goddard sat on the opposite sofa facing them. She rested her elbows on her knees and cupped her hands beneath her chin.

"We are here about Laurence Goddard. What's your relationship to him?" Scott said.

Samantha wrung her hands, her eyes darting between the two officers. She licked her lips nervously.

"He's...my husband."

"And when did you last see him?"

"Erm, this morning before he left for work."

"And where does he work, Mrs Goddard?" Scott asked.

"He has a private tutoring business at the Knoll Business Centre."

Scott gave Abby the slightest of nods.

"Mrs Goddard, there isn't an easy way of saying this, but I'm sorry to say that a body was found just a few hours ago, and we believe it's your husband. We found a driving licence in his name in a jacket, and a picture that resembles that of Laurence Goddard. Of course, we would need you or another next of kin to formally identify that it is your husband."

Samantha Goddard stared at a spot on the floor. Her eyes searched for answers; her brow was furrowed.

Scott and Abby observed Samantha's reaction closely. Relatives of victims often reacted in different ways. Some cried hysterically, others displayed anger, and some fell into a silent shock. Samantha Goddard was in the last camp.

Scott nodded in the direction of the kitchen, a subtle hint for Abby to rustle up some tea. "Mrs Goddard, are you okay?"

"He's gone..." she said in bewilderment.

"At the moment, we believe it is your husband. And we're very sorry for your loss."

"He's gone...He's finally gone. I'm free." Her eyes brightened as her mind processed the news.

Perplexed by her answer, Scott probed further. "I'm sorry, Mrs Goddard. Can you clarify what you meant when you said, 'I'm free'?"

"I'm...*free*," she said in a slow, soft voice. She looked at Scott, pointing to her bruised and battered face. "I'm free of this. He can't hurt me anymore."

"Are you telling me that Laurence Goddard assaulted you and caused those injuries?"

She nodded as she looked down in an effort to hide her face.

Abby appeared in the doorway of the lounge. "Guv, a quick word?"

Scott made his excuses and joined Abby in the kitchen.

She picked up a newspaper from the kitchen table and

handed it to Scott. *The Argus* front page from earlier in the week had reported on the death of Christopher Johnson. It wasn't the story that caught Scott's attention but the fact that the picture of Johnson had been circled in red marker and a few small red crosses had been placed beneath it.

Scott looked at Abby, who simply raised her eyebrows in response.

With the newspaper in hand, Scott walked back into the lounge and sat opposite Samantha Goddard. "Mrs Goddard, did you draw on this?" Scott asked, holding the page in front of her.

She briefly glanced up at the note. Her eyes widened for a moment; then she dropped her gaze to the floor. She nodded once.

"Why did you circle it?"

When she wasn't forthcoming with a reply, Scott pushed her. "Mrs Goddard?"

She opened her mouth but paused for a moment. As she looked away, a tear rolled down her cheek. "Christopher Johnson...was my lover."

"Mrs Goddard, I'll arrange for an officer to take you shortly to identify the body." Scott waved the paper at her. "After that, we'll need to speak to you at the station about why Christopher Johnson's picture has been circled."

39

A dressed Samantha Goddard was taken to the mortuary, where she confirmed the body was indeed her husband. The female officer accompanying her had reported to Scott that Mrs Goddard had expressed no emotion on seeing the body, or since.

Scott and Abby deliberated outside the interview suite.

Abby leant up against the wall. She yawned and stretched. Clocking-off time had come and gone; her shift was supposed to end at six p.m. It was heavy shifts like this that wore her down. She had frantically called in favours from grandparents so the kids were looked after.

With her grey suit now crumpled, her brown hair hanging loosely, the hairband discarded a long time ago, she was in desperate need of a shower and her bed.

"Do you want to lead on this one, Abby?" Scott asked.

"Fine with me," she replied, pushing the door open and stifling another yawn.

Now that Samantha Goddard was dressed, Abby saw a different woman. When they had visited her earlier in the evening, she'd looked a mess with her hair up in a bunch and no make-up. Now her hair was neatly combed. Golden high-lights added a nice contrast to her light brown hair. She wore a light blue blouse with dark-coloured jeans. Abby couldn't help but notice that despite her bruises, she was pretty.

"Once again, we're sorry for your loss," Abby began. "Samantha, your husband was attacked in his office. Had he been in trouble recently, or did he mention anything about being worried?"

Samantha sat upright in the chair, her arms wrapped tightly around her chest. "No, he...we never talked much," she replied softly.

"Had he been in any trouble in the past that you know of?"

Samantha shook her head slowly, unable to offer anything of substance. She shrugged her shoulders in bewilderment.

"Can you describe your relationship with Laurence?" Abby asked.

"We didn't have a relationship. You call this a relationship?" Samantha scoffed, pointing to her bruised face. "After he left Edmunston, things were okay for a while. He was excited about setting up his tutoring business. More recently he changed. He became moody. He'd come home late. He was always drunk. A drink was never far from his hand."

"And you can't explain why there was a change in his behaviour?"

"No. He became horrible. He was always angry, really angry – almost resentful. He'd shout a lot, drink alone, throw stuff around the house and then come upstairs and, well..." Samantha's voice lowered to a whisper. "I tried to avoid him as much as I could. He was a horrible, nasty person by the end. I couldn't take it anymore. After he raped me several times, I just wanted it over. He can't hurt me anymore, and I'm pleased about that."

"Wanted it over enough to harm him?"

Samantha looked up, her eyes wide. "No...no, of course not. Are you thinking that I had anything to do with this?"

Abby pushed. "Samantha, we have to explore every avenue, and you had enough cause to want him out of your life."

"Yes, I did want him out of my life, but that was it, just out of my life and gone. Gone away from me, but certainly not dead. I didn't deserve to be his punchbag."

Abby nodded in sympathy as Scott watched Samantha.

"For the record, can you confirm your relationship to Christopher Johnson?" Abby asked.

Samantha stared into a corner of the room, her pain and anguish clear. "He loved me. We were lovers."

"How long were you in a relationship with him?"

Samantha smiled. "About two years."

"How did it start?" Scott asked.

"We had a school barbecue, which Laurence and I were invited to. Laurence as usual got drunk and made a fool of himself. He turned on me and pinned me by the throat to a tree. He was so angry. He said I was dressed like a tart, that I was desperate for it." Her eyes filled with tears. "Chris saw what was happening and stepped in. He organised a taxi to take Laurence home whilst I stayed on. Chris took care of me, made sure I was all right. He was a handsome, caring man..."

"And you began a relationship after that point?" Scott asked. Samantha nodded. "Did your husband know?"

"I don't think so. I'm not sure. Perhaps. But he was too wrapped up in his own world. If he'd found out, he would have beaten me senseless. And not because I'd met someone else, it would have been out of pride and control. I think he felt like I was his property."

"Why didn't you leave if he was so abusive towards you?" Abby asked.

Samantha shook her head. "I wish I knew. I don't know why I stayed. I guess a part of me still loved him. He was my husband. He was stressed. Don't they say that you always take your stress out on those closest to you?"

Abby interlaced her fingers on the desk. From experience in the job, Abby knew that for many victims of domestic violence, it wasn't simply a matter of walking out the door. Leaving was a process.

It was difficult for many people to understand why a person would stay. Every case was different, and there could be many reasons. Abby knew from her DV training that strong emotional and psychological forces often kept the victim tied to the abuser. Sometimes basic situational realities like a lack of money kept the victim from leaving. They could convince themselves that their abusive partner would change because of their remorse and promises to stop the violence.

She'd even known in several harrowing cases that the victim had stayed out of fear because their partner had threatened to kill them if they reported the abuse.

Victims often felt fearful of change; many carried guilt that it was their fault the relationship had come to violence. They felt helpless and trapped and had nowhere to go. Many women were worried about the harm to their kids, or just plainly believed that the police wouldn't take their claims seriously. That could be the case, especially if the victims were male.

Samantha continued, "I guess Chris threw me a lifeline. He cared about me and made me feel good about myself. I felt wanted, not neglected."

"Where were you earlier this afternoon, Samantha?" asked Abby.

The question took Mrs Goddard by surprise. "Are you still

thinking I had something to do with this?" she asked with a raised voice.

"You had a good reason. Your lover is dead. Your husband drove you away, and you've suffered abuse at his hands. Perhaps you were angry over everything you've lost?"

Samantha shook her head vehemently and denied any involvement in Laurence's death. "Yes, I hated what he'd done to me. He was a bastard to me, but I could never kill him, or anyone for that matter."

"Mrs Goddard, where were you earlier this afternoon?" Abby asked again.

After a lengthy, reflective pause, she spoke again. "Belinda Evans...Yes, Belinda, my neighbour, can vouch for seeing me this afternoon. We chatted after she turned up at my door with a parcel that had been delivered to her house accidentally."

"Is there anything else that you can think of that may help us piece together why your husband was attacked?" Scott asked.

Samantha rested her chin in her hand as she thought. "Wait...Yes, a few weeks ago he collapsed in bed drunk again. A few hours later I was woken by his restless sleep. He muttered something. He said, 'I'm sorry. They made me. It went too far.'"

40

A week had passed since the first murder. Scott and his team were no closer to identifying the killer. He had to admit that a few loose ends had been tied up, but he wasn't even touching the sides of the investigation. With pressure mounting from senior officers, there was a real risk of the case being passed over to a new senior investigating officer if results weren't imminent.

If there was one thing Scott hated more than anything else, it was failure. It wasn't a prospect he liked to entertain. He would go above and beyond to get a result in whatever he did whether it was personal or professional. He would put in extra hours to get the job done. It had even extended to when he'd sat his inspector exams. He had locked himself away in his bedroom for two weeks and learnt PACE, the Police and Criminal Evidence Act 1984, to pass.

His sense of failure was never more poignant than the day he'd lost his beloved family. His life had been turned upside down as he'd stood there helpless, as his wife and daughter were mowed down in a hit-and-run accident. He should have been able to protect them. It had been his duty to protect those he loved most, and he'd failed.

At the time of the accident, friends and colleagues had rallied around to reassure him that he wasn't to blame. After all, it was an accident he couldn't have prevented. But they hadn't been inside his head; they hadn't seen and felt the torture that ripped his mind to shreds. How could they? They'd meant well, but it hadn't made things any easier.

The sense of guilt he felt was now his life sentence. And it was the fear of failure that spurred him on.

The morning hadn't started the way he'd planned. A briefing for nine a.m. had been pencilled into his diary. DCI Harvey and Superintendent Meadows had insisted on Scott giving them an update first thing ahead of their meeting with Assistant Chief Constable Anne Grayling. The pressure was mounting, with both Scott and DCI Jane Harvey becoming decidedly more uncomfortable with the lack of results as the case progressed.

Chief Constable Lennon was worried about how he and his force might be viewed by Masonic members who had a vested interest in Edmunston-Hunt School and were now asking discreet questions. And for this reason, Lennon was demanding answers.

A surprise call from Mary Harrison, the deputy head of Edmunston-Hunt, had meant a change to Scott's plans as he made his way over to Ditchling to meet her. As far as he was aware, she'd been signed off with stress following recent events and was due back to work imminently. A curious voicemail message from her about a development with Matthew Edrington had piqued his interest.

Scott had pleaded with DCI Harvey to cover for him and spin any old yarn about being called away to deal with a development in the case. At this stage, he couldn't be certain if there was anything of value that Ms Harrison had to offer or whether it had any bearing on his ongoing investigations. It was her mention of Matthew that had compelled him to follow through.

The boy was troubled – Scott was sure of that. He'd witnessed first-hand the intimidation that Matthew faced, and for that reason, he couldn't stand by. Maybe it was the paternalistic side of him, but the one thing he hated most was to see any child suffer. His last big case involving the death of Libby Stevens still affected him and the team, even though they didn't talk about it.

They were human. They had feelings and had been deeply moved by Libby's death and the horrors that Sabina and Kelly, two girls who'd been trafficked and abused, had endured. They were crimes that had robbed young girls of their innocence and childhood. Scott couldn't wait until the ruthless individuals behind those crimes had their day in court.

Scott parked just inside the gates of the school, as Ms Harrison had instructed. Her unusual request only fuelled his inquisitive mind. She'd specifically asked him to park out of sight of the main building. Then he was to make his way along the front perimeter of the school to the walled gardens on the right flank, where she'd be waiting. In another situation, the instructions might have been for a clandestine meeting between two lovers.

As he made his way through the gardens, he noticed that each plant, each shrub, and each neatly pruned bush had a brass name plate staked into the ground in front of it. Scott was hopeless when it came to matters of the garden. He couldn't tell a tulip from a crocus, or a daffodil from a dahlia. Wisteria, clematis, star jasmine – they were just plants to him. A floral infusion of scents.

Near the lily pond that formed the central feature, Mary

Harrison came into view. She was partially obscured in the shade of a large tree.

Not far behind her stood the small figure of Matthew Edrington. Scott immediately noticed Matthew had a black eye.

"Thank you for coming so quickly, Inspector," Mary Harrison said, glancing over her shoulder at Matthew.

Scott had briefly seen Mary Harrison at the start of the investigation. He'd forgotten how her soft, southern English accent sounded calm and reassuring. She could easily fall into the category of a typical English rose with her brunette hair, long and flowing with wispy ends that framed her thin face. A creamy-white, clear complexion was complemented by her dark, warm brown eyes.

"Your message sounded important?" Scott replied. "Are you okay, Matthew?"

The boy stood quietly in the background, balled hands pressed firmly into his chest. His round eyes were bloodshot, and he had a pained expression on his face. He pursed his lips and nodded.

Mary sighed deeply. "I've been finding life incredibly stressful following the recent deaths. But needs must, and I'm trying to get back into some sense of normality, but as you can imagine, that's a little hard to do when members of staff are dying around you."

Mary Harrison paused awkwardly, realising that she'd probably said that a little too loud. She turned and called Matthew over. He did, and she placed a protective arm around the boy's frail thin shoulders.

"Matthew came to see me yesterday and confided in me that he's being bullied. And I'm not talking about the usual name-calling or barging into you in the corridor type of thing. Quite frankly, I'm deeply upset by what he's been experiencing and the deliberate oversight by my colleagues. I just felt I needed to take this further. I'm afraid to say, Inspector, that from what I've heard since I've been here, the school has a reputation for bullying and shall we say *taking things further.*"

Scott nodded slowly, his hands in his pockets. Concern hit him as he looked down at Matthew. "Is this true, Matthew?"

The boy nodded hesitantly, looked up at Ms Harrison for reassurance. She responded with a hug.

In the privacy of the walled gardens, Matthew shuffled on the spot, his mind a melting pot of confusion, sadness, and fear.

"I don't want anyone to get in trouble. I just want it to stop," he said, his voice slow and low.

"It's a very brave thing for you to come forward," Scott replied. "Often the first step is the hardest, but I'm here to help you...we both are." Scott glanced at Mary Harrison, who nodded reassuringly. "So how about you tell me what's been going on?"

41

Matthew Edrington looked a disconsolate figure as he sat between Scott and Mary Harrison on a stone bench. With his hands tucked firmly beneath his thighs and head bowed, Matthew nervously swung his feet back and forth as he stared at the ground, looking decidedly unsure of himself.

"Tell the inspector everything you told me, Matthew. It's okay, I promise," Mary Harrison said with a reassuring tap on the boy's arm.

"Call me Scott," he offered.

For children, titles like inspector and constable could be daunting, off-putting and create unhelpful barriers. Children needed to feel safe, and from previous experiences, Scott knew that giving the child space to think and express their feelings and experiences was vital.

Matthew's gazed fixed on the ground. He flicked small stones that formed the path away with his shoe.

To gently prompt Matthew, Scott asked, "How did you get that black eye?"

After a lengthy pause, Matthew said, "They did it...They pinned me to the wall and punched me."

"Well, why don't you tell me what else they've been doing?"

For the time being, he deliberately held back from asking who had hit him for fear that Matthew would clam up straight away if put on the spot.

"They've been picking on me. Wherever I turn, they're there. It started out with a bit of pushing as they walked past, then it went to pulling pages out of my books...and then when I said I'd tell our housemaster, they..." Matthew clenched his jaw.

"They what?" Scott asked gently.

Matthew glanced at Scott, it was just a brief second, but Scott felt like the boy trusted him.

"They just picked on me all the time. First it was name-calling. They said I looked like a girl. They called me pussy; said I didn't deserve to grow up a man..." His voice trailed off.

"Go on, Matthew. You're doing really well," Ms Harrison reassured him.

"After sports lessons, they'd taunt me in the showers. They'd take photos of me and steal my towel, saying stuff like I'm going to regret ever being born."

Scott listened to Matthew's story. The boy's plight touched a nerve. "Why would they say something like that?" Kids could be so cruel.

"Because of this." Matthew pointed to his ginger mop of hair. "I'm not an athlete. I'm not strong enough to play rugby. I can't compete against the others. I'm like the odd one out here, and because of that, they picked on me. They'd come into my dorm and do things to me. I've slept in a wet bed more times than I can remember..."

Scott glanced at Mary Harrison. Sadness made her features heavy, her eyes moist.

He said, "Listen, Matthew, I'm sorry you've been through so much. I only wish you'd spoken to someone earlier, maybe even called your parents? It's not right that they've been singling you out like this. No one should be bullied."

Matthew shrugged, his shoulders drooping forward. He shook his head. "It's not just me. It's been happening for years since the school was founded. I'm not the first to go through this. It's my turn, I guess. It was my turn to get black-balled." He sighed as if he'd been expecting this at some stage in his time at Edmunston-Hunt.

Scott's eyes narrowed. "What do you mean black-balled?"

Matthew hesitated for a moment as he sought answers to Scott's question. The events of that night clearly haunted him.

He replied in a soft voice, "They took me from my bed to the old music room. It's in the old part of the building. I wanted to run, I really did, but I was too scared, and they dragged me there. I begged them to let me go, but they just laughed." Matthew began to cry, tears collecting on the tip of his nose. Each drop fell into his lap.

"They tied me by my ankles and wrists. The more I tried to get free, the more it hurt. They punched me and laughed. I wanted to run away, but even if I could, I had nowhere to go, nowhere to hide."

Mary Harrison put her arm around Matthew once again, pulling him close.

"They...they...then put warm shoe wax on my balls. It hurt so much, Ms Harrison," Matthew said as he cried into her chest.

Mary Harrison winced in sympathy at Matthew's last recollection. She stroked his hair, apologising, promising him that it would be okay.

Scott gently reassured the boy with a few pats on his shoulder. This was a clear case of assault in Scott's eyes. He was lost for words, and here he was now listening to the intimidation and bullying of a boy unable to stand up for himself.

Scott was furious that a boy under the care of an expensive boarding school had been let down by the system, and by people who were there to guide and protect him. The school was supposed to give him the best start in life, to put in place the skills, attributes and abilities that would shape Matthew's journey in life. But he'd been left a fragile, traumatised and frightened boy.

Something Matthew had just mentioned got Scott thinking.

Scott asked Mary Harrison to step away with him for a few moments. "Ms Harrison, can you arrange for Matthew's parents to collect him? I want him checked over at the hospital. We have a duty of care, and I won't allow a minor who's been allegedly attacked like this to remain here for another day. I'm going to deal with this."

Mary understood and nodded as she returned to usher Matthew away.

WALKING through the large front doors of Edmunston-Hunt School was becoming far too frequent an activity. On each occasion, frustration had tinged Scott's visit from the lack of cooperation, the tense atmosphere, and the sheer bloody-mindedness of Collier. On this occasion, it would be no different.

The school was eerily silent as his shoes clicked on the tile floor and echoed around him.

To his surprise, Mrs Hilary, Collier's sidekick and gate-keeper, appeared to be less than her usual cantankerous, bullish self. If anything, he'd swear that she was in a flap.

"Where's Collier?" Scott demanded as he strode up to her desk.

"I-I don't know. You see, he hasn't turned up. I-I just don't know where he is," she stuttered and nervously fiddled with her pearl choker.

"And you've checked his office?"

"Yes! Of course I did. In all the time I've known Adrian – I mean Mr Collier, he's never not turned up. Even if he was unwell, he'd be here bright and early, his eyes full of life, his head held high, his big strong shoulders pinned back, looking perfectly turned out..." Mrs Hilary stopped mid-sentence, and her cheeks flushed a deep red.

"And you have no idea where he is? Did you check with our officer outside?"

"Yes – I mean no, Mr Collier is not answering his phone. I was just about to go over to his residence to check up on him," she replied, hastily reaching for her handbag.

With his suspicions raised, Scott told her to call him the minute she had found Collier or had further news on his whereabouts.

42

"Get me a black coffee, will you, Raj?" Scott shouted across the floor as he marched into his office. He threw his jacket on a spare chair.

Equal measures of frustration and anger now pissed him off as he headed back out to the incident board.

The pictures of the victims stared back at him. Crime scene photos, post-mortem photos and brief descriptions of the victims were spread out across the whiteboard. He still felt like the team was skirting around the edges of the investigation. Something was being overlooked, something glaringly obvious that once identified, would break this case apart.

Various elements rolled over in his mind. *Cowards, white feather, black-balling, bullying...why?*

"Okay, listen, team, we need to break this case, and something I heard today makes me think that the school itself is a key factor. To add to that, Collier has gone missing. Now, we can't be certain if he's a potential suspect or a victim. His disappearance is out of character by all accounts. His car is still on the school grounds at his residence, so we can assume he's either disappeared on his own accord or has come to harm."

"You think he's been had too?" Raj asked.

Scott pursed his lips. "I wouldn't put it in quite those terms, but as I said, I don't know if he's a victim or suspect. He's running the school like it's some sort of military academy. Collier seems too nonchalant about the deaths of his staff members and carries the belief that violent and ritualistic bullying is acceptable."

The team exchanged glances as they absorbed Scott's last point.

"Who's being bullied? The staff?" Mike asked as he twiddled a pen through his fingers and eyed up the Krispy Kreme doughnut that was sitting on a plate near Raj's coffee. He started to reach out for it, but was suitably deterred by a cold, possessive stare from Raj. Mike shrugged it off and thought he'd sneak it from under Raj's nose once the guv was gone.

"No, Mike. The pupils. From information I received this morning, bullying appears to be an accepted practice for as long as the school has been around. And that's got me thinking. How are we doing with chasing up past teachers, Sian?"

Sian cleared her throat as she rifled through a pile of papers on her desk. She gathered a few sheets and placed them neatly in front of her.

"In the main, guv, most of the ex-staff are ex-military."

"That figures," Mike said. "There's always a tendency for the military to look after their own. It's like a kinship, a bond. Once you've been in the forces, you're never on your own. We all stick together."

"So what happened to you?" Sian smirked; brave for her. She wasn't normally so forthcoming with the sardonic digs.

Mike scowled, and Sian raised a brow in defiance. The others smiled.

Sian continued, "The only other teacher I could find so

far other than John Morecombe is Stephen Barrington. Interestingly, he's only the second teacher I've come across so far *without* a military background. He left three years back; he was only there two terms before he resigned."

"Not long, then..." Scott pondered.

"Didn't even see out a whole academic year, guv."

"Where is he now?"

Sian said, "He's at Longhill High School in Rottingdean."

"Call the head and tell them we're coming over to see Barrington this afternoon. Abby, you and I will see him. Sian, keep working through your list. There may be one or two other teachers we're not aware of. Any news of John Morecombe's whereabouts?"

Sian shook her head. "No, guv, still looking."

"Guv, forensics came back with more results on the plastic tape that was used on Goddard," Abby said. "There were traces of food-like substances that they analysed further. It was starchy in composition, which they narrowed down to potato. That may not mean much now, but there was an oil-based compound that was sent away for analysis. It came back as a refined spice-infused oil."

"Can that be narrowed down in any way? Can we identify who supplies it? Where it's distributed? What it's used for?"

"I should think so, guv," Abby said. "We can get on to local catering suppliers and food manufacturers to see if they can shed any light."

Scott murmured his agreement, his mind working overtime to join snippets of information.

"Okay, that could be really helpful. Mike, can you look into that whilst Abby and I are out, and call me if anything interesting crops up? I've also had an email back from forensics. The DNA profile of the feathers I collected from Bennett's aviary match those placed on the victims."

"Is Bennett, the caretaker, in the frame, guv?"

"That's a possibility. I've spoken with him at length. He had access to the entire school, to boundary rope, to white feathers, and...he's just weird. I called him yesterday and asked him to come in to help us with our enquiries. He's downstairs now, so Abby and I will see him now."

43

Bennett had been shown through to an interview suite. The dark grey floor and white walls of the room didn't give it character or warmth. Functional with a solitary square table and two plastic chairs either side. The room always felt too stuffy and claustrophobic during lengthy interviews, and with no natural daylight, Scott found it easy to succumb to fatigue and tiredness.

After Abby had done the introductions and set up the tape recorder, Scott began.

"Mr Bennett, thank you for coming in. This isn't a formal interview, and you're not under arrest. We're recording this interview as standard procedure. You're free to leave at any stage should you wish to. I understand that you waived your right to legal representation, is that correct?"

Bennett nodded.

"Mr Bennett, you'll need to say your answers for the tape."

"Yes."

Scott went through some questions, asking him about his role at Edmunston-Hunt, what he liked, didn't like, to develop some rapport before he probed a little deeper.

"Mr Bennett, how well do you get on with the staff at the school?"

Bennett held Scott's gaze for a moment, his face lacking emotion. For a moment Scott thought he might need to repeat the question in case Bennett hadn't heard.

The caretaker eventually shook his head and shrugged. "I don't really have much to do with them. I don't think most even know I exist. I'm there to clean up after them and make the place look tidy like."

Scott flicked through a brown file. "Mr Bennett, I understand that you did a stretch of twenty-seven months. ABH for glassing someone in a pub in Soho, London, plus a further four months for assaulting a police officer involved in your arrest. Do you get angry often?"

"No."

"So what happened in this situation?"

Bennett paused; his hands were firmly clasped on the table between them.

He looked between Abby and Scott. "Because they kept saying I was thick, said I looked like a retard."

"Who did?"

"Dunno, some blokes in the pub. Then one tripped me up as I went to leave. I fell. I was mad. I hate it when I'm called thick."

"You lashed out and attacked one of them?"

Bennett nodded.

"Mr Bennett, please." Scott pointed at the recorder.

"Yeah."

"Does anyone call you thick at the school? Pupils? Perhaps the teachers?"

"Nope."

"How well do you get on with the head, Mr Collier?"

Bennett stared at his hands and shrugged. "He's okay. He gave me a chance. No one else would. See, I can't fill in those forms the job centre gives us. I can't read or write too well."

"At all?" Scott questioned.

"Depends. Seeing as I only went to school for a few years, didn't see the point in learning after. I had no dad; he left before I could walk. Mum was a pisshead and a tart."

Scott and Abby exchanged a glance.

"Your aviary, do you like birds?"

Bennett's faced softened. "Yeah, they're lovely creatures. Wouldn't harm a soul. They love when I talk to them."

"Who else has access to them?" Scott asked.

Bennett thought for a moment. "Well, anyone, really. I used to have the odd student come and see them. They liked feeding them birdseed."

"Any staff?"

Bennett shook his head. "I don't even think most of 'em know they're there."

"So to clarify, anyone on the site could and did have access to the aviary because it isn't locked?"

"Yeah."

Scott nodded. "Mr Bennett, you've been extremely helpful. I'll get an officer to show you out. Oh, just one last question. Has anyone come to you to borrow any of that boundary rope outside your cottage, or ask for packaging tape?"

"No."

It was worth a try.

SCOTT AND ABBY left the station and drove out of Brighton on their way to speak with Stephen Barrington.

Abby had offered to drive, but Scott said his life insurance didn't cover him whenever she was behind the wheel, much to Abby's irritation. She was a good driver, but it was too easy to wind her up. All he had to say was that men were better drivers, which always hit a raw nerve.

"What are your thoughts on Bennett?" Abby asked him.

"I'm not sure. For starters, he's just said that he can't read or write very well, so the Latin notes may have been beyond him unless he used Google Translate. The aviary isn't locked, so anyone could get in there and help themselves to feathers. And as for the rope, he's got loads of it by his back door. So he had access to those, but so did everyone else. Easy enough for someone to cut off a length without him noticing."

They'd only just passed the marina when Scott's phone rang. He clumsily fiddled around inside his jacket pocket before retrieving it and throwing it into Abby's lap. "See who that is..."

Cara's name popped up on-screen.

"It's the scalpel queen," Abby replied teasingly.

"See what she wants, will you?"

The case had taken up a lot of his time and energy. He felt bad that their relationship was only just taking off, and here he was knee-deep in a case that sucked up most of his time. It was something that didn't sit well with him.

He recalled hearing the phrase "Join the force, get a divorce" when he first signed up, and never really understood its meaning until now. Shift work had a destabilising effect on home life, the earlies, lates and nights, bigger workloads, tighter budgets, staffing cuts, coupled with the stress and pressure of the rank often took their toll. It was a thankless task sometimes. The public rarely thanked the police. The public was quick to blame them for not doing enough, and the senior management jostled in the politics of policing.

A long-serving DS had once taken Scott under his wing and given him an insight into what was to come.

"I speak from experience of two marriages and one divorce," the old-timer had said. "Going to bed early, and getting up at five a.m., or getting in around midnight absolutely drained, or getting home around eight a.m. just wanting to hit the pillow and then getting ready to go out again around nine p.m. was very telling on family and social life," he'd pointed out to a youthful and exuberant Scott.

Recent events at his home, the mortuary, and Cara's apartment had made him more protective of his relationship and of Cara. He wasn't going to let his relationship suffer in that way.

Abby held the phone to her ear and shot Scott a concerned look.

Scott furrowed his brow.

"What's wrong, Abby?"

"Whoa, hold a minute. Calm down; take a few deep breaths," Abby said calmly, tapping the dashboard. She looked across to Scott. "Someone is in her apartment!"

44

A bby kept the line open while Scott turned around and raced back to Cara's flat. On loudspeaker they could hear Cara screaming, a male voice shouting, the sound of glass breaking and loud thuds as bits of furniture were being thrown around. Abby had also called on her phone for a local unit to get there immediately.

Scott's mind raced. His pulse throbbed as images flashed through his mind.

Why did Cara go back to her apartment after I told her to stay away? Who is there? What do they want? What are they doing to my precious Cara?

The moment felt like déjà vu. Another loved one in need of his help and him powerless to do anything about it. This time he hoped he wasn't too late.

He was taking corners like a man possessed. Abby held on to the door handle whilst shooting nervous glances at Scott. She would know what was going through his mind right now and thought better of asking him to slow down. She tried her hardest to reassure him that everything would be okay, that other units were on the way, but her words didn't comfort him. Scott stared straight ahead, his lips pursed, his hands gripping the wheel like his life depended on it.

That was probably an accurate assumption.

Scott screeched to a halt outside Cara's apartment just as the flashing blue lights and wail of police sirens arrived from the opposite end of the road. The sight of four police officers racing towards one of the properties was enough to raise the interest of passers-by and residents. He saw several curtains twitch and front doors open.

More splintered wood and the front door hanging off one hinge greeted them.

Scott tensed, the hairs on his neck standing up. Through rapid breaths and fearing the worst, he barged in.

The lounge was in disarray; ornaments and flowerpots lay scattered around the floor. Potpourri had been trodden into the carpet; daffodils lay discarded on the floor. A bottle had been thrown against the wall, leaving a shower of green glass across the carpet. The evidence all pointed towards a violent episode. But Cara wasn't there.

Scott was instantly confronted by a tall, unshaven white male who stepped out into the hallway, a knife in his right hand. He prepared for the assailant to come at them.

The uniformed officers released their retractable batons and screamed, "Put the knife down now!"

To his surprise, the man's eyes widened. He snarled at them, his jaw clenched tight, then ran for the kitchen and the rear courtyard garden set beyond.

Scott ran after him, followed by the two uniformed officers.

Abby tailed off as she went from room to room, looking for Cara, shouting, "Cara, where are you?"

Scott shoulder-charged the intruder, forcing him into the kitchen table. He lost his balance and fell head first into the rear patio doors. The officers wrestled the intruder onto his front and secured his hands behind his back. Scott knelt over him to see if he recognised the scrote. Perhaps he'd come across him previously, but the face didn't register with him.

He was pulled away from the scene as Abby called out to him.

Scott retraced his steps to find Abby kneeling on the floor by the bed. Cara lay draped across the end of it, her hair knotted and untidy, her T-shirt ripped from a violent struggle, her cream bra partially exposed, and what looked like the red impression of a bite mark on her shoulder. Scott noticed that the top button on her jeans was undone, but the jeans hadn't been removed.

Lying there dazed and confused, Cara glanced towards the doorway; her left cheek was flushed bright red, the corner of her lip crimson with blood.

More officers streamed through the front door, making the small apartment feel claustrophobic.

Scott found a cardigan and draped it around Cara's shoulders.

"I'm sorry...I'm sorry. I tried to stop him." Tears streamed from her puffy, red eyes.

"Hey, it's fine. It's really fine. You're safe now," Scott reassured her as he sat beside her. He glanced at Abby, who continued to rub Cara's knee. "We need to get you checked out to make sure you're okay."

Cara rested her elbows on her thighs. "You don't understand," she whispered through swollen lips. "I-I know him. He's my ex."

Scott dropped his hands. "He's your ex?" he said, sounding confused. "What's he doing here, and why now?"

"He wanted me back. He said he's been following me for weeks. Everything that happened was down to him..." she said.

"Why did you come back here, Cara? I told you it wouldn't be safe for you," he said gently, rubbing her back.

Cara nodded and sniffed. "I know. I thought I'd just pop in to grab a few bits. I didn't know that I'd been followed until there was a ring on the door."

Abby left the room to give them some privacy. Scott's mind raced, and he looked away, trying to make sense of the last few moments.

"Scott, he damaged my car. He scared me at the office, the pig's head...it was all him. He was after me, not you. Even down to the break-in I had here. It's all him." Cara shivered, the shock clearly setting in, her shoulders shaking. "He was the reason I left London. I needed to get away from him. Listen to me, Scott..."

A confused and shocked Scott frowned. "I don't understand...Why did he want to track you down?"

"Because..." Cara paused for a moment. "Because he was a controlling bully and violent. I fell pregnant but knew I couldn't bring a child into the world with that monster as its dad. I walked away from him, but he threatened to find and kill me because I-I had an abortion."

45

The events of the afternoon had meant postponing their visit to Stephen Barrington. The news had left Scott in a state of shock, his mind replaying what Cara had gone through.

Cara had spent several hours at the police station, giving her statement, being prodded and poked at by SOCO collecting evidence, and being checked over by the doctor. It had left her exhausted.

Cara had been quiet when they'd returned to Scott's house, the shocking attack numbing her.

The next morning, Scott made sure Cara had everything she needed and promised to keep checking in with her regularly. At the front door, Cara wrapped her arms around his waist and buried her head in his chest. They both needed the closeness and reassurance.

Scott and Abby said nothing on their journey to Rottingdean to see Barrington.

Scott drummed his fingers on the steering wheel, his lips drawn in a thin line. He tutted and gave the occasional shake of his head. The violent attack had shaken them both. Scott had felt sickened that anyone would have wanted to harm Cara, and he struggled to handle it. A wave of anger flowed through him as he thought of Cara's ex. He wanted the man to feel the same pain that Cara had felt.

He was awash with emotions. One moment he experienced sadness; then, recalling Cara's confession, hurt would flood his body before being replaced with guilt.

Abby clearly couldn't sit in silence any longer. "Pull over..."

"Huh?" Scott asked, confused.

"Pull over," Abby repeated, pointing to an approaching lay-by.

"Why?"

"Just do it, please?"

Scott did, then turned in his seat to face Abby. "What's the matter?"

"You're the matter!" she said, poking him in the arm. "I'm not being disrespectful, guv. I'm talking to you as a friend, Abby to Scott. But an outsider would think that it's you who's been assaulted."

"Abby, we're in the middle of a multiple murder investigation, and you want to give me a pep talk?"

"Pot and kettle spring to mind. I've lost count of the number of times we've talked about my personal life. You've given me some great advice in the past. You've also taken the piss out of me over my poor choice of men...and admittedly, you've had a point. I've always been shit at choosing men." Abby shrugged. "Cara was clearly living in fear of that tosser and decided on a clean break, a new life – a life that now involves you, you big clut! She clearly loves you, and whether you choose to admit it or not, you love her."

Scott made no response. He dropped his gaze and fiddled with the stitching on the steering wheel. A mixture of embarrassment and surprise at her candour had robbed him of his usual confidence.

Abby explained, "Listen, I hung around outside, and I heard what Cara said to you. Do you honestly think *any* woman takes the decision to have an abortion lightly? She made her decision on what she thought was right at that time in her life. I know you're shocked, but probably not as much as Cara is."

Scott shook his head slowly. "I know...I know what you're saying...but..."

"There's no *buts*, Scott. Just zip it for a moment." She pulled an imaginary zip across her lips. "How could she possibly bring something like that up so early in a relationship? Any relationship? 'Oh, by the way, Scott, I was with a controlling psycho who threatened to track me down after I left him, and I've had an abortion. Hope you don't mind.' Get real, Scott."

Abby's voice rose an octave. "The woman is hurting still. It's probably been playing on her mind since that day, and she's been carrying it around with her, afraid to tell anyone, especially a new fella, in case that changes his feelings towards her. And with what you've been through, how could she possibly find the right words *and* time to tell you?"

Abby stared at Scott, looking fearful that she'd gone too far with her lecture.

"You're right."

"I know I am. Just be there for her. She needs you now more than ever. Make sure she knows that nothing's changed between you. Ok? Yes, you're angry, but you're angry at the bloke who attacked Cara."

Scott sat there gazing out at the coast, feeling suitably chastised. He had to admit that everything Abby said was true, but admitting it was another matter. He was feeling sorry for himself when it was Cara who was hurting, not him.

Scott sighed heavily and held his hand out. Abby gently slapped the back of it.

"Thank you," Scott said, then started the car and continued their journey.

What would I do without Abby? Friends like her are hard to find.

LONGHILL HIGH SCHOOL was situated in the middle of a cluster of four small towns that merged into one another, making it hard to determine when one town stopped and another started. The school bore some loose resemblance to Edmunston-Hunt School. Both had a sizeable sports field in front with undisturbed views across the fields, and a large, impressive sprawling, light brown brick and glass main building. But that was where the similarities ended. Edmunston-Hunt had centuries of traditions and memories, architectural grandeur, and it smelt expensive. Longhill, on the other hand, looked functional, boxy, and cumbersome.

"This looks a bit like my old school," Scott remarked as they parked. They made their way over to the main building. "I remember my first day in year seven. I was crapping myself. The sights, the sounds, and a whole bunch of new people around me. I used to literally break out in a sweat trying to find my way from classroom to classroom in my first week. God, it gives me the shivers just thinking about it now." He looked up at the building.

Abby kept quiet. Her experiences of high school had been different from Scott's. The deprived area she grew up in meant her school had a higher percentage of pupils who'd been excluded from other schools. Teachers had often looked weary and disconsolate from the constant barrage of abuse and lack of discipline from pupils.

Yes, her experience of school had been much different. The fact she'd made something of herself was testament to her determination, grit and resolve to crawl out of the urban ghetto she'd once called home.

After a short wait in reception, Stephen Barrington came through a set of swing doors and greeted them with a wide, chubby smile.

"Thank you for agreeing to see us, Mr Barrington. I'm Detective Inspector Baker, and this is my colleague Detective Sergeant Trent," Scott announced as they produced their warrant cards. "We'd like to ask you a few questions in relation to an ongoing investigation that we're dealing with. We believe you may be able to give us some useful insights."

Stephen Barrington glanced briefly at their cards before ushering them to a meeting room off the main reception.

"Please take a seat," he said, guiding them towards a large, oval teak table with silver legs.

Six dark brown leather chairs were loosely arranged around it. Her seat squeaked as she sat, catching Abby by surprise. She looked slightly embarrassed, much to Scott's amusement.

Barrington was a heavy man who clearly liked his food. His belly spilt out over the top of his trousers. His belt did a sterling job of keeping his rotund belly in check. His white checked shirt strained at the buttons, and his collar disappeared into his thick double chin. His hair was cropped short, grey to the sides, with a hint of brown still on the top. He took the full width of the chair as he leant back and placed his arms on the rests.

"How can I help, Inspector, Sergeant?"

Scott said, "We're investigating the deaths of several teachers at Edmunston-Hunt School, and we understand that you were there for a short spell three years ago. Is that correct?"

Barrington's face went ashen. He had the look of someone who'd been told bad news. The man shifted uncomfortably in his chair and licked his dry lips.

"Mr Barrington, are you okay?" Abby asked.

"Yes...yes, I'm okay. I've not heard that name for a long time," he replied, wringing his hands nervously.

"You weren't there for long, two terms, I believe?" Abby said. "Any reason why it was such a short posting?"

"It was never meant to be short. I was delighted to have secured my post there. Not many teachers can migrate from state education to the elite private sector. I felt like all my Christmases had come at once."

"What changed?" Scott asked.

"Everything..."

46

Barrington let out a huge sigh and buried his head in his hands. The memories clearly weighed heavy on his shoulders. "I don't know where to start."

"What was your first impression of the school?" Scott asked.

Barrington glanced up at the ceiling.

"I couldn't have been prouder. I felt like I'd reached the pinnacle of my teaching career. In case you don't know, teachers with military backgrounds are recruited in to the teaching staff," Barrington said.

Scott nodded to confirm he was aware of this point already.

"It was everything I could have ever wanted. It was a big school with big budgets and exclusivity. To begin with, everything was brilliant. The support from other teachers was great, even if a little rigid. The mark of respect that pupils showed teaching staff was amazing...You'd never get that in a state comprehensive!"

"And then?" Abby prompted as she glanced at Scott.

"And then I got to see the real school, something I hadn't

seen when I was given a guided tour during my interview process. I couldn't put my finger on it. Something just didn't feel right. It was the culture of the school. The kids were almost zombie-like, regimented, disciplined – even fearful at times. Beneath the discipline was conformity. You did it their way or not at all."

"Can you give me an example?" Scott asked.

"Yes, Inspector, that's not hard to do. I recall on one Saturday morning, my year group was required – no, *told*, with less than thirty minutes' warning that they needed to prepare for six laps of the school playing field. One lad – I can't recall his name – wasn't feeling well. Had asthma, I think. The school didn't care. It was seen as a weakness to not do as you were told, or not take part because of ill health."

"What happened to him?"

"That evening he was made to stand in the middle of the field from six p.m. until nine p.m. and forego supper as a punishment. He wasn't allowed to move or sit down. Just stand there to attention. Bloody savage if you ask me."

"Did you not say anything?" Scott asked.

"I dared not; I'd not been there long. If I'm being honest, I was scared to speak out. And now I feel like a bloody coward for not sticking up for the poor lad." Barrington lowered his head, shaking it in disbelief.

"Did you notice any bullying amongst the pupils?" Scott said.

"All the time, I'm afraid. I wanted to stop it on more than one occasion, but several times the head caught me as I was about to intervene, and he'd do this thing with his head. He'd shake it slowly and deliberately, almost as if to say don't intervene." Barrington demonstrated for the officers.

"Are you suggesting that you believe bullying was an accepted and sanctioned norm in the school?" Scott asked, leaning on the table.

Abby furiously jotted a few points in her notebook.

"I think so. It seemed like a tradition-type principle carried throughout the ages. It was so weird, like something that was acceptable back then – if you lived in the era of Oliver bloody Twist!"

"What do you think was the head's role in all of this?" Scott asked.

"To be honest, Inspector, I think it was all his doing. He's a dinosaur from a bygone era. It was the way the school was run from the very beginning, even when he was a pupil there. He's doggedly carried on those traditions. All is not well behind those grand walls, Inspector."

"Clearly not, Mr Barrington. As you know, we're examining the case of several deaths amongst the teaching staff. Do you have any idea why those teachers were targeted?"

Barrington stared at a blank wall behind Scott. His eyes shifted as if he was searching for anything that would help. "I don't know. I read about their deaths, and it's both tragic and alarming. But that school seems to be plagued and haunted by mysterious deaths."

Scott shot Abby a curious and excited glance. "Mysterious deaths? What do you mean?"

"If you're digging into the school's past, then you must have come across a death of a pupil many years ago. Probably a good thirty years, if not more, but I can't be certain of the exact date."

"Anything you might know could be extremely helpful to our investigation, Mr Barrington, no matter how small a detail."

"Well, I heard from the caretaker – God knows how he knew – but there was talk of a group of prefects who ruled the school with an iron fist. I mean proper intimidation. Anyway, the image of the school was tarnished after the drowning of a pupil, allegedly by the prefects. At the time the school covered it up and said it was a tragic and unforeseen accident. It never became public knowledge; it was all made to go away. They said formally that he'd taken a midnight dip in the pool, which was against regulations." Barrington paused to reflect on his memories. With a shake of his head, he continued, "Apparently, the boy was naked when pulled out by staff. They, the prefects, had hidden the boy's clothes, and as far as I know, they're still hidden in the old music room."

Scott gave Abby the slightest of nods. She left the room to pass this information on to the rest of the team.

"Thank you, Mr Barrington, you've been extremely help-ful. Can I ask you to keep this meeting confidential whilst we conduct further enquiries? I'll arrange for one of my officers to take a formal written statement from you later today."

———

SCOTT AND ABBY hastily made their way over to Edmunston-Hunt, taking shortcuts around the back of Brighton to speed up their journey to Ditchling. Abby had instructed Sian to meet them there, but to go ahead and start searching the music room for the missing garments.

Scott smelt progress in the air.

More good news had been relayed to them en route. Mike had been calling around food manufacturers and food distributors. He had some interesting news for them about the oil traces found on the packaging tape used in one of the murders. Through his enquiries, Mike had narrowed down the use of the refined spice-infused oil to the production of a halal and nut-free tikka paste that was used to marinate chicken.

Further investigation had identified one particular Sussex-based catering supplier who distributed this paste to schools nationwide. The interesting point that Mike had discovered was that only three schools in the Sussex area used this paste, one of them being Edmunston-Hunt, the others being Ardingly College and Worth School – the latter two not in close proximity.

"Relay that information to Sian, will you, Abby?" Scott instructed. "I want her to also have a look near the kitchens and storerooms, anywhere that tape could be used or has been used. And when she's done, ask her to search for any further evidence over in the old music room. We're looking for some hidden clothes."

47

Sian arrived before Scott and Abby, not seeing any sign of Scott's car. She stood for a moment looking up in awe at the grand splendour of Edmunston-Hunt School. Its impressive red brickwork and windows set into stone surrounds gave it an historic feel. It was like the building had stood firm and resolute through wars, storms, and natural disasters. She imagined that even an earthquake wouldn't shift this old pile of stone.

Unsure of the layout of the school, Sian followed the boundary around the building. She assumed that the kitchens and storeroom would be around the back some-where, tucked out of view, and the refuse area not far from there. She'd start with the bins first before heading inside to the old part of the building, as instructed by Abby.

She snapped on a pair of gloves and found what looked like a coal bunker of some sort with three walls and a tin roof. One side was fully exposed to facilitate easy access to four large, black wheelie bins. She pinched her nose when the waft of rotting food hit her, carried by the light breeze. The warm sun was no doubt accelerating its decomposition.

I get all the glamorous jobs. Should have grabbed a face mask.

Lifting the first lid, she jumped back as a swarm of flies escaped and flew straight at her. She swatted them away.

"Disgusting creatures," she fumed and composed herself once again.

Peering into the first bin, her day didn't look like it would get any better. A slurry of decaying food greeted her. Hastily dropping the lid, she held her sleeve up to her nose in a desperate attempt to stem the stench creeping up her nostrils.

The next bin offered no respite and more shit.

She breathed a sigh of relief when she opened the third bin. Crushed and flattened cardboard boxes were stuffed into it. Cartons that had once contained fruit juices, boxes that once held fresh chicken pieces, and cereal packets were all piled upon one another.

Result.

Sian found some packaging tape inside a box that once had chicken tikka paste from a manufacturer called Ashrafs.

This could be what we're looking for.

Safely storing away the packaging tape in clear plastic evidence bags and placing them in the boot of her car, Sian checked for Scott. With still no sign of him and Abby, she went into the main school and followed Scott's instructions to find the old part of the building. Pushing through a store-room door, she found herself staring at a crumbling and dusty corridor.

Patches of plaster had crumbled from the walls covered in damp. The odd strip of parquet floor that had probably once adorned this well-trodden and magnificent corridor now lay loosely discarded to one side. In its place was an exposed, dusty, uneven concrete floor that felt lumpy through the soles of her shoes. A heavy stench hung in the air. Sian scrunched up her nose once again. The eeriness and silence sent a shiver down her spine.

Sian found the door that Scott had described, the same door that creaked open once again, its lower swollen edge dragging on the uneven floor. Her eyes adjusted to the semi-darkness, dust from years of neglect drifting aimlessly in the air, dirt gathering in a fine layer like grey snow on the windowsills. The place felt creepy to Sian. She clenched her teeth, trying hard to fight off the urge to shiver with fear. *Spiders...I hate spiders. Where there are cobwebs, there has to be spiders.* She was only grateful Mike wasn't here, or she'd never hear the end of it. The great lumbering oaf would have had a field day taking the piss out of her and playing cruel tricks on her like shutting the door behind her or throwing a spider at her.

There wasn't much for her to look at. A few wooden crates were stacked upon one another. Discarded tea lights were on the old mantelpiece above the fireplace. There were a few cupboards that she plucked up the courage to peer into, just wide enough to shine the light from her phone in. She closed them with a sigh.

No clothes.

Sian became increasingly frustrated. She didn't want to stay here any longer than she needed, and as for any evidence of clothing, she'd turned up a big fat zilch after peering into several cupboards, looking under the fire grate and turning over wooden crates. The silence in the room was briefly broken by a sound.

"Hello? Guv, is that you?" Sian called out, making her way out into the corridor.

She looked in both directions and saw nothing.

Probably a rat...oh, shit, if I see a rat, I'm out of here.

"Hello, it's the police. Anyone here?" she said, raising her voice.

The silence continued.

A loud, crackling static noise caused her to jump as her Airwave job radio sprang into life. "Shit," she hissed with fright.

"Sian, it's Abby. Blimey, we've been trying to contact you for ages."

"Sorry, Sarge, must have been in a dead spot. My phone didn't have any signal. Where are you?"

"We're on our way; we got stuck in traffic. We're just approaching the gates of the school now. How you getting on?"

"Nothing to report so far. I've searched the music room. There's nothing of interest that I can see, Sarge."

"Okay, well, stay put, and we'll be there in a few minutes. We've got a searchlight in the boot we can use to do another check. Hold tight."

The odd sound came again. Sian couldn't place where it was coming from. It seemed to echo off the walls of the corridor.

"Stand by, Sarge. I can hear something."

Sian crept forward carefully and slowly. "Hello, it's the police. Anyone here? Identify yourself."

The silence continued.

"Everything okay, Sian?" Abby asked. "We're just parking up; will be with you in two minutes."

A sharp pain spread across her back, shocking her. She froze when she saw a knife sticking out from beneath the bottom of her stab vest. Sian crumpled to the floor, her face hitting the dusty concrete.

Her mind willed her to move.

Get up, run, run, you idiot.

But her body stayed frozen. Everything around her moved in slow motion. Shock kept her a spectator.

Footsteps. She heard them slow and steady. Someone stood by her face.

Black shoes, I can see black shoes and green trousers.

She willed herself to look up, to identify her attacker. She tried but couldn't. A spot of blood dripped to the floor next to his shoes.

My blood. Help me, help me, she pleaded silently as she stared at his shoes.

He didn't move. He stood there for what seemed an eternity but, in reality, was only a few seconds. Then it dawned on her.

He's going to kill me, that's why he's still here, he's going to kill me.

Panic washed over her, her heart thundering in her chest, her lips drier than a desert. A gurgle emanated from her throat.

And then he was running away. Disappearing into the blackness that was his camouflage.

"Sian, are you there? Sian?" Abby called out over the radio.

A sudden rush of adrenaline numbed the pain a little. From somewhere deep within, Sian's fingers found the radio. She probed for the emergency button.

Sian mustered all her strength and pressed down clumsily with her index finger.

Nothing's happening...press harder...work, you fucker.

Her mind willed her on, but her body felt loose, limp and lacking strength.

Press again; you can do it...I don't want to die...come on, try, try again.

She found it. *Yes.* The control room kicked in, barking orders, trying to locate her whereabouts using GPS. The officer's voice faded in and out. Confusion clouded her thinking.

Was the shouting coming from the radio? Or was someone coming to her aid?

Drawing on all the strength she could muster, she yelled, "Help," in the vain hope they could hear her before darkness took her.

The commotion of the control room trying to reach her and Abby's voice screaming found her.

The sound of heavy footsteps racing towards her, followed by the words, "Officer down...officer down," before Sian's world fell silent.

48

Scott stood behind Abby as she knelt on the cold, hard floor, cradling Sian's head for what felt like an eternity.

"Stay with me, Sian. You hear me...stay with me. Don't you go anywhere," Abby repeated.

The control room diverted all available units from Brighton and Lewes to the area. Officers were being pulled off all non-essential jobs and were being diverted to Ditchling.

Scott was torn between staying with Abby and Sian and finding the assailant. He knew he needed to stay with his officers, but the assailant was here somewhere, and vital seconds were being lost. He knew it would be too late once units had made their way towards Ditchling. Even on blues, the journey would take at least fifteen minutes, and the nearest NPAS helicopter wouldn't get here much sooner.

His fists clenched, and his breathing came out in rapid pants.

Think...think.

He was already treading a fine line with his superiors, having been branded reckless and cavalier on more than one occasion. He'd been criticised for putting results over officer safety, a claim that he'd fiercely refuted. He'd never seen himself as reckless, more pragmatic and energetic.

Abby shouted, "Go...go, Scott. We'll be fine! Go get the bastard who did this."

Scott hesitated. "You sure?" he said, glancing at Sian's pale, lifeless face.

"Yes, we'll take the flack later – together if we have to."

Scott turned and raced down the corridor, his loud footsteps rupturing the silence. He felt like shit. He struggled to think straight.

In the back of his mind, a hazy, haunting image flashed up, almost stopping him in his tracks. It was the lifeless figures of his family sprawled across the road, the car that had mowed them down disappearing into the distance. History seemed to be repeating itself once again, as if some higher power was putting him to the test once more.

A fire raged in his belly. His eyes narrowed.

"Not this time," he said through gritted teeth as he sped up, racing through several sets of double swing doors before shoulder-charging a fire exit door that took him outside.

He stopped for a moment to gather his bearings and to rub his sore shoulder. He couldn't see anything. The only sounds he could hear were of birds singing and chirping innocently in the trees that backed onto the school.

Had he left it too late to pursue? Had the suspect taken a different turn somewhere within the building?

"Fuck!"

Scott raced back inside the school to Abby and Sian. Abby looked a disconsolate figure; her eyes were heavy with sadness.

She glanced up, hopeful.

Scott shook his head. "He got away. How's Sian?"

"Not good, guv. Her pulse is weak," she said, pressing her

jacket over Sian's wound. Paramedics are coming off Coldean Lane. There's a fast response unit a minute away as well."

For a fleeting moment, a change in the direction of the wind carried the sound of an approaching siren.

SCOTT BARGED into Collier's office, seething, his anger threatening to engulf him. If Scott was being honest, he was to blame. The job always carried risks for his officers, but he had been responsible for sending Sian alone.

Any enquiry an officer went out on had the potential to turn nasty. They never knew what would be around the next corner or who would open the next door they knocked on. A seemingly innocent visit to follow up on ongoing enquiries had the potential to go horribly wrong no matter what risk assessment was undertaken beforehand.

He knew all that. Christ, he'd drummed that into all his officers, but now an innocent check had gone horribly wrong, and it had been on his watch.

Now, he needed an outlet for his anger, and Collier was in Scott's cross hairs.

In Collier's office he panted, feeling on edge, his muscles tense. Adrenaline coursed through his veins like a raging river, spiking his fight-or-flight response, and he knew that he was moments away from doing something that he'd later regret.

He didn't give a shit.

Scott searched for Collier but couldn't see him. But then, from the corner of the room, Scott heard the red leather Chesterfield creak.

"Ah, Inspector...I wondered how long it would take until you appeared at my door," came the measured tone of Collier.

Scott could see a few wisps of grey hair poking up over the top of the chair. He stalked over to Collier, grabbed the back of the chair, and spun it round so hard the chair shook. Collier clung onto the armrests, his eyes widened and his lips parted in a gasp. A fine sheen of sweat glistened on his forehead. Their eyes locked in a gladiatorial battle, with Scott sending invisible messages of hate to him.

Collier smiled, a poor attempt at masking his defeat.

"Do you know I have an officer fighting for her life on *your* school premises, and you have the gall to sit here as if everything is okay?" Scott said through gritted teeth. He gripped the man's lapels, pulling him even closer until their faces were inches apart. "At every opportunity you've skirted around my enquiries, spun me yarns and held back information from me. You're going to tell me everything now, because if you don't, I'll throw you out the window, so help me God."

Scott shook with anger. And fear. Fear for Sian.

If she died, he couldn't be held accountable for what he might do to Collier. Cold shivers raced down his spine. His hands trembled through a heady mixture of emotions. But the fear worried him the most: the fear of going too far, even though he knew he'd already done that.

49

C ollier looked a resigned and disconsolate figure. He dropped his gaze, afraid to look Scott in the eyes any longer. Outside, the wail of sirens echoed as emergency vehicles converged on the school. The fight had left the old man. He no longer look like the firm, disciplinarian head that Scott had known to this point. Collier now looked tired, weary, and helpless.

"There's no way back from this, Mr Collier," Scott said. "I think it's high time you were straight with me. You and I both know that you've been holding back on me. You've sidestepped answering my questions from the very beginning. This school is in lockdown now. The school's reputation has been damaged beyond belief, and you've just spent your last day as the head of Edmunston-Hunt School. The school governors will issue a vote of no confidence in you. So that's it, it's over."

Collier gave a thin smile and shook his head. "Checkmate, Inspector. It appears that my options *are* limited. This school has been my life," he said, waving his hand lazily in the air. "It's been my home, my castle, and my establishment since I was a boy. I've protected it fiercely; I would have laid down my life for this school."

But Collier had already done that. He knew nothing about the world outside these four walls, and Scott doubted that Collier had been past the gates of the school much in the last decade.

"Mr Collier, I'd love to sit here and reminisce, but I've got to track down a violent criminal and identify the person who's attempted to murder one of my team," Scott said sternly.

There was a lengthy pause while Collier reflected.

With a heavy sigh, he then said, "This has always been a school that prided itself on discipline. *Keeping boys in line* is built into the fabric of the school, and it's taken as a given. I saw it with my own eyes – and, to be frank, was on the receiving end of it when I was a young lad here. But it set me up for what I was about to experience in my military career. Even when I came back here as a teacher and housemaster, I knew the bullying and initiations were still carrying on."

"Right under your nose and you never did a thing? You turned a blind eye?" Scott asked.

Collier pursed his lips and shrugged, "I guess so. It was the done thing."

"And the pupil who drowned – what happened?"

Collier nodded slowly. "Peter Jennings. The name has stuck with me. The prefects at the time took their initiations and discipline a little too far."

"More than a little too far," Scott remonstrated. Collier ignored his jibe.

"It was they who were responsible for Jennings's death," Collier said. "They threw him into the pool, but they knew full well that the lad couldn't swim. They pushed Jennings away every time he tried to get to the side. They laughed as he fought to survive. After he drowned" – he paused for a moment – "we covered up the unfortunate incident. We blamed it on Jennings breaking school rules. An unavoidable accident was how it was described."

"I understand he was found naked. Where were his clothes?"

"In the old music room. Hidden behind some loose bricks in the flue of the chimney. It was a very dark period in the school's history, but we did well to manage the situation."

Scott couldn't believe it. Collier sounded as if he was pleased by the school's damage limitation strategy. He shook his head in disbelief. Collier seemed to be operating in a parallel dimension where the boundaries of respect, decency, ethics, and moral responsibility had been distorted beyond recognition.

The heavy sound of footsteps behind him broke the temporary silence. Scott glanced over his shoulder to see Mike and several uniformed officers at the door.

"Why Jennings?" Scott asked.

There was another lengthy pause. Collier was in no hurry to explain. In a perverse way, he appeared to be enjoying the attention he was receiving. "He was allegedly having an unhealthy relationship with another pupil."

Scott's brow furrowed as he glanced at Mike, who looked equally perplexed. "Unhealthy relationship?"

Collier cleared his throat and shifted in his chair. "He was a poof, Inspector."

"Why does that matter?"

"He was always seen with another boy. They both were frail, weak and effeminate, always shying away from playing manly sports like rugby. They'd both find excuses not to participate and were always the last in inter-house cross-country competitions. Had poor grades, spent all their time together... You get the drift."

"And on that set of traits, you questioned his sexuality?" Scott asked.

"Well...yes, but the prefects had seen them in an embrace."

"So the prefects were judge and jury?"

Collier glared at Scott.

It was all starting to become very clear. Homophobia ran rife within the school. The physically weak in the school were also punished. Those unable to defend themselves became soft targets for the bullies. The last image of Matthew sobbing ran through Scott's mind.

How many others suffered over the years?

Scott crossed his arms. "And the prefects were?" he asked, knowing full well what names would be put forward.

"Christopher Johnson, Giles Rochester, Alex Winterbottom..." Collier paused for a moment. "And Laurence Goddard."

Scott shook his head in frustration. "This all could have been stopped before it got this far. And who was the boy that Peter Jennings was allegedly involved with?"

"Timothy Marchant, a weak individual with no backbone. Plump, round face, dark hair, large forehead. There was no place for his kind in my establishment."

"And what happened to Timothy?" Scott asked.

"The very next day we shipped him out of here. His father was a government official based at the British consulate in Turkey. But the lad wound up staying with his mother, who resided in England. Kent, I believe. Tonbridge, to be precise."

"More damage limitation?"

"Hmm, something like that. I'll give him credit. He showed his mettle in the end and didn't go quietly. He was angry, didn't want to go, but equally was too upset to stay. Dithering idiot. I would have wiped the scowl off his face had it been under different circumstances."

"And this was sanctioned by the governors as well?" Scott asked.

A look of remorse came over Collier's face as he turned in his chair to face the window. The silence that ensued suggested otherwise.

Scott turned Collier back around. His eyes shot daggers at the head. Every fibre in his being hated the man, but he was here to uphold the law.

"Mr Collier, you are under arrest for withholding information and perverting the course of justice. And that's just for starters."

50

S cott left Collier in the capable hands of Mike and the
uniformed officers whilst organising other officers to
do a more detailed search of the old music room in
the disused part of the school. He left Collier's stuffy room for
the front of the school, currently the scene of frenetic activity.
Police vehicles littered the front drive, parked at curious
angles in the drivers' haste to bail out and assist. He could
hear police dogs barking in the distance and fast radio
chatter as new information came in.

The school was in full lockdown. Armed officers assisted
their unarmed colleagues who were stationed on the front
gate. Other officers roamed the grounds, looking for any
evidence of the assailant or his weapon.

Scott quickly headed towards a cluster of ambulance
vehicles to get an update on Sian's condition. An officer
caught up to him. "Sir, one of the dogs has picked up a scent
heading into the forest behind the main building."

"And where does it lead?" Scott asked in mid stride.

"The scent enters and leaves the forest about a hundred

and fifty yards farther down, seems to double back in the direction of the school."

It was likely the assailant was still in close proximity and was attempting to throw them off by heading into the forest. "Ok. Get more officers on the trail. Follow with caution."

Scott approached the nearest ambulance and saw Abby standing there. Time froze. The commotion around them dropped away. Streaks of salty tears zigzagged down her pale cheeks. Her arms hung loosely by her sides; the top part of her light grey trousers was stained dark crimson, as were the sleeves of her cream blouse.

Abby took a few steps towards Scott, her eyes bloodshot and heavy with tears. She didn't need to say anything; she couldn't say anything. The words wouldn't come. She tried to tell Scott, but her mouth stayed frozen in shock.

"Abby?" Scott asked, knowing in his gut the news wasn't good.

Abby shook her head and cried. "We lost her. Sian's gone. They tried to save her. Paramedics worked to try to stabilise her, but she'd suffered too much blood loss..."

Scott stepped in and pulled Abby in close. She sobbed heavily into his chest. His mind raced, thoughts tumbling over one another.

Sian's dead...I shouldn't have let her go in alone...This was my fault.

A cold chill raced through his body. A mixture of shock, fear and sadness made his stomach flip. A thin veil of sweat broke out on his forehead. Nausea came in waves as he fought to keep the bile down.

SCOTT REMAINED AT THE SCENE, partially because of shock but mostly because of a burning need to oversee the search for

Sian's assailant. Forensics had the grisly task of combing the crime scene for evidence as well as visually cataloguing the last few moments of Sian's life.

It was a few hours before Scott returned to the station at the DCI's insistence.

Officers watched in silence as Scott made his way through the station towards DCI Harvey's office. A sombre mood cast a pall over everyone. Officers spoke in hushed tones, huddled in corners, digesting the information that trickled out in dribs and drabs. None of the usual station banter, mickey-taking or shouts echoed across the office. The subdued silence only amplified the ringing noise from desk phones and mobiles.

The odd sympathetic pat on Scott's arm from some was matched with cold looks from others.

Had he gone too far this time? Had his reckless actions led to an officer's death? His mind swirled. His skin got hot under his collar as he wearily made his way up the stairs and entered DCI Harvey's office.

DCI Jane Harvey sat at her desk, her fingers interlocked on the table. The presence of Detective Superintendent John Meadows seated in one of the two chairs opposite her only added to Scott's tension. Meadows appeared to be struggling as he ground his teeth in anger. The DCI glanced nervously between Meadows and Scott.

"Scott, take a seat," she said, nodding at the only spare chair in the room. "Firstly, I'm sorry about Sian. We're all devastated at the loss of such a young, promising officer."

Scott gave a slight nod, knowing the sentiment was genuine, but a prelude to much worse.

"We'll need a full report from you about what happened, and of course there will be an internal investigation to assess whether procedures were followed correctly. We need to ascertain if there was an error in any part of the chain of command that could have prevented her death."

"Basically, you're trying to find out if I messed up?" Scott said flippantly, then instantly regretted his anger. "I'm sorry, ma'am, sir. I didn't mean that, and I apologise for speaking out of turn."

Scott saw Meadows shifting in his chair, his face an unhealthy shade of red.

"Let me remind you, Detective Inspector Baker," Meadows said, "DC Mason was a member of your team and a member of the Sussex constabulary. We lost a young officer today. I've already had several calls from the chief constable, and I'm due to give him a further update in an hour before he holds a press conference. You're more than welcome to take the call for me should you wish," he said, goading Scott. "This is a sad day for Sussex Police, and I don't give a shit how you feel. All I'm interested in is finding out exactly what happened and whether it could have been avoided. The chief constable has the unenviable task of contacting DC Mason's parents to inform them that their twenty-seven-year-old daughter has been killed in the line of duty."

Meadows rose from his chair, shooting Scott a grimace before turning to DCI Harvey and barking, "Sort it."

An uneasy silence settled in the room after Meadows stormed out.

"Scott, off the record, could this have been avoided?" Harvey asked.

Scott thought hard for a moment as feelings of sadness and guilt blushed his face. "I don't think so, ma'am. I'd instructed Sian to follow a line of enquiry at the school. At no point did I think her life would be in danger. Had I thought that, then I certainly wouldn't have sent her alone. But now, I regret it now. You have to believe me, ma'am. Abby and I were on our way to meet her, so she would have had backup. Unfortunately, we got stuck in traffic, so we were late getting there."

The DCI sighed heavily. Scott knew her hands were tied. She trusted him implicitly, and his past results were a testament to his intelligence, tenacity and need for justice. However, the spotlight was firmly fixed on him, and indirectly on her. She fixed her gaze on him. He knew what she had to say next.

"Scott, I have no choice but to suspend you whilst a full investigation is conducted into the death of DC Sian Mason. You'll be relieved of your duties immediately, and we'll appoint another investigating officer to take over from you."

Scott sat in stunned disbelief. His whole world had just been flipped on its axis. The investigation was standard procedure, but the suspension was harder to stomach.

"Ma'am, I appreciate you must do this. It's standard operating procedure, but I've done nothing wrong. I'm getting closer to wrapping up this case. I've got motive, and I've now got a name for the potential suspect."

Harvey shook her head. "Scott, you know the rules. Any information you've got regarding this case will be passed on to the next SIO. Whoever's assigned as the senior investigating officer can review your information and evidence and decide whether it needs a follow-up."

A desperate need to see this through tightened his throat, threatening to choke him. He'd spent the last ten days working tirelessly with his team to get a result.

Chancing his luck, he asked, "Ma'am, just give me until the end of the shift. Let me get a result. Let me do this for Sian, please?"

DCI Harvey shook her head vigorously. "Scott, you know I can't do this! Both of our careers depend on this."

"Ma'am, don't you think I know that?" Scott asked.

Silence hung in the air for a few moments. He looked around and saw a grey-coloured box on the floor, half-filled with a few files, personal photographs, and certificates.

He nodded at it. "What's going on there?"

Harvey gazed at the box for a few seconds and sighed. "It's been a long time coming. They've been at me for months to take retirement. I'm not stupid. I know I'm old school and a bit set in my ways. I'm hardly the poster girl for modern-day policing, am I?" Harvey paused for a moment. "I'm retiring with immediate effect. Someone more *their type* will take over the reins. Someone whose thinking and leadership is more in line with what they expect."

"They're kicking you out?" Scott asked.

"Well, I wouldn't exactly put it in those terms. It's more like a gentle shove to the edge of the cliff, with a ball of concrete attached to my ankles," she said sarcastically.

"Then give me just a few more hours to wrap this case. I've got a name, and I've got a hunch. Just cover for me a few more hours, that's all. Let's both walk out of here with our heads held high, and one last good result under our belts. Please?"

DCI Harvey shook her head slowly. She blew out a deep whistle of air.

"Shit, I'm going to regret this. You've got a few more hours. Prove them wrong, Scott. And do this for Sian."

SCOTT BURST through the doors of the CID room. Raj cast a sad and lonely figure as he sat there reeling from the news and staring at a blank computer screen. With his team numbers dwindling by the minute, his officer was the only one currently holding the fort.

"Raj, how are you holding up?" Scott asked, placing a hand on his shoulder.

The officer jolted. "Sorry, guv, I didn't know you were there. Must have been away with the fairies."

"I know. Listen, I'm only here for a few more hours, and then I'm on suspension pending a full investigation. I need you to hold the fort with Mike until Abby gets back tomorrow."

Raj's eyes widened, and his mouth dropped open. "Sorry to hear that, guv. If there's anything I can do to help, you know you can just ask."

"I know, and I appreciate it. But I'm in enough trouble as it is. The last thing I need is you getting into trouble, too. Actually, come to think of it, there is something you can do for me. Have a look through the Edmunston-Hunt School website and look at the gallery section. See if you can find class photographs or year photographs going back about twenty to twenty-two years."

"No probs, what am I looking for?"

"I'm looking for a name. Peter Jennings. He was fifteen when he drowned at the school. If you find it, ping it through to me in the office."

Scott entered his office and thumped down in his chair, his body aching. He could barely remember the last few hours. Today was just a blur.

His neck ached, and his legs felt heavy. He glanced around his office, hoping that this wouldn't be the last time he'd be sitting in his chair. He grabbed his phone and dialled Cara's number. In all the melee of today he'd barely had the opportunity to call her.

She picked up. "Scottie, are you okay? Just heard about Sian. My God. I'm so, so sorry," she said, her voice shaky with emotion.

Scott felt numb. He'd been running on adrenaline for the past few hours and was now coming back down with an almighty bang.

"I've had better days. Think we're all still in shock about Sian. And...I've been suspended pending an investigation."

"Well, just remember, it's not personal. They have to follow procedure. Listen, we can talk; we need to talk. I've missed you. I know you're busy, but I can't stand the thought of you going through this alone."

Scott agreed. "I've missed you too, and I'm sorry for everything. I'll see you later."

He hung up, not entirely sure exactly what would happen over the next few hours, but his hunch was starting to crystallise into a plan. The screen on his computer beeped to signal an incoming email from Raj.

Good man!

Raj had managed to take a screenshot of an old black-and-white photograph that showed two rows of students posing for a house photograph. The second row stood on an elevated platform. Beneath the photograph were the names of all the boys listed by their position. Scott scanned the names and found Peter Jennings. He looked just as Collier had described: thin, slight-framed, pale skin, red hair and freckles.

If anything, Peter Jennings had similar characteristics to Matthew Edrington.

Scott continued staring at the list of names as they appeared in the photo. Beside Peter's name was Timothy Marchant's. On closer inspection, he noticed they were standing very close to each other, their shoulders overlapping more so than with any other pupils in the photograph. Timothy Marchant was slightly chubbier, had a round face, dark hair and a large forehead with small eyes. But a charming, large radiant smile lit his face that made him stand out amongst the crowd.

He hit print, and the printer in the corner of his office whirred into action. His next stop would have been the geeks in the high-tech unit, but it was likely they'd know about his suspension and refuse to help him. Heading over to Sussex HQ in Lewes would be risky, too.

He only had one option left. Sussex University would have to do.

51

Simon Barrett, the lecturer in modern languages at Sussex University, waited by the visitors' car park as Scott pulled up.

"Inspector Baker, good to see you. I wasn't expecting to hear from you again so soon, but it's a welcome surprise," he said, extending his hand.

"Yes, sorry for calling you out of the blue and so late in the afternoon, but my investigation is moving quickly, and the next few hours are critical."

"I'm sure, Inspector. I gathered that from the urgency in your tone when you called me."

"As I said on the phone, I need an image adjusted. We do have the capability to do it in-house, but I couldn't get it turned around in less than twenty-four hours, and I really need it now."

They walked through the corridors of the university towards the Centre for Photography and Visual Culture. "I've spoken to one of the lecturers there, and he's assured me that they have specialist facilities and multiple edit suites with Adobe Premiere Pro alongside a Pro-tools suite. They'll have the Photoshop thingy you asked for," Simon said, cycling his hand as he tried to convey the terminology that had likely been explained to him by his colleague.

As they swung through some frosted-glass doors, Scott observed crisp clean lines and modern whitewashed brick walls, which created a fresh and exciting atmosphere. Small clusters of prints dotted the walls at random intervals. Scott's shoes squeaked on the highly polished, dark red tile floors that offered a contrast to the light colour of the walls.

They turned into a small studio situated off the main corridor. The high-tech equipment surprised Scott. Several large LCD screens sat on stands above a long row of laptops and boxes that had a bewildering display of dials, switches and buttons. It looked like something from NASA launch control.

A middle-aged man, thin, with lanky, dark hair and thick, black box-framed glasses swivelled around in his chair but didn't bother to get up. He seemed friendly enough as he gave Scott a nod whilst Simon did the introductions.

"Craig, this is Detective Inspector Baker from Brighton CID. He needs our...well, *your* help on a rather urgent matter. Can I leave him in your capable hands?"

After thanking Simon, Craig offered Scott the seat next to him. "Simon said you needed some Photoshopping?"

"That's correct," Scott replied, handing over a USB stick containing the image. "I need to age an image if possible."

"I would have thought you'd have access to more sophisticated age-progression software than our Photoshop?" Craig said, loading up the stick and navigating through the file structure until a solitary image appeared on the screen.

"We do, but the turnaround is a bit slow with bureaucracy, paperwork, cost centres and all that stuff. You know how it is..." Scott said, trying to sound convincing. He pointed with a tip of a pen. "It's that boy there I want aged up."

"That shouldn't be a problem."

"Does this type of thing take long?"

"Depends on how much detail you need, the degree of accuracy and, of course, the quality of the original," Craig said, pushing his glasses onto his head to get a closer look at the quality of the image. "It's not great, I'm afraid. It's an old picture. It's grainy and more pixelated because it's been blown up."

Scott nodded. "Anything is better than nothing, to be honest."

Craig appeared to have everything within arm's reach, and Scott wondered if it had been set up deliberately like this for convenience. He watched as Craig lifted the lid on a scanner next to him, placed the photo face down on the glass, closed the lid and pressed the black start button all in one deft, slick movement.

The image started to appear on a screen behind them. Craig swivelled around another forty-five degrees to face the screen.

Scott watched in fascination as Craig used a piece of software to outline the boy in question and then remove him from the picture, leaving a square hole. The sound of rapid mouse clicks made it hard for Scott to follow exactly what was being done.

"I'm just cutting out the image so we can work on just that," Craig explained. "I'll save it first before opening it up in Photoshop."

He flicked through a few screens before the image reappeared in Adobe Photoshop surrounded by rows of editing features and tools. "Do you know much about Photoshop?"

"I've heard of it. I think I've even got it on my laptop at home, but I've never used it. I'm already lost just watching what you've done so far," replied Scott.

Craig let out a small laugh. "Yeah, it has that effect on

people. I'm going to blow up the image, which will make it a bit grainy to begin with, but that will get sorted as I work on it. Then I'll refine the edges as we go. How does that sound?"

Scott nodded in agreement.

"Age?"

"Sorry?"

"What age do you want him to be?" Craig clarified.

"Thirty-seven, thirty-eight?"

"Sounds good for starters."

"I'm going to add some puffiness to his face, a few wrinkles. What about hair?" Craig asked as he clicked furiously with the mouse, using one editing tool after another.

"Keep it dark, the same with maybe a little bit of creep?"

"So full head, but larger forehead," Craig verified before he selected the brush option to work on the eyebrows.

The heat of all the equipment made the room feel stuffy. Scott felt his eyes getting heavier; he stifled a few yawns, hoping Craig wouldn't notice.

"How's this looking?"

"Could you elongate the nose? It's quite a young, boyish, thick nose at the moment and doesn't suit the rest of the face."

"Sure, no problem."

"Beard, moustache, earring, glasses, scars, spots?" Craig asked.

"Not sure, to be honest. Leave them off for the time being."

"Once I've got the image the way you want it, I can knock up a few more with a beard, without and some specs too?"

"That would be great. Could you email those to me if that's okay, as I'll need to shoot off."

An older face formed on the screen that piqued Scott's interest. "On second thoughts, can you add a beard in?"

Craig nodded and delivered the request in a few extra clicks. "Bushy, long, tight, neatly trimmed, colour?"

Scott's eyes narrowed from the confusing number of choices. "Tight, trimmed and the same colour as his hair."

With a few final rapid clicks, Craig leant back to admire and show off his handiwork. "There you go. That's probably as best I can get it with the little time we've got. Does that help?"

Scott smiled. "One hundred per cent."

52

Why *does traffic always move slower when I need to get somewhere?*

Scott fumed as he turned right into Coldean Lane and raced back towards Ditchling. Every learner driver, red traffic light, bus and slow-moving lorry seemed to be in his way, testing his patience.

Scott called Mike's number, the ringing tone on loud-speaker filling his car.

"Come on, come on, pick up, Mike," Scott barked. The evening sun hung low in the horizon. A long, eerie line of red tail lights snaked up the hill and past the University of Brighton's halls of residence.

The visit to Sussex University had been more fruitful than he had expected. Whilst he'd watched in awe as Craig manip-ulated the image, Scott's excitement had expanded within his chest, threatening to overflow. He'd only recently seen that face.

His revelation had not only opened a new line of enquiry, but it had helped lock various pieces of the jigsaw together.

Revenge was a plausible motive for the murders, but it still left the unanswered question as to why Latin wording and white feathers had been left at all the crime scenes.

Were they a clue? A calling card?

Simon had said that the English interpretation of the inscriptions was in reference to cowards, but the why was becoming clearer. There was the belief that bullies felt more powerful in numbers, but get any one of them alone, and their power faded. Most bullies were weak individuals, in Scott's opinion. They lacked self-confidence, had low self-esteem and more often than not lacked intelligence. Rather than have these faults exposed or exploited, it was easier to hide behind a wall of violence, fear and intimidation.

"Guv?" Mike picked up.

"Mike, are you still at the school?"

"Yes, guv. Why? What's up?"

"We still got Collier?"

"Yes, we've got him detained. I hadn't heard back from you, so uniform was just about to take him back to the station. guv, I heard the news about you being taken off the case. Pardon my French, but what the fuck's that about?"

"I can't explain now, Mike, but listen to me. Keep Collier there. Do not let Collier out of your sight. Yes, we're charging him with withholding information, but he's not our murderer. I believe that the person who attacked Sian is still on the grounds of the school, and Collier could be the next target. I'm just a few minutes away," Scott continued. "The man we need to find is Timothy Saunders. He's the catering manager for the school. Keep your eyes peeled, and get uniform to check and double-check everything, search the grounds, search the school, his home...find him."

"Will do, guv. See you in a bit."

"Mike, how are you holding up? We've all had a massive shock."

"I'm okay, guv. Yes, it's hard. I've been in shit like this before, but we've got a job to do."

53

An NPAS helicopter hovered overhead as Scott approached the school. Its bright searchlight flickered in the darkened sky, widening to illuminate the grounds of the school. A state-of-the-art thermal-imaging camera would help to identify any heat sources not visible to officers on the ground. The on-board camera system and the video downlink capability would be beaming back real-time information to the control room.

The grounds were awash with officers undertaking controlled sweeping arcs, their torchlights dancing in the darkness of the evening. The rhythmic high-pitched whirring from the helicopter engine as its blades cut through the air.

Mike was standing beside a police van when Scott drove up alongside and parked.

"Any sightings, Mike?" Scott asked as he got out.

"Nothing yet, guv – well, nothing concrete. The dog picked up a scent coming out of the forest and back into the school, but it seems to end in and around the entrance to the school kitchens and where the school food bins are. The dog was going back and forth. One minute it picked up a scent, and the next it lost it. The handler thinks that something's been smeared on the ground to confuse the dog."

"Anything else from Collier?" Scott asked, peering into the side window of the van. Collier sat solemnly between two uniformed officers; a third officer who was armed sat opposite them. Collier held his head high and stared straight ahead, choosing not to look at Scott.

"No, guv, I've kept him here until you arrived. Though I'm not sure why. Surely, if he's in danger, then we need to get him away from here, pronto?"

"One simple word, Mike: bait. Whilst Collier is here, our man still has unfinished business. If Collier is the last target on his list, he'll want to get to Collier, and that means he'll still be close by."

"He'd be stupid to try to get to him," Mike said, nodding towards the van. "We've got half the force here."

"I know, but I needed Collier on site for when I got here. For all we know, Saunders could be watching us right now. He knows this place better than we do. It's safe to say that if he wanted to get to Collier, he would have done so by now. Get Collier back to the station, and as much as I hate to say this, make sure he's well protected."

"Want me to go with them?"

"No, Mike, you stay with me. We're going to look for Saunders."

"He can't have many places to hide out, guv. The grounds are swarming with uniforms. We've got the helo up there, a dog unit down here, and the roads leading to the school are cordoned off."

"The old music room is being combed over by SOCO. The corridors and rooms are being searched. So where else would he feel comfortable or safe, Mike?"

Mike looked unsure.

Before Mike had a chance to answer, Scott headed off

towards the back of the building. Mike jogged the few steps to catch up, trying hard to keep up.

Scott stepped through a white uPVC door that led to the kitchens. A mixture of smells that were reminiscent of being back at school greeted him. It was a warming mix of meaty aromas that reminded him of the school meat pie or shepherd's pie. Then wafts of sweetness from a different part of the kitchen drew him in – the smell of chocolate chip sponge and custard. Above it all was an overpowering odour of cleaning fluids that clung in the kitchen air and along the corridors.

Another, distinctive strong smell assaulted his nostrils. "Pepper and chilli powder."

"And a lot of it too," Mike added, trying not to sneeze. "Uniformed have...have...swept this area already, guv. Back outside is where the dog kept losing the scent." He released a thunderous sneeze.

"Bless you. What does that tell you, Mike?"

"That I need a tissue. Sorry, dunno, that he's trying hard to lose us?" He sniffed loudly.

"Exactly...and that means?"

Mike took a guess. "He doesn't want to be found?"

"That's certainly true, but more importantly, it means we're close. We're close to him, and he doesn't like that. Look around you, Mike. The metal work surfaces are spotless, the shelves neatly stacked, but the floor is covered in footprints and spices. Admittedly, some of the prints will be the work of uniform traipsing through here, but Saunders is not going to go far. This is an area of the school he's most comfortable with. It's his territory."

"You think he'd come back here?"

"Probably. Just in the way that Saunders wouldn't go into a classroom or interfere with teachers, teachers wouldn't come in here and interfere, so he feels safe."

"Right, I get you, guv." Mike nodded, looking around.

"On the face of it, he's just disappeared, but as it stands, he's not in the school building as far as we know. Nothing showed up on the heat sensors in the forest or grounds. Officers are sweeping the surrounding area, *but* we know he's back here somewhere."

Scott paused. He crossed his arms and looked from one set of footprints to another. *Where are you, you bastard?*

Heavy imprints from Magnum police boots criss-crossed the dark, shiny red tile floor. Dotted in amongst them were paw prints from the search dog. The dog had probably lost some of the scent due to the pepper and chilli powder mix. Nothing stood out; nothing made sense.

Then he spotted it. Scott stood still as his eyes tracked them. A different set of footprints.

The prints headed towards a corner of the kitchen farthest away from the door.

"Mike, let's check these out," Scott said as he gingerly stepped around the prints and followed them.

"Saunders?"

"No idea, but it's likely if we can't fit them with anyone else. And as far as we know, no one else has been in here apart from officers."

"Kids?"

"Tread is too big for kids."

The footsteps stopped by a large, industrial double-door fridge-freezer that was pushed up against the far wall. Scott glanced around the sides of the unit, then behind it, before kneeling.

"This has been moved, Mike. Look, there are rubber marks on the floor. Give me a hand."

Mike and Scott leant into the side of the unit, expecting that, due to its size, it would barely move. They both exchanged curious looks when the unit smoothly glided with little effort. Scott knelt again and peered underneath to see the unit was resting on a set of roller gliders.

After pushing the unit aside, the men noticed the footprints carried on and up to the wall. Again they both shot each other a glance before scanning the wall. There was no discernible or designated doorway. However, they could make out a thin line that had been cut into the wall towards the bottom.

"Just enough to crawl through?"

Scott nodded as he stuck a finger into the hole that had been drilled into the wall. Giving it a hard tug, a small section of the wall came away, revealing a large dark space behind.

"Fairly easy for someone to crawl into and then pull the fridge back towards the wall. Crafty," Mike murmured as he knelt and peered into the darkened space. He reached for his phone and switched on his backlight to offer more illumination. "It goes on a bit, guv. Judging from the stud wall partitioning, it looks to be an old corridor that's been sealed up."

"Well, the building is old enough. I wouldn't be surprised if there's a warren of hidden walkways and corridors beneath the school and behind these walls."

Mike lifted a hand to silence Scott before sticking his head farther into the gap. He waited for a few moments before withdrawing. "Think I can hear something, guv. Could just be rats, or the big rat we're after?"

"Only one way to find out. Call it in and get backup," Scott replied, squeezing past Mike and crawling into the dusty dark hole.

Mike followed him whilst relaying their findings and position to the ops room. The corridor was wide enough for just one person to walk through, so Mike followed behind, the lights on their phones barely strong enough to illuminate their way.

The corridor smelt damp and musty; years of no ventilation and natural light gave the space an eerie, cold feeling. They walked slowly, feeling their way. Scott's hands were cold from the dampness in the air.

A rustling up ahead stopped them in their tracks.

Scott strained his eyes to focus in the dark and identify the source of the noise. Mike stood by at Scott's shoulder, ready to barge past in his usual heavy-handed manner.

For a brief moment, a glimmer of brightness bounced back at them. Then it happened again as they inched farther along.

An outline loomed ahead. The outline of a man holding an object in his hand.

54

"This is the police! Identify yourself!" Scott peered into the darkness.

The silhouetted figure remained still and silent.

As the light from Scott's phone hit the man's hand, the object became clear. A knife.

"This is the police; identify yourself now!" Scott repeated. "We're armed officers! Put the knife down!"

"Now, now, Inspector, we both know you're bluffing," Saunders said. "CID officers don't carry arms unless they're specially trained."

"Come forward now, Saunders!" Scott barked again upon recognising his voice.

"Inspector, Inspector, that's not how we do things around here. There's a pecking order. You have to toe the line, *oh, the wonderful line.*" Sarcasm tinged his cold, measured words.

"Put the knife down. Let's talk about this and see how we can help you."

Saunders started to retreat slowly, the darkness swallowing up his outline.

"Bit late for that, don't you think, Inspector? You have an annoying habit of sticking around, and that doesn't help me."

Before Scott could say anything else, Saunders disappeared into the darkness, the sound of his footsteps fading.

"Proceed with caution," Scott whispered to Mike as they followed in pursuit. They started out slow to begin with, watching their footing in the semi-darkness.

Their laboured breaths drowned out the sound of Saunders's footsteps. Scott was unsure what direction they were heading in and what would greet them at the end. Each cautious turn delayed them further as they headed deeper into the warren of hidden passageways.

Scott knew that confronting and pursuing an armed suspect required tact, backup and caution. The very same elements he'd discarded as he'd gone after his man. He knew he was putting his life at risk as well as Mike's. But adrenaline coursing through his veins spurred him on. His desire for a result and justice overshadowed any logical reason to stop the pursuit now.

A soft glow from an open doorway up ahead punctured the darkness. Scott put out his arm to slow Mike, then placed a finger to his lips. The light from inside the room flickered and danced on the walls of the corridor.

Alarm bells rang in Scott's mind as he pressed his back to the wall. He peered around the corner and through the doorway. Saunders stood in the centre. The overpowering smell of fuel hung in the air.

Scott entered and glanced around the room that was dimly illuminated by an assortment of tea light candles placed around the edge. His eyes darted over to the fireplace mantelpiece, where several Molotov cocktails had been placed, primed with fuel-soaked rags. His heartbeat accelerated to match the fear racing through his body.

Scott's anger boiled as he realised they had been lured

into a trap. With so many tea lights the fumes from the fuel could ignite at any moment. He and Mike could have seconds or minutes before the whole room went up.

Shit.

Scott looked around nervously, seeing small pieces of paper had been pinned to the walls, all bearing the same Latin words as the notes in the victims' pockets.

Saunders stood behind a wooden chair in the centre of the room. Its worn seat had been covered in a liquid that Scott assumed was more fuel. Several lengths of rope lay loosely around the chair's legs; handcuffs dangled from the armrests, ready to receive their captive. A green plastic fuel can and a box of matches sat close by.

The whole damn place has been soaked in petrol.

"Saunders, it doesn't have to come to this. We can end this peacefully, come out of this alive," Scott said, hoping to reason with this psychopath.

Saunders sniggered and inhaled deeply through his nose. He closed his eyes briefly.

"It's a little too late for that, don't you think, Inspector?" He pointed the knife in their direction.

In the soft light, Scott saw what looked like blood on the blade.

Sian's blood?

He clenched his hands at his sides, itching to squeeze the life from this prick's body. But Scott needed to keep Saunders talking whilst he analysed the situation.

In a matter of minutes reinforcements would be arriving, and if the situation went horribly wrong, the fireball created by the Molotov cocktails would race down the corridor, taking out everything and everyone in its path.

Scott turned to Mike, his eyes wide with fear and anger. "Get out of here. Get *everyone* out of here."

"Guv, I'm not –"

"It's an order, Mike. Get out of here. Now!"

Mike stayed put, struggling with the need to be compliant versus his military instincts to stay, defend and fight. He glanced between Saunders and Scott.

Scott glared at him. Mike took a few tentative steps backwards out of the room, his eyes firmly fixed on Saunders.

"That's a good boy." Saunders sneered. "You run along like the good inspector's told you. Save yourself because the inspector has a nasty habit of letting down those who matter – don't you, Inspector?" Saunders flashed Scott a cold steely glare. "This isn't your battle. But I'm willing to make you a deal. I'll exchange you for Collier."

"It doesn't work that way," Scott said. "Listen, I know what happened. I know about Peter Jennings."

55

"You know nothing!" Saunders yelled, his face turning from relaxed to red with rage. "You know nothing. You'll never know what it feels like to lose someone you love."

"I do, Timothy. I do, trust me," Scott said softly. "I know what they did to Peter, but revenge killing isn't the way to resolve the situation."

"They killed him. They punished him. They bullied him."

"Is that why you were so protective of Matthew? Because he was being bullied? You felt his pain?"

"He's just a soft soul." Saunders began to cry. "He's done no harm, but that's the problem with this place. It's wrong; the weakest don't survive." Tears rolled down his cheeks and into his beard.

Fearful of an imminent explosion, Scott pleaded with Saunders to leave with him now. But his request seemed to wash over Saunders.

Saunders said, "Do you know how hard it was living this secret life?"

"No, why don't you tell me, Timothy?"

Saunders sobbed as snot ran down over his lips. "I've known since I was a young boy that I was different."

"And then you met Peter? Someone who felt the same way you did?"

Saunders nodded helplessly, the fight leaving him. "I could handle what they threw at me, but Peter couldn't. He became a soft target. Johnson, Rochester, Winterbottom, Goddard – they all used him as their punchbag. They were scum. They were cowards and deserved to die. And yet they could do no wrong. Collier loved them, loved how hard and manly they were."

"Why now? Why after all these years?"

He curled up his lip in a sneer. "It's taken me this long to get close to them. I've been planning this moment for most of my life. I wanted to see them up close. I wanted to live around them and see them living their lives without a care in the world. Goddard was the only one shitting himself, and rightly so. And what did he do? He got pissed and beat the crap out of his wife!"

As Saunders spoke, Scott had slowly inched back towards the door.

"Do you think I wanted to be a chef...or a bloody catering manager? I wasted years learning how to cook. NVQs for this, NVQs for that. Going from one restaurant to another, one school to another 'til I landed this job. My position allowed me to blend into the background and bide my time."

"And Collier?"

"It was entirely his fault!" Saunders yelled again, clutching his head. "It was always him. He was the housemaster. It was his prefects. Then he brought them back as teachers. It was always Collier, and now you've spoiled the main event. Collier's seat was all ready for him...'til you spoiled it, Inspector. And now you must pay the price...or you can give me Collier."

Saunders rocked on his heels, mumbling incoherently. He shook his head from side to side.

"Taking Collier's life won't solve anything. You're better than them. Give up now, Saunders."

Saunders raised a finger to his lips. "I've done what I came here to do. I've nothing to live for. My time will come again, another life, another being." He reached into his pocket and pulled out a lighter, then proceeded to taunt Scott with it. "Justice will prevail; the weak will die. Justice will prevail; the weak will die –"

"No!" Scott shouted as he backed away quickly. "Don't do this."

Scott's words fell on deaf ears. Saunders stared at Scott. The emotion had drained from his eyes. He looked solemnly in Scott's direction before a small smile broke out on his face. The scratch of the wheel on flint was the last thing Scott heard before he was thrown back into the corridor by a searing surge of orange fire.

He scrambled to his feet. His face and skin felt hot. His eyes stung. He stumbled to the side of the door and glanced back in, holding up a hand to shield his face from the intense heat that prickled his skin.

A yellow and orange flame consumed Saunders's body. A human fireball. No cries or screams pierced the air. The man didn't even drop to the floor in an attempt to extinguish the flames. Saunders stood motionless as he was engulfed by a golden inferno. The chair in front of him crackled and creaked as the fire took hold. Saunders's skin melted, his clothes offering the perfect kindling for the flames.

Scott began to run. There was nothing he could do now other than save himself. He knew that once the Molotov cocktails exploded, the ensuing fireball would be moments away. That would be catastrophic for him, as the fireball only had one way to travel, and that was back down the corridor.

He stumbled as he desperately tried to retrace his steps. He wasn't sure if it was the smoke or his injuries that slowed him down, but the passageway seemed to go on forever.

He fell to his knees as smoke choked his lungs, robbing him of air. His chest felt like it was burning; his eyes stung as a thick acrid sea of black smoke smothered him. He could feel the heat bearing down on him.

Fire. He needed to get away.

He checked his surroundings, but confusion tightened its grip on him. He coughed. Disorientated and succumbing to the smoke, he fell to the floor.

56

Mike kicked through the ashes. He shook his head in bewilderment.

Blackened walls gave a chilling reminder of the fireball that had ripped through the room. The noxious smell of fuel hung in the air, stinging his nostrils. Sweat beaded on his forehead from the heat that lingered. Columns of steam rose from the charred wood, spiralling upwards gracefully towards the ceiling.

It was nothing he hadn't seen before in conflicts. The charred remains of Afghan houses and those who had once lived in them had exposed him to the horrors. Parents, children, young and old – none of it mattered. Fire didn't discriminate; it took anyone who stood in its path.

He stared at the charred, blackened body of Saunders lying in the middle of the room.

Shit, that smell of burnt flesh.

He'd seen enough bodies to be unfazed by the smell. It was an acrid stench in your nose with a hint of earth and burning flesh. It didn't smell like meat, but you knew it was human.

It was a smell that etched into your brain and could not be erased.

The coroner's van would be there soon to remove the body. From where Saunders lay and what was left of him, it would be impossible to distinguish any discernible features, let alone if it was male or female.

SCOTT LIFTED his left hand up and gazed at the white gauze dressing wrapped around it.

He blinked hard as tears escaped from his stinging eyes. When he coughed hard, mucus rose to the back of his throat. He pulled away the oxygen mask for a moment. His hand stung as his fingers gripped it.

"I guess you like living on the edge," DCI Harvey said. She was perched on a chair alongside Scott in the back of an ambulance.

He tried to talk but winced when no words came out. His throat stung from inhaling smoke. He glanced at the DCI and shook his head in resignation.

In a faint crackled whisper he managed, "Well, I'm definitely on suspension now."

Scott was exhausted, but his mind desperately processed the events of the last few hours.

The ambulance rocked when the large hulking figure of Mike clambered in. "You had a lucky escape, guv. You okay?"

Scott blinked furiously, desperately trying to clear the fuzziness from his mind. "Saunders?"

Mike shook his head. "I've seen more meat on a barbecued spare rib."

Both DCI Harvey and Scott shot him a disparaging look, which Mike met with one of his nonchalant shrugs as if to suggest, *what's the big deal?*

The DCI patted Scott on the shoulder. "The good news is you'll survive. You've got a few superficial burns to your left hand, a bit on your face. You've lost a bit of your eyebrows, but nothing an eyebrow pencil won't sort out." Mike fought to contain a laugh. "And you inhaled a bit of smoke. They're taking you to the hospital for a check-up."

"And how's Abby after...?"

"Abby is doing okay. We'll be offering her a counsellor if she needs one, but our Abby is made of strong stuff. She'll pull through this. We've all been affected by Sian's death, not just CID and Brighton, but the entire Sussex constabulary. It's going to take a long time for all of us to come to terms with it." DCI Harvey sighed.

Harvey's words brought forward the reality of Scott's situation. He'd lost a good member of his team. A young, vibrant, intelligent officer who he had no doubt would have gone on to bigger and better things. He had been her commanding officer. It had been his responsibility to ensure her safety as well as the safety of others on his team, and he had failed.

Failed yet again to protect those around me.

No doubt the internal investigation would determine what part he'd had to play in her death. Had procedures been followed correctly? Had a suitable risk assessment been conducted, and more importantly, could her death have been avoided?

57

Scott had endured an overnight stay for observation at the Royal Sussex County Hospital. He'd been surrounded by geriatrics and the infirm who had their own inter-ward competition for who could cough the loudest or shout "nurse" the most times during the night. His only consolation after a poor night's sleep had been a visit from Abby the following morning at home. She had been a welcome visitor. They'd sat together sipping tea whilst talking through the events of the last twenty-four.

The DCI had been right.

On the face of it, Abby appeared to be strong and coping well. It might have just been a front, a defence mechanism to get her through the trauma. They still had Sian's funeral to go. It would be a difficult moment for all to deal with, and Scott really didn't know how he'd be able to face Sian's parents and family.

The eyes of the force would be looking at him. Judging him. He would no doubt face some difficult questions from friends and colleagues, and that was something he wasn't prepared for. He didn't have the answers. He wished he did.

Two days later

THE COOL SEA air cleared Scott's head as he and Cara walked along the beach. The waves lapped over the stones as seagulls floated above, swooping down to grab a discarded chip or half-eaten sandwich.

They walked hand in hand. An awkward silence marred most of the walk. Neither knew what to say, and neither was willing to start the conversation, afraid of where it might end up.

Scott stopped a short distance from the Brighton i360, the city's newest attraction, a one-hundred-and-sixty-two-foot-high observation tower with a viewing capsule. On a clear day, it offered spectacular views of the marina, and from the white cliffs of the infamous suicide spot Beachy Head in the east to Worthing Pier and Portslade in the west. It was a modern feature on the old Brighton landscape.

Cara turned to face Scott, holding both of his hands. She rubbed the backs of them with her thumbs. "Scott, listen to me. I'm sorry for not telling you more about my past. You and I had only just got together, and I wasn't sure how to bring up what happened with my ex. I put you – us, in danger. But now you know why I had to leave London. Jason was a violent bastard.

"It all started off really well between us. He was really kind, caring and generous. Then he started staying out later and later. He started drinking and coming home and being aggressive towards me. He criticised me over my job. He tormented me about it, saying it was creepy, that there must be something wrong with me. One minute it was my weight; the next it was what I wore or what I cooked for him. He always found something to have a go about. He hit me a few times. Stupid me, I didn't leave. I was too scared. And...then I fell pregnant.

"And trust me, I really wanted a baby. I have always wanted children, but the thought of bringing up a child in that abusive environment...I knew it wasn't safe for me or the baby. It wasn't fair."

"So why didn't you just leave and still have the baby?"

Cara looked into his eyes. "Jason would have always been in my life because of the baby. As long as I had his child, he had a way of controlling me. He'd told me on plenty of occasions that if I left him, he'd track me down and put me in a wheelchair for life."

Scott nodded and looked out at the sea, his eyes drawn to the emptiness of the ocean.

"I'm sorry for keeping you in the dark and not telling you sooner," she said. "When an amazing relationship like ours creeps up on you, coupled with what you've already been through, I genuinely didn't know how to tell you. I guess it took me by surprise."

She continued, releasing his hands, "I fell in love with you, Scott, and the deeper I fell for you, the harder it became to tell you." Cara rubbed her temples and squeezed her eyes tight. "I'm not making a lot of sense... I hope you understand my reasons at the time. I guess I ran away. I tried to get as far away as possible. To start a new life, but I was always looking over my shoulder, fearful that Jason would have found me... well, sadly, he did."

Scott closed his eyes and rested his forehead on hers. He gave her soft Eskimo kisses. Cara had filled a void in his life, and for that he was grateful.

"Cara, I'm sorry for not being more understanding. I just didn't know how to process it at the time. You mean too much to me, and I can't imagine my life without you in it."

"Well, you're stuck with my ugly mug, then!" Cara replied, planting a soft kiss on his lips.

Scott smiled, his heart beating hard in his chest.

"I love you, Scott Baker," Cara said as her bottom lip trembled.

"No more secrets," he whispered.

"I promise."

WE HOPE YOU ENJOYED THIS BOOK

If you could spend a moment to write an honest review on Amazon, no matter how short, we would be extremely grateful. They really do help readers discover new authors.

ALSO BY JAY NADAL

TIME TO DIE

(Book 1 in the DI Scott Baker series)

THE STOLEN GIRLS

(Book 2 in the DI Scott Baker series)

ONE DEADLY LESSON

(Book 3 in the DI Scott Baker series)

IN PLAIN SIGHT

(Book 4 in the DI Scott Baker series)

Printed in Great Britain
by Amazon

44715322R00182